STONE COLD SOBER

Cindy Davis

Cover and Interior Design by Jennifer Carson
www.princeandpauperpress.com

Copyright © 2015 by Cindy Davis. All rights reserved. No part of this publication may be reproduced, stored in a retrieval system or transmitted in any form or by any means, electronic, mechanical, photocopying, recording or otherwise without the prior written permission of the copyright holder, except for brief quotations used in a review.

This is a work of fiction, and is produced from the author's imagination. People, places and things mentioned in this novel are used in a fictional manner.

Visit Cindy on the web at www.cdavisnh.com or
www.fiction-doctor.com

ISBN: 978-1-62251-023-8

Enigma Books, an imprint of

Prince And Pauper Press
South Sutton, NH

Printed in the United States of America

This one goes to my dad,
for encouraging my life-change, and for
being there when I needed him.

*Never get married in the morning,
because you never know who you'll meet that night.*
~Paul Hornung

CHAPTER 1

The Olde Bay Diner bustled with early morning activity. Angie Deacon almost had to shout to be heard over the clank of plates and chatter of voices. "I don't miss Tyson one single bit." She leaned back and crossed her arms in an exaggerated manner. Then she laughed and leaned across the table, almost head to head with best friend, investigative cohort, and sometimes-lover, Detective Colby Jarvis. Just Jarvis to those who knew him well.

He laughed and wiggled his eyebrows.

"Okay, huge lie," Angie said. "I've needed him no less than ten times and he's only been gone two days. Seriously though, things are looking good so far. You'd be proud of me. Drum roll, if you please."

He obediently rapped his index fingers on the table.

"I selected the leading man for Prince & Pauper's first performance of the year." She waved her hands in the air as if she'd scored a three-point shot—a term she'd learned from basketball freak Jarvis.

Now it was his turn to lean forward. "So, what's wrong?"

How was he always so in tune with her? "I'm not sure I made the right choice."

"Why are you second guessing yourself?"

She shook her head and gave a short bark of laughter. "It's

not because of his talent. All the ladies, and even one of the men, are google-eyed over him."

"Is he that good looking?"

Angie stopped to choose the right words. If she described him using one of the cast member's words—that he was like Tom Cruise and George Clooney rolled into one—Jarvis's infamous jealousy would rear up like a wild mustang. Okay, she wouldn't color the truth; any lie told now would come out when he and the leading man met.

So Angie pulled in a breath and let it out as she said, "The play's a comedy set at a construction site. The star's perfect for the role of the foreman, self-confident, tall and good looking, and he oozes charm. He throws out comedic lines as if he was born to it. He's friendly and helpful around the set."

"He sounds perfect. What's the problem?"

"I'm afraid he might be too much of a distraction. In the few days he's been here, the women are falling all over him and the men are his best buddies."

"How is that a distraction? Seems it's a good thing for everyone to get along."

"Stone is always laughing and telling stories." Many of the stories were funny. Some involved risking life and limb. Angie couldn't imagine they were all true. How could so many things happen to a person who hadn't reached his mid-forties? Yet, he told each tale as if he'd lived it in glorious Technicolor.

"Seems like it's good to have them getting along. Remember that diva you had to deal with last summer…"

Angie groaned. "Don't remind me."

"Exert your authority, my lady. Remind them they're there to work and they can tell stories at the bar afterward."

The glass door of the diner opened. Angie's costume designer snuffed out a cigarette in the snow, stomped goop off her feet, and came in. Blanche Powers was a quiet woman, talented at costume design, and in great demand around the state. She'd been working on Prince & Pauper's costumes since the theater opened nearly two years ago. Blanche had deep green eyes, dark brown hair that swung freely to her slim waist, and a free, easy disposition. She ordered a hot tea to go then spotted Angie and Jarvis. "Good morning, you two."

Angie slid over and patted the cushion beside her. Blanche eased herself into the seat. "What a tan! I'm jealous," Angie cooed. "How was your vacation?"

Blanche assumed a wistful expression. "Tahiti was great. Sorry to say this but I think I have to quit all my design jobs and move there. Coming back to this snow is like culture shock." She greeted Jarvis with a hearty good morning.

"So, you really had a good time?" Jarvis asked. "Is it someplace we should go?"

"Only if you like crowds, free-flowing alcohol, and rampant debauchery."

Jarvis frowned. Angie laughed. "She was kidding, Jarvis." To Blanche, she said, "Weren't you?"

Blanche shrugged. "I went with three girlfriends. We danced and drank and swam—sometimes doing all three at once. It felt like we were single again."

"No men?" Jarvis asked.

Her comment, "None were our husbands," had Jarvis burying his attention on his breakfast, which made the women laugh. "Seriously though," Blanche said, "it's the best climate."

"You'd better not be leaving us," Angie said.

"Wish I could afford it. Maybe when I retire."

The waitress set Blanche's tea on the table. Blanche popped the top on the waxed cardboard cup and dipped the teabag up and down while blowing on the steamy contents. "I'll be stopping by the theater in a bit. I want to pick up a copy of the script. I'll spend the afternoon at home scribbling notes for costumes. If you have any free time tomorrow, I'll show you what I've come up with."

Jarvis laughed. "Free time? I was lucky to get her to take time to eat a bagel."

He was right. Since Tyson left, Angie's head had been spinning with ideas, solutions, and prayers that things would run smoothly. "I left you a copy of the script on the green room table."

"Great. I'll stop as soon as I pick up a few groceries. I have no idea what my husband ate while I was gone. Everything in the fridge is green except what's supposed to be. Those are brown."

The diner door opened again. In stepped Angie's new leading man. Stone Powers was everything the cast members claimed—charismatic, handsome, and a bit of a flirt. He shot Angie a wide smile. Jarvis kicked her under the table. She flashed him a stop the jealousy scowl, then realized Jarvis thought she was making eyes at a total stranger.

Stone spotted Blanche beside Angie. His perfect face practically glowed. Blanche gave a tiny squeal. She launched from the seat, screeched, "Stony! What are you doing here?" and threw herself into his arms, burying her face in his neck.

He swung her in a circle, somehow avoiding a man trying to exit, then set her feet on the floor. "When did you get back?" His deep, late-night radio voice gave Angie goose bumps.

"The girls and I got in about an hour ago. I popped in for a shower and to dump off my luggage." Her, "Careful not to trip on it when you go in the door" made everyone laugh. "No. Really. I did just dump it inside the door. I thought you were on the road this week and wouldn't notice—um, I mean fall over it."

Wow. Angie had known Blanche was married, but never met her other half. And if anyone had asked her to guess whom it might be, she never would've considered Stone. These two seemed like such opposites. Blanche was outgoing and hardworking, Stone flirty and hard working. Well, maybe they weren't so different after all.

"My flight got changed. I leave first thing tomorrow morning." Stone removed his gloves.

"Damn. You'd think since I just got home…"

"I know sweet pea, but that's the way it is."

"All right, all right. I'll look on the bright side. We'll make tonight special. I'll cook your favorite dinner. And"—she wiggled her eyebrows—"your favorite dessert."

"With whipped cream?"

Their innuendos left Angie feeling like a fifth wheel. She shrugged at Jarvis who shot her a *two could play that game* look.

The happy couple finally seemed to notice they weren't alone. "In case you haven't realized it yet, Stone is my husband," Blanche said.

Angie laughed. "Has he mentioned he's our new leading man?" She said it for both Blanche and Jarvis's benefit.

Blanche swung her hair back over a shoulder and tilted her head to look up at Stone. "You got the part?" she squealed.

Angie had known the woman for two years and never once heard her squeal. Now, in the space of two minutes, she'd done it twice. Blanche linked fingers with Stone, tiptoed up and kissed his cheek. "I'll see you later." She turned to Angie. "What time should I come with the sketches?"

"Ten-thirty?"

"Okedokee smoky," Blanche called over her shoulder as she left. Stone went out behind her. They stood on the stoop talking.

"Okedokee smoky?" Jarvis asked.

Angie shrugged. "I learned a lot about her today. Funky vocabulary is only part of it." She crumpled the paper napkin and jammed the wadded ball into her empty cup.

"You looked surprised to see your handsome leading man."

She laughed and heaved an inflated sigh. "I guess I left out a few details about him, but that's your own fault for being so jealous all the time."

He held up a hand. "Don't say it. I know." His gaze flicked toward the door then back. "How the hell can anyone be that good looking?"

Angie laughed and aimed the conversation along a different route. "I was surprised to learn they were married. I guess I should've made a connection between their last names both being Powers."

"The name isn't that uncommon."

"No, but the point is, I should've noticed."

"Can't stand to miss a single detail, can you?"

Angie opened her mouth to disagree but he had a point. She hated not knowing things. She always dug, upended and juggled till answers became clear. Okay, fine, one got past her. Big deal.

The door opened and Stone returned to their table.

"Stone Powers," Angie said, "this is Detective Colby Jarvis. Jarvis, this is Prince and Pauper's new leading man."

The men shook hands. "Join us?" Jarvis said.

Stone began to slide in next to Angie, but she waved for him to stop. "I'd love to stay longer, fellas, but I have to get to work." She stood and left room for Stone to take her seat, bent and kissed Jarvis under the left ear. As she grabbed her briefcase from the seat, Stone drew a container of hand sanitizer from his pocket.

"Thanks for breakfast," Angie told Jarvis.

"What do you want for lunch? I deliver," Jarvis said

When he made a scrunchy face Angie almost made a comment about whipped cream, but said only, "Surprise me."

CHAPTER 2

Jarvis watched Angelina until she was safely in her Lexus. He'd never been able to think of her as Angie like everyone else, including her mother. The love he felt for her went beyond any emotion he'd ever experience. Beyond even, he realized recently, what he'd had for Liz, rest her soul.

"You're a lucky man," Stone said.

"I was just thinking the same thing."

"How long have you two been married?"

"We're not—yet."

"Anything planned?"

"No. I asked. She turned me down."

"I only just met her, but I get the idea she's had a hard time of it."

"That's an understatement." Jarvis wouldn't get drawn into a discussion about Angelina's past. It was none of her employee's business. While he slathered jelly on the last morsel of toast he tried to think of a change of subject. "So, are you an actor by trade?"

Stone bent forward as if sharing a momentous secret. "This is my first acting job. I've always loved the theater. I once did grunt work at a marina in Newport, Rhode Island where they have a great theater. I used to sneak in and watch rehearsals. Never had the balls to try out for a part though."

"You don't seem like the shy type to me."

Stone gave a hearty laugh. "People change."

STONE COLD SOBER

The server refilled Jarvis's coffee, then poured a cup for Stone. She greeted him as though she knew him, which was hard not to—Alton Bay, New Hampshire's population was only five thousand.

Stone ordered breakfast and orange juice. "In my regular job, I'm a pharmaceuticals salesman." He doctored his coffee with cream and four sugars. "I'm on the road two weeks out of every month."

"That's got to be tough."

Stone shrugged. "The pay makes it worthwhile."

Jarvis frowned. "Wait a second. You're the leading man—how can you fit in the strenuous rehearsal schedule?"

"The schedule is very flexible. This week though, I need to go to Chicago to take care of a client—my best one. Then I'll be back here to begin rehearsals."

"What did you do for work at that marina?" Jarvis poured cream into his cup, then, thankful Angelina had gone, added three heaping spoons of sugar.

"I'd just gotten out of the Marines. I planned a career around boats and the water so the marina seemed a natural starting point. I didn't expect to start at the very bottom." He laughed. "And I mean bottom. They had me scraping hulls. Anyway, it wasn't long before I realized being around the water wasn't where I wanted to be. I heard about the sales job...I didn't want to do sales—"

"But the money was too good to turn down."

"Exactly. The job doesn't require heavy selling—I sell only to pharmacies. Usually all I have to do is let them know the availability of a new product, give them the pros, cons and bennies, then let them decide."

"I assume bennies means benefits?"

"More like kickbacks." He shrugged. "Nothing to do with me. Anyway, the hardest part of the job is getting hold of the buyer."

"Seems like the hardest part would be the travel."

"I enjoy it. I get bored easily."

"So, what do you do for fun?"

"I'm a big fitness buff. I work out every morning— Thanks hon," he interrupted himself as the server slid an omelet onto the table. "I'm a vegetarian. I love sports—especially basketball and fishing."

At the word basketball, he had all Jarvis's attention. "You like the Celtics?"

"Big-time. 'Bout time they let go of Garnett and Pierce, huh?"

Jarvis nodded. "I thought they'd keep 'em till they needed walkers to get down-court."

"Yes. They still need a forward who can score." Stone pointed his fork at Jarvis. "I think they should draft Zach Collins."

"If I remember right, he's just out of high school, but isn't he only six-seven?"

"No six-ten. For me though, I really like that St Stephen's Episcopal center—Jerrett Allen. He's six-ten also."

"What do you like about him?"

"He can run the floor with the best of 'em. He's a good rebounder, which we need in the worst way. Too bad you're leaving town, there's a game at the high school tomorrow night—Alton's playing Sanborn Regional."

"Do you go to all the games?"

Jarvis pushed away his empty plate. "Many as I can."

"Angie's okay with it?"

Jarvis laughed. "Angelina doesn't care for sports. She goes to some games to keep me happy. Besides, for the next few months, all her energy will have to go into this production. Not sure you're aware, her partner got a job on Broadway, so there's a ton of extra responsibility heaped on her shoulders."

Jarvis's phone rang. Rickie Kennedy's number showed on the caller ID. Rickie was Angelina's mom's toy-boy. He was young, athletic and handsome. Word around town was that Rickie was after Gloria's huge lottery winnings from a couple of years ago. What the locals didn't know was that Rickie's family was already wealthy.

Though he and Rickie had attended a few sporting events together, they rarely spoke on the phone; something must be wrong with Gloria. "Sorry Stone, I have to take this call."

Stone nodded, turned away, and removed a vial from his pocket.

"Where are you?" Rickie asked.

"At the diner." Jarvis watched Stone douse himself with nose drops.

"You have a few minutes to spare?"

Okay, it didn't sound like an emergency. "Sure."

"I'll be right there."

He must've been around the corner because he whooshed into the building along with a gust of cold air.

Stone replaced the vial in his pocket and dabbed his nose with a napkin. Rickie motioned to the waitress for coffee and slid into the booth beside Stone. As usual, Rickie was bundled in leather and fur, not a concession—as some townspeople thought—to extravagance, but to his inner workings. Being from southern California, and having spent most of his life in Hawaii, the young man was cold all the time. Jarvis made introductions between Rickie and Stone Powers.

"Hi. Nice to meet you." Rickie used his teeth—bright white and perfectly straight—to pluck off the fingers of black leather gloves. They shook hands.

"You too. Unfortunately, I have to get going." Rickie stood so Stone could climb from the booth. "Sorry to race off. I hope to see you again so we can get acquainted."

"Same here."

"Maybe we can do that tonight," Jarvis said. "There's a game between Alton and Sanborn Regional."

"Great," Rickie said.

"I can't make it—celebrating with Blanche," Stone said with innuendo-laced words. "Keep me in mind for the next game though, 'kay?" Stone said seeya and left.

Rickie dropped the gloves on the bench seat. "I know you're

probably on the way to work so I'll talk fast." He inhaled. On the exhale, he said, "Gloria and I are having problems."

Jarvis hoped his internal groan didn't show on his face. This was stuff he shouldn't be hearing and he told Rickie so.

"I have nobody else to talk to."

"What about your parents?"

Rickie spooned sugar into his coffee. "They're part of the problem."

Had he missed something? Didn't Rickie just say the trouble was with Gloria?

Rickie aimed a thumb out the window.

Jarvis leaned around the frame and looked. Snowbanks; parking lot with a few cars, none familiar; seasonal restaurant across the street. "Not sure what you want me to see."

"Check out the red car."

Jarvis couldn't stop his eyes from popping wide. Rickie bought a Ferrari? He must've said it out loud because other patrons turned to peer out also.

"Yeah." Rickie lowered his voice. "Here's the problem. I'm sure Gloria told you my family has money. What she didn't tell you, because she doesn't know, is that all my money is in trust. I get a yearly allowance."

Had he spent it already? How could that be—the new year was only three weeks old.

"I'll tell you about it sometime, but I know you're in a hurry. The problem is that I let Gloria encourage me to buy the car." He put up a palm to stop Jarvis from speaking. "Before you pass judgment—we both loved the car." He gestured at it. "Who wouldn't? So it didn't take much to be talked into it." He gave a smirky grin. "Okay, I admit it, I didn't have the balls to tell her no."

Jarvis nodded. "I think I see your problem. You can't pay for it."

The server arrived pad in-hand. "That's okay," she said. "You can bring the money later."

Rickie and Jarvis laughed. "Thanks for the offer," Rickie

said, "but—"

"You weren't talking to me, right?"

"Right." Once she left with his breakfast order, Rickie lowered his voice. "Not being able to pay for the car is only part of it."

Jarvis saw the problem. "You can't ask Gloria for the money because she thinks you already have it, and if she finds out you lied by omission she'll think you're with her for her money."

"Right. Enough people around town are calling me a male gold digger as it is." He gave a long-suffering sigh. "I'm trying to get my father to give me a raise. I've texted and called but he won't even discuss it. I got so desperate, about a week ago, I sneaked away to see him in person."

"I thought they lived in LA."

"They were heading to Europe via Boston. Seemed like the perfect time to do the son-ly thing." He raked the fingers of both hands through his hair just above his ears. "This is making me a nervous wreck."

"So, what is it you want from me? I sure has heck don't have that kind of money to lend you."

"Advice. I guess I just want you to tell me what to do."

How the heck to give advice to a not-even forty-year-old ex-surfer dating his girlfriend's mother? He settled for a shrug and, "I think you should be honest with Gloria."

Rickie gave a nervous laugh. "Is that the cop or potential in-law speaking?"

Potential in-law! Whoa. That would be a whole other pile of pooh to add to Angelina's woes. "Okay, I have to interrupt to say: in-law?"

Rickie waved a hand as if to say that was a subject for when they had more time.

Jarvis had trouble focusing after that. "This is the friend talking," he managed. "There's a reason they say honesty is the best policy."

"I know. But Gloria will go crazy. You've seen her

condescending attitude toward Angie, well..."

"It's worse with you?"

"Sometimes. She's got an awful inferiority complex."

Jarvis squinted at Rickie. He'd never seen Gloria act inferior about anything.

"She's so jealous of Angie's accomplishments..." Rickie said.

"She ought to say so now and then. Their relationship would be miles different."

"Tell me about it." Rickie finished the last of his coffee and waved off an offer of more. "If Angie knew Gloria's life story..." He sighed. "They really need to have a long talk."

"You mentioned having two problems," Jarvis said.

"We touched on it a second ago. Gloria is pressing for us to get married."

CHAPTER 3

Angie drove to the back lot behind the theater. She hadn't lied to Jarvis; with Tyson gone, there literally were a million things to do.

Last year, to help pay the mortgage and to try to attract new theatergoers, she and Tyson had sectioned off the second floor of the old factory building for rental units. The back half of the structure overlooking the now-frozen Alton Bay would soon be an Italian restaurant operated by a man named Anthony Quattro, owner of three other restaurants in New Hampshire. The street-side of the building had been divided into four smaller spaces for local shop owners. She was careful to park out of the way of the construction vehicles here to work on the restaurant.

As if in response to her thoughts, Mr. Quattro's green Lincoln Navigator appeared in the parking lot. It came to the lower end but didn't pull into a space. It swung in an arc around Angie and stopped. Gray-haired Mr. Quattro left the vehicle idling, climbed from the driver's side, and shut the door. The passenger door opened. A tall, thirtyish woman with long, bottle-blonde hair pulled back in a hairclip made of seashells, strode around the car—gosh, Angie would kill for those boots; they looked like snakeskin—and climbed into the driver's seat. The door shut. The tinted window slid down. The blonde head with cheeks made plump by the big smile, popped into view. An arm, with a bling-covered ring finger, rested on the sill.

Quattro leaned forward and kissed the woman on the cheek. Gee, what was the big deal with May-December romances these days? Was it that hard to find someone closer to your own age?

"See you in two hours!" the blonde called. The big engine gunned and the SUV started up the hill, but stopped almost immediately when Angie's mother's Mercedes appeared on the hill. Had to be Rickie driving; Gloria rarely went that fast.

Mom's car stopped beside Quattro's SUV. Both driver's side windows went down. Angie couldn't understand what was being said, but from the tones, it was clear the two knew each other. Their conversation was short. The Lincoln's window went up. The woman continued on her way. The Mercedes came toward them, now moving slower. It stopped beside Angie. Rickie poked his arm out. Along with it came a bundle of envelopes, mostly manila ones. "Your mother sent me to deliver the mail."

"Where did she get it?"

"At your house. She was there looking for you. She thought you might need it."

Angie was a little confused. And more than a bit peeved. Rather than begin a discussion that would put Rickie in the middle, she thanked him. He raised the window and pulled away, sliding a little on the way up the hill.

Angie started toward the theater.

"So..."

Darn. She'd forgotten Anthony Quattro.

To avoid a discussion with the too-forward man, she continued walking, though slowed a bit.

"Where are you going in such a hurry?" he called.

She stopped and waited for him to catch up. "Good morning, Mr. Quattro."

The well-dressed man shook a gloved finger in the air— the act of a person repeating something for the umpteenth time. "Anthony. Call me Anthony."

Angie wasn't comfortable being on a first-name relationship

with the elder Italian. This man was her tenant. Without Tyson as a male buffer, it was best to keep things formal. Another reason for the formality was because her mother kept inferring that she and Anthony Quattro would make a perfect couple. Which was a total irritation because the idea so blatantly disrespected Angie's relationship with Jarvis.

Angie would be the first to admit she and Jarvis were the quintessential city-girl/country-boy pairing. But it worked for them. Gloria—who had no right at all to criticize other people's relationships—had to accept that. Besides, Mr. Quattro was clearly taken—by the blingy blonde with to-die-for boots.

Angie shook off the distracting images and gestured at the forklift raising a pallet of lumber to the second floor where a deck was being added to the back of the building. "Looks like the work is going well."

"We'll be open for the Memorial Day crowd."

"A lot to get done in five months."

"It's not a problem. I only hire the best crews."

A beat-up green Toyota cruised over the rise at the top of the parking lot and slid into a spot beside Angie's Lexus. The Toyota looked vaguely familiar but it wasn't until the driver got out that she, with conflicting measures of disappointment and delight, recognized the driver as Montez Clarke. Angie hadn't seen him in over two years. All muscles and a Jamaican accent that perked up her hormones, the guy oozed sexuality through every word, nerve ending, and hair follicle.

He'd changed a lot. In particular, he'd cut off his dreadlocks. Montez now sported a buzz cut that let his scalp show through. He wore a black wool pea coat and had grown a new appendage on his left arm: a woman with cocoa color skin and shoulder length hair that looked to have been professionally straightened. The appendage's short skirt displayed way too much leg for the forty-degree temperatures. She leaned into him gripping his hand.

It took Montez a moment to recognize Angie. Had she changed too? A happy expression creased his smooth-skinned face. He stepped forward, easing out of the appendage's grasp, and pulled Angie into a hug. "It's great to see you," he whispered in her ear.

The friendly contact shot pulses of unbridled sensation through her. The pulsations reacted with regret when he let her go and stepped back beside his now-seething girlfriend.

Mr. Quattro's well-groomed mustache turned up at the corners. "I was about to introduce you two, but clearly you already know each other."

The woman mumbled something in a tone everyone ignored.

Montez nodded. He said, "Angie once suspected me of murder," the same time she said, "He saved my life."

For several seconds, the pair of vague explanations hung in the air. Mr. Quattro's eyebrows shot up and then down, his only outward reaction to the ambiguous and yet telling descriptions. Montez's girlfriend though, displayed a series of emotions—none of them positive. Her deep brown eyes had gone to ebony. Her pretty mouth pinched up like she'd eaten a kumquat.

Montez introduced Angie to the girlfriend, who was named Chia.

Really? Chia—like the clay objects people slathered in seeds and waited for them to sprout greenery? Nowadays didn't people eat chia seeds?

"Montez is installing my computer system," Mr. Quattro explained.

"So, you still own the computer shop. That's nice," Angie said. "How's your sister doing?"

"Great. She runs the place now. I spend most of my time on the road doing repairs and installations."

"How is she doing physically?"

"Took a long time, but Shanda's adjusted to being in the wheelchair. Emotionally…" He shrugged. "I told her I might be seeing you—Tony mentioned you owned the building—and she said to say hi."

"Hi back." She turned to Chia. "Do you work with Montez?"

"No, I'm a librarian in Manchester. I started the children's reading program there. Didn't I, Montez?"

His hesitant nod told Angie he had no knowledge of a children's program.

"I used to be a model, didn't I, Montez?"

Another nod and a slight eye-roll from the sexy black man left another awkward pause in the conversation. While the pause stretched, Angie took note of Chia's designer coat and boots—way too expensive for a librarian's salary.

"Tony," Montez continued, "I came to take measurements and draw up some diagrams so I can order supplies."

"Good. I'll show you around. Talk to you later, Angie."

"Nice seeing you," was all she could think of saying. Chia tottered beside Montez on high heels that, in this slush, were broken bones waiting to happen.

Most days, Angie entered through the back entrance, using the two-story stair climb as part of her exercise regimen. Today her mind was awhirl with emotion and two-year-old memories. Montez first appeared in her life on a sunny summer day. He'd awakened emotions that had lain dormant for a very long time. Over the next months she'd thought often of what might've transpired between them if her world hadn't spiraled out of control that same day.

To keep from walking up the stairs behind Montez's oh-so-perfect Levi-clad rear end, she slogged through driveway slush up the hill to the front of the building. Once inside, business as usual ousted further conscious thoughts of Montez Clarke. The answering machine contained several messages: two advertisers requesting copy before the afternoon deadline; the cleaner announcing the drapes for the ticket booth were ready; and the printer reminding her that the new business cards needed proofing.

In her office, while fifteen copies of the latest script printed, Angie responded to the messages. Then she stapled the scripts together and carried them into the main theater. The cast had arrived.

Prince & Pauper Theater maintained a payroll that included costume designer Blanche, a technical director, a carpenter, a janitor, and a half-dozen actors. The six actors were assigned most of the roles in every performance. But to involve the general public, and to keep things fresh, parts were assigned to outsiders, people who lived and worked in the community. For this show, they'd only cast one outsider—Stone Powers.

The leading man now sat with his feet dangling over the edge of the stage facing the rest of the cast, who either sat or mingled around the front row. Everyone was laughing. Angie would bet it was over some story Stone had told.

He drew a small vial from his shirt pocket, opened the top and tilted back his head to deposit a drop in each nostril. He sniffed to draw the drops deeper, then closed the cap and returned the bottle to his pocket. Stone greeted Angie's arrival with an enthusiastic wave.

She pulled in a breath to help keep her nerves from spilling over. Till now, Tyson had tackled the production end of things. He had a talent for handling people and knew the ins and outs of play structure better than she did. Angie sucked in another breath. This was her baby now. She could put on her big-girl panties and do it.

At least that's what everyone kept saying.

Angie blew out the breath and moved down the aisle, every eye watching her approach.

Before a cascade of emotions sent her running back up the aisle, Angie spent a few minutes describing the basic plot, most of which took place at a construction site, and the theme— that anything could be accomplished if you put your mind to it. A perfect lesson for her. As she answered various questions, she realized a second thing: the nerves were gone.

Emboldened, Angie passed out scripts then pulled herself up to sit on the stage six feet to Stone's right, tucking her skirt around her thighs.

STONE COLD SOBER

They wouldn't read any lines today. That was scheduled for tomorrow once everyone had time to go over the script. While the cast thumbed the pages, she discussed the characters and their relationships to each other. Angie, about to call the meeting to an end, re-stressed the play's theme, which sent Stone into a short story of his own experience in accomplishing something through hard work. It—as did most of his stories—ended on a humorous note.

A door opened at the top of the auditorium, putting an abrupt halt to the cast's laughter. Daylight carved a trapezoid of light on the right side of the room. A silhouetted female figure stopped in the doorway as if waiting for her eyes to adjust to the darkness. Then she strode down the aisle. Angie didn't miss the fact that Stone had turned—no pun intended—into stone.

Angie slid off the stage and met the newcomer at the end of the first row of seats, not recognizing her until she stepped into the circle of light thrown by a bulb in the orchestra pit. Montez's Chia pet.

"I got bored upstairs," she said. "I was wandering around. I hope you don't mind."

Her animosity toward Angie seemed to have disappeared. "Well, this is a closed rehears—" Angie started to say, but Chia's attention focused on something behind Angie.

A smile broke onto her face. She laughed. She brushed past Angie, jostling her arm. "Oh. My. God!" Chia flung herself at Stone. The script clutched in his left hand, fluttered to the floor. "I can't believe you're here," Chia crooned.

After a short reunion, Chia and Stone broke apart. He stooped to retrieve the script.

Angie repeated Anthony Quattro's words from earlier, "I'd been about to introduce you, but clearly you know each other."

"Well, of course we know each other. Rocky is my husband!" Chia announced.

CHAPTER

Rocky? Stone? Husband?

Angie felt like she'd stepped into an episode of Twilight Zone.

No. She cast the thoughts aside. She didn't have time—and if she were honest, didn't have the courage—to ask questions about Blanche and Stone's marital status. Or Chia and Rocky's relationship. She also did not want to know how Montez fit into the picture. She did want to think about how it might all affect the theater. Chia's left ring finger was bare. No pale skin from which one had been removed. Same thing with Stone.

Angie made direct eye contact with him as she sent the cast home to study their scripts. He didn't avoid her. Didn't look embarrassed to have been caught with a second woman. Man, the guy had balls. Either that or there were extenuating circumstances. Yes, that must be it. One of the couples was divorced and had remained friends. It happened all the time these days.

"See you tomorrow at nine," Angie said to the cast, who shouted goodbyes and scattered in all directions.

"I have to get my things in the green room," Stone said, mostly to Chia.

The green room was a catchall area. It spread the width of the building behind the stage; it was connected to the stage and the theater via identical hallways on each end. The hallways ended in three steps on either side of the stage that descended into the audience area.

Stone and Chia took the ones to the left of the stage. Their silhouettes were swallowed in the dark hallway.

Angie started up the aisle to proof the sample of business cards that waited in the ticket office. A large figure blocked the doorway. The figure cleared its throat. Unless Angie missed her guess, it was Mr. Quattro. She continued toward him. "What's up?" she asked.

"Two things. I have your rent check. Totally forgot earlier."

Probably because he was distracted by High-maintenance Blingy-boot Lady. "Thanks. I'll get you a receipt from my office."

"You can give it to me tomorrow. I really came back for a quick question. Will you have dinner with me tonight?"

A combination of thoughts zipped through her. First: how dare he? Second: what balls. Third: How dare he!

"There's a great new place up in Meredith," he continued. "I thought we could try it."

"Mr. Quattro…"

"Anthony."

She shook her head. The movement broke the anger-bubble into smaller, less noxious, pieces. "I have to say I'm tongue-tied. That woman…in your car…"

Quattro threw back his head and laughed. "She's my daughter. Amber has just moved back to New Hampshire from California—she's an avid surfer. Was coach of the team there."

"Surfer?" Angie grasped onto the topic change like a drowning swimmer to a life-ring. "My mom's boyfriend is from California, born in Hawaii. He was a surfer too." They looked to be about the same age but Angie didn't say anything, mostly due to questions that would arise regarding her mom's age.

"I bet they'd have a lot to talk about. We'll have to introduce them."

Wait. They had met, this morning. Rickie bringing the un-asked-for mail; Amber dropping off Daddy.

"Anyway," Mr. Quattro continued, "Amber's husband's job

keeps him mostly on the east coast. They figured they could see more of each other if she moved out this way. Luck was on her side. She's an ER nurse and, as coincidence will have it, Lakes Region General had an opening."

"It must be nice to have her close again."

"I'm loving it. She's on her way to do some furniture shopping. She rented an apartment in Northwood."

"Until now, you must have gotten to know her husband pretty well."

He nodded. "Allen and I have become quite close. Ms. Deacon, now that we've cleared the obstacle of my daughter, what about dinner?"

One of Angie's anger-bubbles refueled. "I guess you're overlooking the fact that I'm seeing Colby Jarvis."

He tilted his head at her. "Your mother indicated the relationship wasn't that serious."

Angie shook away the anti-mom words that wanted to spew forth. "My mother is wrong. I'll have the rent receipt for you later." She headed for her office, feeling Mr. Quattro's eyes on her backside. The irony of the fact that she'd done the same thing with Montez earlier wasn't lost on her.

She didn't want to go through the green room right now. She didn't want to hear what might be going on between Stone and Chia—but couldn't get to her office any other way. But Angie stiffened her spine, adjusted her big-girl panties, and went backstage.

Stone and Chia stood in front of his locker on the left-side wall, talking softly. Their manner seemed congenial. Angie walked past them. Her office was off a small hallway at the back of the green room. The old office, that is. A new one was being constructed on the second floor next to Mr. Quattro's soon-to-be restaurant. The new office would have two things the old office didn't—a view of the bay and privacy. This office was tucked into a space the size of a closet. Once she moved upstairs, this area would be turned into a kitchenette. Appliances and cabinets had already been ordered.

Angie filed the rent check for deposit, wrote out a receipt, then printed two more copies of the script to give the set builder who was due to arrive in twelve minutes. With the scripts tucked under her arm, she locked the office door but stopped at the sound of Chia's voice talking to Stone. "I thought you were on the road."

"Delayed it a bit while I tried out for the show," Stone answered.

"Where have you been staying?" Chia's tone wasn't curious; it was accusatory.

"Motel," he said. "I didn't want to drive back and forth to Manchester."

"It's not that far."

"It's too far to commute."

"Okay, I'll accept that—grudgingly. Now tell me why you didn't let me know."

"I thought I'd surprise you. Now can we go?"

When there was no response, Angie moved into sight. Stone hadn't moved from in front of his locker. He wore his jacket and had a briefcase of sorts—okay, a man-purse—slung over a shoulder. Chia stood close to his side just as she'd done with Montez earlier. Wow. And she dared act as though Stone—no, wait, she called him Rocky—had been doing something less than kosher by staying here in Alton! Some days she thought she'd never understand people.

Footsteps sounded in the hall. Angie expected the carpenter/set designer—a squat thirty-five year old man with a bushy red mustache—to enter, but Montez stepped into the room.

Oh gosh. She wished Tyson were here. He wasn't big and burly, but he'd make a better buffer than her fearsome thoughts.

Montez spotted Chia and smiled. Looked like he'd been searching for her. Seeing her standing up-close-and-personal with Stone, his lips flattened into a straight line. Angie remembered that same tightness the night he'd saved her from a mugger. He'd focused that anger first on the mugger and then on her for letting herself get caught in such a situation.

The air in the room changed. Stone's face morphed from friendly to confused, lips clenched between his teeth. Chia's hands jammed into the pockets of her coat. Angie considered stepping between the three people in case they decided to take things out on her green room. But then elected—quite wisely, she thought—to stay where she was. Insurance premiums had been paid.

Questioning, Stone glanced from Chia to Montez, to Chia and then to Angie.

Montez's tight face was making the same back and forth shifts. Chia simply stood there wearing a mask of confusion. No wait—that was terror.

Those accusations she'd thrown at Stone must be circling in her head like a tornado. And they were about to be vomited right back at her. Montez's eyebrows went up and then down—a question to Chia: what the hell's going on?

"I guess I forgot to mention." Her voice was meek. "Rocky is my husband."

With no change in expression or demeanor, Montez gave a nod and stood back a half step so the couple could pass. Stone flinched, probably expecting to be clobbered from behind by a muscular black man carrying a loop of cable wire over a shoulder.

Angie had only known Montez for a short time two years ago. At that time, even in the face of his best friend's murder and his subsequent arrest, he'd kept his emotions under tight rein, but in this situation, she wondered if those emotions might break free.

To his credit, he remained there, arms stiff at his sides, until the sound of Chia and Stone's footsteps faded out the front of the building.

"Shit, that was a surprise," he said.

Understatement. "Are you all right?" she asked.

"You ever know me not to be?"

"No. I guess I never have." There was always a first time.

Especially where love was concerned.

More footsteps sounded in the hall. What now?

Had Stone returned to gloat, or maybe to fight for his woman? Montez's only reaction was a single clench and unclench of both fists by his sides.

This didn't bode well. But it was Jarvis who stepped in.

Just what she needed, more testosterone in her air space.

Jarvis carried a tray of drinks in one hand and a bulky white to-go bag in the other. Was it lunchtime already? She guessed the saying was true, that time flew when you were having fun. Argh.

Jarvis set the containers on the table, removed that ever-present deerstalker hat, and stepped forward, hand extended to Montez.

Montez shook his hand. "Nice to see you, man. How's the copping business?"

"Same old, same old." Jarvis shrugged. "Till we get all the bad guys..."

Was that comment directed at Montez? She wouldn't be surprised to find out that it was. Men!

"Well, it's been nice to see you again, Angie," Montez said. "I'll be going."

"You don't have to leave on my account," Jarvis said.

"I was on the way out anyway."

"Sorry for what happened," Angie said.

"Wasn't your fault." Montez wiggled two fingers in the air at her. "See you 'round."

Once he'd gone, Jarvis seated himself at the long green room table and opened the paper sack. "What did you have to be sorry about?"

"Hold on. Be right back." She hurried to the front door and locked it. Then she did the same to the back door waving to the departing Jamaican. Locked doors would provide time to relax, and make decisions. If Stone was truly a bigamist, he was breaking the law. She was pretty sure multiple wives was illegal in every state—except maybe Utah or Nebraska. Wasn't that where Mormons lived?

In the green room, she sat and watched with great consternation as Jarvis unwrapped two enormous sandwiches and laid them side-by-side on the table.

"Your eyes are wide as saucers," he said. "You can't be surprised by these, we've had them many times before."

"Yes."

"So, what's got your panties in a wad?"

She laughed at his comment—being that it so closely related to her recent thoughts of big-girl panties. "If I tell you something, will you promise, as a cop, to do nothing about it?"

He raked his fingers through thinning hair. "Can't lie to you. It depends."

"Could you at least promise to put a hold on reporting it?"

"For how long?"

"Let's not battle over semantics. This could be serious. Might be." She shook her head. "I'm not sure. What I really need is your advice."

He gave a phony long-suffering sigh that made her laugh. Angie explained about Stone's suspected marital goings-on. At first Jarvis laughed. Then he realized the dilemma facing them.

She explained how the information had come to light. "Montez took the news well. I can imagine how he felt. I mean, I'm furious with Stone myself. I don't even know what to do."

He got up and paced, eating the sandwich as he walked and talking through mouthfuls. After about a mile around the long, narrow table, he said, "I get why you're confused. So am I…" He left the sentence hanging but it didn't need closure.

"Believe me, I'm really angry he could do such a thing, but what good would it do to report him?" She thumped the heel of a hand on the table. "They're really not hurting anything." Angie cupped her face in her hands. "Can't believe I just said that."

"You're thinking about the show."

"If we could just get through it…" She looked up. "Besides, right this minute, we aren't sure he's a bigamist. There might be an explanation."

"Could be. But you also know this could blow up in our faces..."

She did. The last case they'd been involved with ended only two weeks ago, and had ruined several lives. Emotionally it sucked her dry. Now, with Tyson gone and full responsibility of the theater on her hands, not to mention her mother and toy-boy still in town, Angie didn't want to employ what Hercule Poirot called "zee leettle gray cells" on anything more than reading the bundle of script submissions that arrived every day.

"So, what brought Montez here?"

How very carefully Jarvis worded the question. In the past, they'd had trouble related to his jealousy—so much so that he'd was seeing a therapist.

"Mr. Quattro and the new shop owners hired him to set up their computer systems." Might as well say it—she knew he was thinking it. "He'll be back and forth a lot in the next few weeks."

They ate in surprisingly companionable silence for several minutes. Her mind was abuzz with thoughts of Stone's possible bigamy. She couldn't tell what was going on in Jarvis's head, but he didn't seem upset or suspicious, or jealous. Maybe those sessions with the therapist were helping. Or maybe, like her, he couldn't stop thinking about Stone. Still, he was usually more talkative, relating things that happened at work, family stories his friend and co-worker Ambrose Wilson told...

"You going to eat that whole sandwich?" he asked.

"Um, no. I'm not sure I can even finish this piece."

He snagged the untouched half.

"You're very quiet today."

"Uh, yeah. Before you ask, nothing's wrong. Just stuff going on at work."

The squeak of the front door presaged another person's arrival. It had to be Kiana, Angie's seventeen-year old protégé, the only other person who had a key.

With her dark skin and regal bearing, Kiana Smith was

perfection in motion. Tall, with a grace belying someone much older, she looked like an Indian princess. They had met while Angie was standing in for a murdered drama teacher and been so impressed with Kiana's drive and abilities that she offered the girl a job. Her first performance had garnered no less than three ovations. Angie's inbox had been engorged with raves, not to mention reviews in two local papers had attracted reporters from the southern part of the state, an area much more popular for community theater.

Kiana flourished her big furry hat from her head and fluffed her shiny black hair. She greeted Jarvis and turned down his offer to go pick up more food.

"Sorry I missed the meeting this morning," she said. "I was at my old high school."

"How's the play coming along?" Angie asked.

"Pretty well. We were working through a few glitches and sort of lost track of time."

"No problem. You didn't miss much." Liar! "I got the cast members acquainted with each other. Passed out copies of the script. Everything went smoothly."

Jarvis's bark of laughter had both women turning to him. "Only you would consider this morning as smooth."

Kiana regarded him a moment then pursed her lips at Angie, who explained about the appearance of Stone's two wives.

Kiana's first reaction was to giggle. "Wow. That could create some major fireworks."

"I'll make sure there's a fire extinguisher in every corner," Angie said.

"Wait. Isn't that illegal?" Kiana asked.

"I think fire extinguishers are a requirement," Jarvis said. Both women shot him a smirk.

"What are you going to do?" Kiana asked him.

"Nothing. For the time being."

"Maybe you need to talk to Stone."

"Yeah," Angie said.

"Okay, so, what do you need me to do today?"

"You could take inventory of the storeroom, and the office, and place an order. All I know for sure is that we need printer paper. Maybe you pick up the draperies at the cleaners. They're ready. Otherwise, things are under control for the moment."

Kiana tilted her head toward Angie.

"What's that look for?" Angie asked. "You dare disbelieve me twice in a row? You don't think I can handle this?"

"I not only know you can, I have seen you in action. I also know there are things you'd rather not do. Things I can, and want, to do. So, bury me."

Angie couldn't help laughing. "Okay. I guess there are some things." She named a couple of menial tasks: a trip to the post office, proofing the business cards, and a phone call to the recycling company, then added one she knew Kiana loved: a visit to a local thrift shop to seek out jewelry, hats, and handbags—inexpensive accouterments for their inventory.

Rather than appear pleased at the new responsibility, Kiana threw her a smirk. "Is that the best you can do?"

"All right. You asked for it." Angie went to her office and retrieved a box, which she thumped on the long green room table.

Kiana's face lit with glee.

Probably afraid Angie would change her mind, Kiana yanked on her hat and picked up the box. "I'll see you at nine in the morning," she shouted over her shoulder.

"That girl is a whirlwind," Jarvis said around a mouthful of roast beef.

"A treasure. She wouldn't complain if I asked her to clean the bathroom at your house."

"Very funny. What was in the box? She acted like you gave her diamonds."

"Scripts. We receive two or three every day. She's been begging to pre-read them—you know, filter out the bad ones."

Jarvis nodded, probably recalling the wonderful play Kiana had written last year—her senior year—for her school to perform. A play intended to bring in revenue to save the drama program. After Kiana's graduation, and Angie's offer of a starring role in their fall production, she'd elected to defer college for a year.

"Will she write rejection letters too?" Jarvis asked. He knew it was a chore Angie hated.

"I sure hope so."

They ate in silence for a moment. Angie's mind wandered back to Montez Clarke. He'd come to New Hampshire when he was young, so he didn't speak with a Jamaican dialect, but the accent still infused his words and turned Angie's insides to goo. She wondered how he'd felt learning his girlfriend was married. The fist-clenching showed the emotion was there in spite of his denial. She prayed it would remain under wraps. Things would probably be okay if Chia stayed away from the theater.

The sound of Jarvis crumpling paper and jamming it into the to-go bag made her turn.

"What'll you do if Kiana goes off to college in the fall?" he asked.

"I'm thinking of sending her."

Jarvis frowned. "Say what?"

"She was offered a partial scholarship to go to Greensboro College—they're the ones who agreed to defer for a year. Seeing that Kiana is adopted and her parents can't afford to send her, I'm thinking of paying the rest of her tuition."

"Greensboro? The one in North Carolina? That'll seriously affect her ability to commute." Then he seemed to realize what Angie meant. "Oh, I get it. You want her to bring that education back here." He ate another bite of lunch. "Aren't you afraid she'll move on to greener pastures?"

"It's a chance I'm willing to take. Personally, I think she'll remain loyal. I'd be happy if she even stayed a few years." Angie wondered if he was thinking the same thing—that she'd expected Tyson to stay around too. Then at Christmas, he'd dropped the bombshell about heading to Broadway.

Angie pushed away the last of her sandwich. Like a vulture searching for road kill, Jarvis snatched it up and finished it in four bites.

Something told Angie there was another bomb about to hit the building. She hoped for as little fallout as possible.

By three o'clock, nothing had happened. She called it a day and went home to the condo. She'd just started a load of laundry and hauled the vacuum from the hall closet when her mother whooshed in. Gloria rarely showed up without calling first. And she never came without a specific reason. Hopefully, this had nothing to do with Angie and a relationship with the rich, handsome Anthony Quattro. God knew she'd fielded that argument often enough.

By the time Angie brewed a pot of herbal tea, it was clear her mother hadn't come as a matchmaker. Something else was about to detonate. And it didn't take long for the grenade to go off.

"I think Rickie is seeing someone else."

If anyone had offered a million dollars for her to predict her mother's words, these never would've been on her lips. Months ago, if something had happened to separate Rickie and her mom, she would've been glad. Their near-thirty-year age difference had bothered her immensely. But Jarvis helped her realize it was their business. Their problem. And though totally mismatched they got along well. Apparently, until now.

Okay, Mom came to unburden herself. Angie wondered if she had time to run to the bathroom and don a clean pair of big-girl panties. "Mom, Rickie loves you." Angie slid onto the stool next to Gloria. "He wouldn't cheat on you."

Gloria sipped and set the cup on the counter.

"What makes you think he's up to something?" Angie asked.

"Last week, he sneaked off. He was gone a whole day."

"And?"

"When I asked where he'd been, he said he went for a drive in his new car and got lost."

New car? Nope, don't ask. "Mom, people do that sometimes. And remember Rickie doesn't know the area. He might really have gotten lost—"

"The car's got built-in GPS."

Uh-oh. "You know how men are. He probably took the longest route possible. Maybe he stopped for gas and got into a car conversation. You know how long those can last. Wait. New car?"

Gloria broke into a grin. "He bought a Ferrari."

"A Ferrari. In New Hampshire?"

"We won't always be here."

Thank you, God.

"He hasn't wanted sex lately."

Oh man, Angie didn't want to be having this conversation with anyone, most especially her mother. Once, as a teen, she tried to have a sex talk with her, Gloria made an excuse that she needed milk and rushed out to the corner store. She was gone two hours.

Okay, big-girl panties—do your job. "Mom, there are a lot of reasons people might not want to…to do it. You don't need me to tell you that."

"I know."

"Why not set up a romantic evening? You know: candles, dinner. Put on your best perfume and a sexy evening dress. You know, a strapless gown—like you wear for opening nights."

"Does that work with Jarvis?"

Yes! "Our sex life isn't up for discussion here. You need to talk to Rickie."

"I tried. He walked out."

"Try during a calm moment. When you're doing something mundane like watching TV." And not while you're anywhere near this house or the theater. "Surprise him with it, if you know what I mean."

"There's another thing."

Damn.

"He won't introduce me to his family. In spite of his

assurances to the contrary, I think he's embarrassed about our age difference."

An hour later, Gloria left. They hadn't resolved any of her issues, but hopefully she felt better for having gotten them off her chest.

Angie for sure didn't feel better. Now, every time she saw either of them, she'd think of sexless evenings. And new cars. When had that happened? Could Rickie be having a mid-life crisis in his forties? Was it too early for a stiff drink?

Or four.

CHAPTER 5

Jarvis spent the rest of the afternoon in solitude at the station. He felt almost guilty knowing the chaos Angelina was going through at work. Nothing he could do about any of that though. He considered calling her at home; she should be there by now. But she needed downtime to relax and not think. About the theater, about bigamy, or even about himself.

Trouble was, besides Angelina, all he could think about was Montez. There was something about him—and Angelina—but until the situation was clear, it was best not to think about him at all. Then there was Rickie and his money troubles. Oh, to have that kind of problem.

It was almost his quitting time when a call came in from dispatch. "Jarvis, there's some trouble at the pharmacy. A car just crashed into the building."

"Anyone injured?"

"No but there's a shouting match going on in the parking lot between the driver and the manager."

Jarvis slapped on hat and jacket, scurried to his Jeep and sped to the location. Sure enough, a man wearing a white shirt and a nametag that identified him as a store employee waved him toward the commotion—which was pretty dumb because other than the crowd in that one spot near the building, the lot was just about empty.

Jarvis leaped from the vehicle, elbowed through the crowd

of gawkers, and hurried toward the pair of shouting people in the center. The woman was about thirty years old and very short. His first thought was that she probably had to sit on a box to see out the windshield. He wouldn't be surprised to learn her height was the cause of the accident.

She shook her fist at the man who also wore a nametag with the store's logo. He heaved a sigh of relief seeing Jarvis. "Look what she did." The man—the nametag indicated he was Manager Kelton—gestured redundantly at the car resting several inches inside the cinder block wall, which indicated it had hit at a pretty good clip. The clear, dry pavement said the accident wasn't weather-related. The impact must've shaken the building to the core; thankfully, the thick blocks remained in place.

Jarvis pulled out his notebook and a pen, and used his cell phone to snap some pictures.

"I told you I didn't mean it."

When the man only shouted four-letter words in her direction, the woman turned her attention to Jarvis.

"My foot slipped off the brake."

"You did it on purpose," Kelton said.

On purpose? What was that all about? Jarvis aimed a quizzical expression at the man. "For two days she's been fighting with one of my clerks."

"That's not true!" She lunged at Kelton, fists flying. Jarvis got hold of them and pulled them behind her back. In a flash, the cuffs kept her in place.

"She caught him cheating on her," the man went on, undaunted, though a smirk twitched the corners of his mouth.

"Did not."

"Yesterday she was chasing him up and down the aisles. I had to throw her bodily from the building."

"That wasn't me. I was at work all day yesterday."

The man heaved a sigh that must've cleared every ounce of air from his lungs. He spun on a heel and went into the store. Jarvis busied himself writing down the woman's pertinent information. Then he took statements from two witnesses and phoned headquarters for a tow truck. When Kelton had been gone ten minutes, Jarvis wondered if he'd absolved himself of the situation altogether. He was about to go inside and retrieve the man to get the store's information when Kelton towed a red-faced clerk by the shirtsleeve.

"Tell the cop what happened yesterday."

The man related a situation similar, but in more colorful detail, than Kelton's. Before he finished, the woman launched herself at him calling him some names even Jarvis didn't know and tried to head-butt him. Jarvis grasped the woman's wrists before she could hurt someone, then helped the woman into his Jeep. He'd just locked the door when the tow truck pulled in. They all stood around as it—over her screeches about injustice—hooked onto her car.

Once back in the Jeep, he was subjected to a screaming tirade from the small woman. He climbed from the vehicle, made a show of shutting the door, and completed the paperwork on the still-warm hood. The sound of shouting—two voices at a distance this time—intruded on his thoughts. Without moving his head, he glanced up. On the far side of the parking lot stood a man and woman in a heated discussion across the hood of their vehicle. They didn't seem ready to come to blows so he finished writing the report. Jarvis figured he'd cruise past the couple on the way back to headquarters.

When he got back in the Jeep, the woman in the backseat, and the couple at the end of the lot were still shouting. Jarvis shot a frosty glare into the back. "If you don't stop that, I'm going to lock you in a cell with the town drunk. He gets amorous when he's been drinking."

They didn't have a town drunk but the threat worked. She clammed up, sagged in the corner, and found something to look at outside the window.

He drove toward the other couple, stopping to let a car pass. The arguing couple had crossed around to the front of the car. The man's back was to him. Jarvis had a full-on view of the woman, a tiny thing—couldn't have stood over five feet. A little on the plump side, with long black hair and Asian features. She had one fist in the air and was shaking it at the man. About to strike him or driving home a point?

Jarvis lowered the passenger side window and leaned across. "Everything all right here, folks?"

She lowered her hand and gripped the strap of her shoulder bag. "Yes, I was just leaving." Her voice, with its Boston accent, was as small as her size. She spun around, heaved the shoulder bag through the window of a blue mini Cooper with a British flag painted on the rooftop, and flung herself inside. As expected, the door slammed.

Jarvis waited for some acknowledgement or reaction from the man. Finally he turned and bent his head into the window. "Just a little exuberant conversation."

The men recognized each other at the same time. This was none other than Prince & Pauper's new leading man, Stone Powers.

"That's the first time I've heard such a loud fight called an exuberant conversation," Jarvis laughed.

Stone gave a combination palms-up gesture and two-shoulder shrug. Jarvis's "Who is she?" came out the same time as Stone's, "Seeya." He slithered into a silver BMW and sped away before Jarvis could say anything more.

"How come you didn't arrest them?" asked the woman from the backseat.

She had to be kidding. "They weren't beating on each other."

"I wasn't— Well, he deserved it."

Jarvis didn't reply, mostly because he remained in a baffled state all the way to the station. Stone Powers arguing with an Asian woman. He didn't like where his thoughts were headed.

It was after midnight when he let himself into Angelina's condo. He tiptoed into the foyer, holding tight to Red's collar. The big Irish setter wiggled all over in anticipation of seeing her mistress. Normally Angelina would still be awake, but with such a hectic schedule, she'd been sleeping deeper and longer. He made the dog sit on the ceramic tile so he could wipe her feet. One thing Angelina would not stand for was paw- or footprints on the white carpet.

As he unzipped his jacket, the hallway light came on. He suffered a moment of guilt for waking her but, god, she looked gorgeous silhouetted there—the light made a halo above her naturally blonde hair. He told her so, which made her laugh.

Jarvis gave Red permission to get up. She ran to Angelina for a hug.

"How was the game?" she asked.

"We won." He pulled her close, tussled her sleep-tousled hair, then kissed her deeply.

"You go alone? Want a beer or something?"

"No thanks, we stopped for a couple after the game."

"Who's we?"

"Rickie. After that, I went home to walk Red but she said she wanted to see you."

Angelina laughed, shuffled to the fridge to pour some juice for herself, then she got a treat for the dog. "What was it you wanted to tell me?"

"What gives you the idea I had something to say? Isn't it possible that Red really did want to see you?"

She rubbed the dog's head. "Totally possible. But you're too considerate to wake me so late unless there's something on your mind." She sat on one of the barstools. "Want a beer?"

"I'll get it." He went to the fridge, ignoring her smirk. Jarvis took the other seat while twisting the top from the beer. "Are you saying I've been thoughtless to you?"

"Oh stop. You know what I meant."

Should he tell her about Rickie's visit that morning? He hadn't been sworn to secrecy or anything. It had bothered him all evening. How did couples keep secrets like that from each other? He didn't recall a dilemma like this while he was married to Liz.

No, Rickie's secret should probably remain between them

for now. But Jarvis could talk about Stone's wives, which he knew would have Angelina's complete attention.

"I told Rickie about Stone and the wives."

"I bet he thought it was cool."

"How much would you bet?"

She laughed. "By the way you said that, I'd better back off while I'm ahead."

"Good, 'cause you'd lose. He was mad—said it was… what'd he say—sacrilegious."

"What did you decide about it."

"I'm waiting until I have more information."

"What did Rickie say?"

"I got a lecture about the sanctity of relationships." He waved the hand holding the bottle. Some beer sloshed on his sleeve." He wiped at it with a finger but only made the spot wider. He grasped her free hand resting on the counter. "He really went into a rant over it."

"You think he did it for your benefit? Because of the trouble between he and Mom?"

"You know about that?" He was excited for a second hoping to get the issue off his chest. Not that Angelina would have any more answers than him…

She frowned. "Yes, but I-I don't think we should talk about it. If they wanted us to both know, they would've mentioned it while we were together." She shook her head. "I can't believe the man's spent a years keeping two wives hidden. I can't stop thinking how stressful that's got to be."

Talking about stress—that should be an easy conversational slide into talk about Rickie and his car troubles. Especially since she already knew. Still, something held Jarvis back. The information had been divulged in confidence. Wasn't it?

Just then the phone rang. He and Angelina frowned at each other. She stood and moved toward the wall phone. "I always go into a panic when the phone rings this late. It's never good news." She lifted the cordless handset. "Hello…hi Mom." She rolled her eyes at Jarvis who turned away so she wouldn't see his grin. "He's not? Wait, Jarvis is here, I'll ask him." She moved the phone aside. "Did you drop Rickie at home?"

He shook his head. "We went in his car."

Angelina relayed the information to her mother. Jarvis mimed phoning, which meant he'd call to see if anyone had been in an accident or, heaven forbid, arrested. She nodded.

"Jarvis is phoning headquarters. I'll call you back, okay?"

Jarvis made the call to the dispatcher who said she'd had no reports but would send someone to check the road leading to HeavenScent, and she'd also get in touch with the hospital and let him know.

They sat in nervous silence, waiting for the phone to ring again. It did within five minutes. The news was good, but not satisfying. Rickie's Ferrari hadn't been found; no accidents, arrests or hospital admittances were reported.

Angelina called her mother back.

So, where was Rickie Kennedy? When he dropped Jarvis at his house, Jarvis assumed he'd go straight home. Actually, he said he was exhausted. That made sense—emotional stress took a lot out of a person. Sure was doing a number on him tonight.

"Want me to come there and wait?" Angelina asked her mother. "You sure? I can throw on some clothes and be there in ten minutes…No, Jarvis only got here a few minutes ago from the game…They stopped for a couple of beers…Are you sure?…Okay, let us know when he gets home, will you? Doesn't matter what time."

"What a day," he said after she hung up. She was still gazing at the phone. "So, go over anyway," he said.

She faced him. "No, I know it sounds inconsiderate, but I couldn't face being with her right now. Somehow this whole thing would turn into my fault."

He started to ask how, then realized: he'd invited Rickie to the game. If Angie had been a better girlfriend, she'd have him there at the condo with her, or would've gone to the game. Jarvis couldn't help grinning.

"It's not funny."

"You'll laugh about it tomorrow."

"Where do you think he went?" She dropped back into her chair.

"Probably took a joy ride around the lake. That car moves like a dream."

"Don't get any ideas."

He laughed. "Can't afford ideas like that." Would it be the wrong time to change the subject? He didn't want her to think he was insensitive but he had a pretty good idea this thing between Gloria and Rickie wouldn't solve itself quickly. "Had an interesting call at work today. A car drove into the pharmacy building."

She rose from the stool and headed toward the bedroom. "I hope nobody was hurt. Thanks for telling me."

They shared a chuckle over the inane subject and Angelina sat back on her stool. "What were you going to say?"

"Nobody was hurt—the point I was leading up to was, as I was leaving, two people were arguing across the other side of the parking lot. I drove past assuming they'd break it up when they saw me, and they did. The woman got in her car and left. The interesting part is the man's identity—Stone Powers."

Angelina pushed the glass of juice aside and sat up straighter. "Who was the woman? I assume since you didn't mention that either of them was Blanche or Chia, it must've been someone else."

"Yup."

"Did you ask him about her?"

"Tried to. He was in the car and shooting from the parking lot before I got the words out of my mouth."

"So you went back to the station and checked her license plate number."

He grinned. She knew him so well. "The car is registered to Miata Lin Powers. Age 29. Born Wilmington, Delaware. No arrests or warrants."

"Dare I suggest, maybe she's his sister?"

"She's Asian."

Angelina didn't reply. That meant her brain was working double-time. He expected a revelation, anger, or something from her but all she said was, "Is there such a word as trigamist?"

He shrugged, knowing she didn't expect an answer. She had a thousand times better vocabulary than him. If there were such a word she'd know before him.

"This is so…amazing. No—wrong word—this is shocking."

"It could be just coincidence, you know. The woman could be somebody he works—or worked—with."

"Sure. And she just happens to have the same last name."

Jarvis let a shrug be his answer. "I saw Stone again tonight. He and Blanche were at the bar where Rickie and I stopped. They were in a corner, heads bent together over a couple of drinks. Looked like they were enjoying themselves. I went over to talk for a second because I knew you'd pump me like an oil well once I mentioned seeing them."

She gave him a smack on the arm.

"They'd gone to a movie, then stopped for dessert and drinks on the way home. He didn't seem concerned that he had an early flight in the morning."

"Not a big issue. You can nap on the plane."

Jarvis laughed. "Yeah, because once you're home—in whichever house—the wife isn't gonna let you sleep."

"Jarvis, I get the point. You think it's possible the Asian lady is really another wife?"

"Well…" Jarvis channeled his logical, calculating side. "He said he's on the road two weeks a month. I bet most of his job can be done on the phone and online." He pointed an index finger at her. "There are four weeks in most every month. If he spends a few days with each wife…"

"Or sleeping." Angelina finished her juice. "This afternoon the Chia pet—the one who arrived glued to Montez's left arm—seemed surprised to see Stone. She asked where he'd been staying and why he hadn't come home. He used the excuse that it was too far to commute."

"To Manchester? What did she say to that?"

"It was clear she didn't believe him, but didn't want to argue in front of us. She just asked why he hadn't called."

"Is it possible he's not actually married to any of them? That there's another explanation? You know—wife in name only." Jarvis was having a hard time wrapping his head around being married to more than one woman. Though his devilish side thought it might be fun, there'd be far more problems than it could ever be worth.

"I know sometimes people divorce and still refer to each other as husband and wife. I could accept that possibility if she hadn't expected him to be home with her."

"It does sound like they're married," he admitted. "I can't think of any other explanations. Except…"

"Maybe Miata is a sister. Adopted or foster."

"Tomorrow—er, later today—I'll check marriage records."

"Remember, you promised to keep this private."

He kissed her cheek. "I'm doing the best I can. I hope you realized that if there's a chance of three wives, and they're all right here in town—"

"I know but—"

"Wait. Not finished. And some developing conflict…"

"I know what you mean. What do you think we should do?" Angelina took the glass to the dishwasher, a signal the discussion was moving to the bedroom. He polished off the rest of the beer and followed her down the hall.

"I don't know yet. My gut says report it. What they're doing is illegal. It's just that I'll feel awful if I'm the one to ruin your first solo production." He kissed her again, this time on the lips. "I just hope this mess doesn't explode in all our faces. Especially not in your theater.

She removed her robe and hung it on the back of the bathroom door. Moonlight shining through the slatted windows made the nightgown just about invisible. It silhouetted her body in gold. Thoughts of trigamists popped like champagne bubbles.

CHAPTER 6

Seven o'clock, Angie had finished her morning run, was showered and heading out the door when her mother's car swooshed in beside hers, throwing up slush and just-shoveled goop. The way she was driving said that Rickie must not have returned home last night. Rather than be worried, Gloria—typical of her—was angry. Angie went back inside to make coffee. It turned out to be a smart move because it was clear before Mom had her coat off that she'd been crying.

"He didn't come home?"

She nodded.

Does that mean yes he came home, or yes he didn't come home? Angie busied herself getting out cups, cream and sugar. If Mom had time to gather herself, she might provide a sensible reply.

"He did come home."

"I thought you were going to call. I couldn't sleep for worrying about him."

"I did call. You must've been out jogging."

Angie managed to stifle a raise of her eyebrows and a shocked, "He didn't come home till five in the morning?" She said instead, "Did he say where he'd been?"

"Said he was driving around." Gloria focused on doctoring her cup. "The worst part is that I prepared a special dessert for when he got home from the game. I did my hair up with that new rhinestone butterfly. I wore my new black gown and the diamond necklace. I put on Johnny Mathis."

If she mentioned whipped cream Angie was dashing back to the bedroom and hiding in the closet.

It was hard, and awkward, seeing her mother in this condition. She'd given her best suggestion for handling Rickie's disinterest in bed. What else was there to say?

"Mom. I don't know why Rickie didn't come home but I will not believe he's cheating. There's one thing I found when I was married to Will, when men cheat they work harder at home, give you more sex, bring flowers—so you won't be suspicious. More than likely there's something else going on with him. Something of a personal nature."

"Do you think he talked to Jarvis?"

"All I know is he and Jarvis went to the game last night. I have no clue what they said during those times. Maybe they only talked about basketball." Angie was very close to walking to the wide archway between the kitchen and living area and beating her head against the wall.

"You're saying Rickie does have something on his mind?"

Grrrr. "I wasn't saying anything."

"I don't see how he can have a problem. We tell each other everything."

"Mom, nobody tells each other everything."

Gloria shifted the chair so they were facing each other. She scowled. "You told me you and Jarvis talked about everything."

As usual, she'd taken the comment out of context. In murder cases, they did talk about everything—but how to make it clear without getting her more upset? "We do for the most part. But gosh, Mom, you never tell everything. It's just not…natural. One thing I do know—if Rickie said anything to Jarvis of a personal nature, he wouldn't have repeated it to me." Although last night, it seemed like he had something on his mind. "Jarvis is loyal to his friends. You tell him something, it's like going into a confessional."

Gloria's well-plucked brows rose in disbelief. For some reason she wanted to argue. Okay, it was time for Mom to leave. Or…time for Angie to get to work. She stood up and began clearing the coffee mess.

Gloria never moved from the barstool. Oh well.

For a moment, Angie thought about bringing up the multiple wives—to change topics. But Mom wasn't in the mood for a discussion that didn't involve her personal life.

"Mom, I have to go to work. You can stay here as long as you want." But please be gone by then. She had enough crap going on in her life without this.

"What do I do?" Gloria's voice turned to a whine of desperation.

Angie sponged down the counter. "Like I said yesterday, talk to him."

"I tried that last night—this morning. We ended up fighting."

"That's because you tried during an emotional time. He was already on the offensive. He knew you'd be angry he stayed out all night." Angie leaned across the counter to try one last time. "IF he has a problem in the sex department, maybe he's embarrassed to talk about it. You nagging—" oh god was that the wrong word— "him about it only makes it worse. You have to be understanding and supportive. Maybe last night he suspected you had something romantic planned and couldn't face…whatever: the confrontation, the truth, the guilt. Maybe he's trying to figure out how to tell you."

Gloria stood from the stool. Her scowl had disappeared.

By george, maybe she's finally got it. Thank goodness. Angie picked up her coat from the arm of the living room chair where she'd tossed it. She retrieved Gloria's too, but her mother had gone into the bathroom.

"Good luck, Mom," she shouted. "I hope things work out for you. I love you." And she left.

Angie stopped at the fast-food joint for what Jarvis would call a keg of coffee. On the way inside, she met up with none other than Rickie Kennedy coming out. It wasn't even seven-thirty and her day was already on a downhill swing. That closet was becoming more intriguing by the moment.

Rickie was wearing dark glasses—really out of place so early in the day; the sun had barely crested the mountain. He stopped, seemed to recognize her and lowered the glasses. His eyes were red rimmed—from crying or driving around all night?

None of her business.

"Good morning," each said.

Rickie waggled a bag of food in front of her. "Woke up starving this morning."

"I've heard that happens when you've had too much to drink."

He gave a shy smirk. "After the game, Jarvis and I stopped for a couple of beers. I met your new star. He's an odd fellow."

First time she'd heard Stone described in less than glowing terms.

Rickie lowered his voice. "I can't believe he's got three wives!"

How many beers had Jarvis drank last night, anyway? He wasn't one to talk about cases. Strike that—this wasn't a case. Yet.

Still, to let Rickie know he was aware of something illegal and hadn't reported it...

"Stone's marital status hasn't been officially established. Be good if this didn't go any further for now."

He made a locking motion with his fingers to his lips. "Disgusting. That's all I can say."

Maybe not disgusting but definitely weird. "Gotta run. Take care."

Angie carried her coffee to the second floor of the theater and let herself into her new office. The white sheet-rocked walls were taped and ready for paint. The windows that met at the corner of the building gave a panoramic picture all the way up the bay—she would never tire of this view. Today the bay was empty of skaters or ice fishermen. A few stray brown leaves skittered across the surface.

Lately, the theater building had been like Boston's Route 93, wiring completed, and the builders had finished the handicapped entrances. They had also sheet-rocked the walls and installed doors in the four shops so the new tenants could take over decorating. So, although some of the confusion had stopped, since all the shops had been rented, it would soon multiply many times over.

Angie spun in place, imagining the completed office with the new furniture including a foldout sectional. The right hand wall that abutted the restaurant's north wall shook with the force of the air hammers shooting nails into where the deck was being attached to the building. Funny, it appeared the crew was working in front of her windows also.

She set down the cup and went to find Mr. Quattro to bring the mistake to his attention. She spotted him in the hallway inspecting the new elevator. His daughter, the blonde woman from the parking lot yesterday, stood next to him. She wore a long flowing skirt that shimmied when she walked. As Angie approached, Mr. Quattro lit up. He performed introductions. Angie shook hands with Amber, who must've taken her light skin from her mother.

"How did the furniture shopping go yesterday?" Angie asked.

The green eyes widened. "Very well. I found a great shop in Meredith."

"I hear you work in the ER at the hospital," Angie said.

"Yes, it's mostly reception work, but it pays well."

"I worked there too for a long time." For a moment they spoke of the trials and pressures of their jobs.

"From what my father tells me, the pressure isn't much less here in the theater."

Angie spread her arms, palms-up. "Who'da thunk it?" She handed Mr. Quattro his rent receipt.

"Well, I must be on my way," Amber said. "It was wonderful meeting you Angie. I hope to see you again soon."

"Likewise."

Amber pecked her father on the cheek and left using the stairs. Mr. Quattro didn't make any move to follow.

"I had another reason for coming here besides the rent receipt," Angie said.

"Oh?" He wiggled his eyebrows. "Come to accept my offer for dinner?"

"No, I just wanted to mention that…well, it looks like your men are making the deck too long. It's extended all the way past my office."

"That's not an oversight. I thought you might like your own outdoor space. I've instructed them to erect a divider though, so the restaurant's customers won't disturb you. This afternoon the crew will cut in your door. Will sliding glass be all right?"

Angie thought the idea a wonderful one, but was shocked at the man's gall. "Mr. Quattro—"

"Anthony."

"Mister Quattro, I—"

He held up a hand. "I see I've made you angry. I assure you, it wasn't my intention. I seriously thought you'd love the surprise."

Stand your ground, she told herself. "I appreciate the thought. I really dislike surprises in my building though. Next time I would like to be consulted first, Mr. Quattro."

"Anthony."

The name battle was one she obviously wouldn't win. "I want you to remember that this is my building. You are a tenant…renting space. All changes and decisions must go through me. Are we clear on that?"

He gave a wistful smile and a half-bow that could have been taken as condescension or contrition. For now, Angie opted for the latter.

The arrival of the painter cut off further discussion. She bid Mr. Quattro good day, turned on a heel and led the painter to her office. On the corner of her desk were paint swatches—a bright pumpkin for the largest wall and three shades lighter for the other two, the fourth wall being all windows. The darker shade accented colors in a very ugly painting Tyson had given her for Christmas: Kratos—a man with a shaved head, armor, and a loincloth—was the Greek god of strength, which was the reason Tyson made the gift. Kratos, the old fellow, had already been her sounding board several times.

Leaving the painter to his work, Angie went downstairs to meet with the cast and found that Stone was the only one who'd arrived. He sat at the green room table, his copy of the script and a pair of to-go cups of coffee before him. As Angie dropped her coat on the back of a chair, he shoved one of the cups toward her.

"Thanks. How'd you know I needed this?"

"Word around here is you never turn down a cup. Word also says you like milk rather than cream in it. I hope those particular rumors are true."

"They are. I thought you were leaving for Chicago this morning. I'd planned for Jacoby to stand in for you."

"The meeting got postponed—from the other end. Something came up with the client. I appreciated him letting me know before I got all the way out there."

She clamped her lips tight to keep questions from squirting loose. The first and foremost had to do with wives. Was it kosher to ask someone's religion? After all, if he said he was Mormon, that'd change the situation, wouldn't it? Angie wasn't sure; did New Hampshire recognize the Mormon religion?

Okay, she would mind her own business. If he wanted more than one wife, so long as it didn't affect Prince & Pauper's production schedule, why should she object? A small part of her said to keep him talking, maybe he'd let something slip. She took a seat on the opposite side of the table and opened the coffee. "So, tell me about yourself. Are you from around here?"

He regarded her a moment, then said, "I was born in Secaucus, New Jersey." He laughed. "I bet you thought nobody was born in Secaucus."

"I never really thought about it. Did you grow up there?" She took a long sip from the cup.

"Yup. Graduated from high school. Left when I was seventeen to go in the Marines. Spent two years there, declined to re-up, and also declined to return to New Jersey. Mom and Dad weren't happy but I had to spread my wings. You know?"

"Sure. I did the same thing. I was born in Massachusetts, went to nursing school in Rhode Island."

"I had a stopover in Rhode Island too. Worked for a marina in Newport for two summers. I wonder if our paths ever crossed." They each shrugged. "The marina owner bought a place in Portsmouth, New Hampshire and asked if I wanted to transfer."

"So you did."

He nodded. "I seem to suffer from wanderlust. I get bored easily."

The sort of explained the wives. He needed variety. Why did he have to marry them? Stop! None of your business. Concentrate on the theater.

"Just about that time my parents were killed in an auto accident. A cement truck crushed their car."

"Oh, I'm so sorry."

"Worst part? They were on their way to vacation. Their first time in Europe." Stone smoothed a lock of sandy blond hair behind one ear. "So, you went to nursing school and ended up running a community theater."

She shrugged. "It seemed like a natural progression up the ladder of success."

Stone chuckled.

"Long story."

"Is how you met Jarvis also a long story?"

"No. That's short. I was a suspect in a murder investigation. He was the detective on the case. Period." She told him about the murder on board the fishing tour boat, and how she ended up in business with Tyson Goodwell. She left out the stuff about the divorce. It was still painful—though not in an I'm gonna die kind of way. Now, it just carried the dull ache of failure.

Stone drew out his vial of nose drops and dosed himself. "Sorry about that," he held up the container, "I have a sinus condition." He shook his head. "Wow, that stings." He read the prescription label. "Doesn't usually burn like that." He put the container in his pocket then pinched his nostrils for a moment. Then he apologized again. "I would've been here a lot earlier today, but I couldn't find the darned bottle. I always keep it on my dresser. This morning, you wouldn't believe where I found it—on the kitchen floor."

"Do you have a cat who could've been playing with it?"

He shook his head. Now he came up with a container of hand sanitizer and squirted a liberal amount on his hands.

Kiana burst through the back door in a whirlwind of jasmine-scented air. She carried her ever-present cup of cocoa in one hand and a large envelope tucked under the other arm.

Angie nearly leaped up and ran for cover since it was clear the girl had something on her mind. But Angie was the boss now, supposedly the grownup. Later she'd place an order for a case of those big-girl panties. For now, she stifled the urge to run, told Stone thanks for the coffee, and preceded Kiana to the office. "What's up?"

"I read two of the scripts last night. I wrote rejection letters for them. Here they are for you to look at." Kiana dropped the envelopes on the table. "The plays are written well enough, but aren't something that'll fit our stage environment." Kiana's face lit up. "But they did give me an idea."

Though she probably should've felt a twinge of fear for what was to come, Angie couldn't help thinking how glad she was to have this girl in her life. "Go on."

Kiana pointed a finger at her. "What if we present our summer performance outdoors? Tyson's backyard at Heaven Scent would be perfect. It has a huge flat area. The front yard is big enough for a hundred cars to park comfortably. Might squash the lawn a little but it'll grow back. We could use the garage to store sets and the house for changing rooms, so all we'd need is a stage. I've already contacted the Girl Scout troop who's willing to clean the house once we're through—for one of their merit badges. I'm sure we could borrow the stage the high school built for homecoming last year," Kiana gushed. "Which means the only expense would be trucking it up here. And I think I've got that covered too." Kiana paused for a breath so short that it didn't leave time for Angie to interject a comment—that the idea was awesome. "My uncle has a flatbed. I already asked and he'd be willing to donate the truck and a driver to bring it here."

"Sounds like a done-deal," Angie said.

"Well, only if you're agreeable."

"Did you have time to sleep last night at all?"

"A little." Kiana grinned, showing two rows of perfectly straight, white teeth. "I was so hyped about the idea that I was wide awake."

"It'll catch up to you later."

Kiana shrugged. Of course. When Angie was that age, nothing as mundane as sleep mattered either.

"What do you think of the idea?" Kiana asked.

"You knew I'd love it," Angie said.

"So, we can do it?"

"Do what?" Blanche asked as she stepped into the room. Kiana explained about the summer show.

"If we can get the permits from the town." Angie hugged Kiana. "Let's discuss it further over lunch."

Kiana wasn't finished yet. "Blanche, I wondered if you'd be willing to do some kind of demonstration there—something like costume making or design."

Blanche shook her head, amazed at Kiana's exuberant description of the future plans. "Love to talk more about it."

"Okay, going now. I'll bring something for lunch. Grinders?"

"Sounds good. Meet back here around noon. Where are

you headed now?"

"To pick up office supplies."

Angie spent an hour with Blanche who was as bubbly as Kiana over her vacation. She oohed over photos of the tropical scenery, how happy she was to be back with Stony, their plans for tonight, and then she lamented why Angie couldn't—or wouldn't—take time off.

"My last vacation almost killed me and Jarvis. Not ready for another."

"Trouble does seem to follow you two." Blanche made the sign of the cross over her chest.

Catholic, huh? Not Mormon.

That meant, no way she knew of Chia and Miata. Angie chastised the infernal amateur detective, the one who wouldn't accept the possibility that Chia just might be an ex wife who'd remained friends. And that Miata Lin was a foster sister. Or— heaven forbid—Blanche was the proverbial other woman.

Blanche's designs were, as usual, excellent. She had a knack for knowing what mood needed to be achieved and what fit the character to best advantage. Angie okayed all but one, which they tweaked color-wise to fit what Stone would be wearing in that scene.

After Blanche left, Angie met with the cast. They read through the lines twice to could get a feel for the flow of the plot. She fielded questions about mood and timing.

The set designer was next on the appointment list. Before leaving, Tyson had given Angie a run-down on everyone they dealt with on a regular basis. He'd said the set designer rarely needed much official input, and he'd been right; Fred was a dream who seemed to have things totally under control.

Just before noon, the UPS guy delivered a box of glossy tri-fold brochures. Angie stood against the wall in a long triangle of winter sunshine to read one through, praying she and Tyson hadn't missed anything while proofing during the holidays.

She was putting away the box when Kiana arrived carrying a bundle of office supplies. She thumped it on the floor near the ticket booth then raced back outside. "Got the curtains too," she called over her shoulder. A moment later, she returned toting a clear plastic bag that held forty-eight feet of cranberry colored velour. It must weigh a ton. They stood on stepstools to hang the fresh smelling draperies inside the ticket booth.

As they pushed the last hook into the slot and dropped it over the rod, the front door opened. Drat. Today wouldn't be any quieter than yesterday. The off-season was supposed to be just that—off. Quiet. Restful—lounging around the condo reading a mountain of scripts. Angie thought about going home and cocooning under a duvet in front of the television—then remembered her mother might still be there.

Real grownup, Angie-girl. Really mature.

So she dove back into work.

A petite Chinese, or maybe Korean, woman with mousy features stepped into the foyer, blinking at the change in lighting. Her head turned left and then right. Her demeanor said she hadn't been here before. Kiana asked if she needed help. In a New England accent, the woman said she wanted to purchase a pair of season tickets to the theater. Angie let Kiana handle the transaction so she could gain experience at every level.

Kiana gestured for the woman to meet her at the ticket booth window, then moved inside to locate the box under the counter.

Angie busied herself nearby, just in case Kiana needed help. Angie changed the vacuum cleaner bag. She went outside coatless and heaved the old bag into the dumpster. When she returned, the woman, who couldn't stand more than five feet tall, was bent over the counter filling out the application form. Angie installed the new bag, then put the vacuum away. As she ducked back out of the closet, Kiana said, "Welcome to the family, Mrs. Powers."

Angie stopped in her tracks.

CHAPTER 7

The woman stood erect, tucking straight black hair behind her ears. Dark eyes gazed at Angie who forced a smile to her face. "Welcome aboard." *I think.* "Did I hear Kiana say that your surname is Powers?"

As she said this, she remembered a conversation with Jarvis. The woman Stone was arguing with in the parking lot was of Asian descent. Could this be her?

"Yes, I am Miata Lin Powers." The woman pronounced the last name as Powahs. "I am a gynecologist. I just opened a private practice in Rochester." Pride shone in her eyes.

"Our new leading man is named Powers also. Stone Powers."

"That's an interesting first name, isn't it?" When she said, "My husband's name is Martin," Angie relaxed a little—so the last name was just coincidence. But the addition of, "He's out of town right now. He is a salesman for Marrick Pharmaceuticals," had Angie's goose bumps groping for fresh air.

Kiana knocked the box of season ticket holder cards to the floor. It burst open and cards flew in all directions. Had she realized too? Or was the explosion of cards a coincidence?

Somehow, Angie managed to keep from plugging the teen's mouth shut with both fists. This was indeed the woman Jarvis had seen arguing with Stone. What the heck was going on?

Kiana disappeared behind the counter as she gathered the cards, and probably her composure.

"Martin is on the road three weeks out of every month," Miata Powers continued. Angie wished she'd shut up. This was definitely TMI.

"That's got to be difficult for you as a couple." Wait, wait, she told the Judgment Police. Maybe this was all coincidence. Illegal yes, but none of her business. She inhaled a long breath and then let it out.

"Yes," Miata was saying. "The upside is that the time we have together is the best. Anyway, he's enamored with your community theater. I've heard wonderful things about Prince and Pauper from my friends and thought season tickets would be a great gift for his birthday."

"Er, how long have you been married?" Again Angie wanted to cram her hands in her mouth. Why couldn't she just shut up?

"Six months." Miata Lin's smile widened. "Another nice thing about being apart. It makes the reunions that much nicer."

"I can imagine."

Was it really possible all these women 1) didn't know about each other or 2) did indeed know, and 3) accept each other?

Yesterday, Stone hadn't acted the least bit embarrassed that Angie met Blanche and Chia within a ten-minute period. Jarvis said Stone hadn't acted self-conscious at the meeting with Miata Lin. What—as Jarvis would say—balls the guy had.

Kiana placed the box on the counter and began arranging the cards into alphabetical order.

Mrs. Powers opened a red leather handbag and drew out a matching wallet. "I assume you take credit cards."

Angie stepped into the main foyer. "We do."

"Martin and I met at a Red Sox game in New York. Isn't it amazing how fate works? Two people from New Hampshire meeting in New York in a crowd of however many thousand."

As Miata Lin drew out the credit card, a square of paper fluttered to the floor. Angie crouched to retrieve the paper, saying, "It definitely seems as you two were fated to meet." She handed back the photo of the couple in wedding garb thinking that big trouble—like a hurricane shooting straight toward Prince & Pauper—because there was now no doubt that Miata Powers' husband Martin, and their leading man were one and the same. Unless they were identical twins. And they were both pharmaceuticals salesmen. Maybe that was it. Stone was an identical twin—no, that would be triplet…

Kiana poised, ready to swipe the credit card through the machine. The photo caught her eye and she picked it up. "Look Mrs. Deacon, she has a picture of Stone." The girl's confused gaze switched to the small Asian woman.

"That's my husband."

"But—" Kiana stopped talking.

Angie was thankful because it was clear the wrong words were about to erupt from her mouth.

"My husband's name is Martin." Miata Lin tapped the counter, indicating the photo in Kiana's hand.

"But this is—" Again the teenager caught herself.

Maybe it was better not to stop Kiana's verbal thought-detonation. Maybe it'd be better to let the situation lava to the surface on its own. Get things out in the open now because sooner or later it would come out. Big-time. With cops and lawyers involved. Maybe if it came out now, she and Kiana could—what? Not sure what could be done to douse the potential firestorm.

"Maybe they're twins." Kiana suggested the idea with the naiveté of a person inexperienced with deceit.

Mrs. Powers took the picture and waved it toward them. "This is my husband Martin. He's not a twin."

Mrs. Powers Number 3 jammed the photo in her purse, stomped toward the door, slammed it so hard the glass rattled, and marched across the parking lot to a blue mini Cooper. Twice on the way, she slipped in the slush.

Angie turned to find Kiana standing at her elbow. "What made her so mad?" the teen asked.

"I'm not sure." It dawned on Angie that perhaps potential

Wife Number 3, as Wife Number 2—the Chia pet—had been suspicious of Stone's behavior. Otherwise wouldn't she have voiced amazement instead of annoyance at the coincidence?

"Wow. Three wives."

Was this the sort of thing a seventeen-year-old girl should be witnessing? Would her adopted parents hold Angie responsible when—because it surely would—it all came to gushing out? It definitely was time to do something about this.

Kiana's, "I wonder how he remembers which shelf the toothpaste goes on," pushed Angie's anger into a burst of laughter. Maybe the girl had a better handle on the adult world than she'd given her credit for.

Kiana had a point though. The implications were mind-boggling.

As if choreographed, Angie and Kiana moved toward the door and peered through the tiny window. Out in the parking lot, the blue car slipped and slid just like its owner. It struggled up the grade toward the main road where it didn't stop before launching into traffic. Angie squeezed her eyes shut as two cars barely missed hitting the escaping vehicle.

"I wonder what she would've done if she knew he was right here in the building."

"Kiana my dear, you're being way too bold for your own good today. Come on, let's get to work. Everyone should be here by now."

"I think I'll skip the meeting," Kiana said, "and go shopping for fire extinguishers. Or one of those bomb-disposal robots. I have the feeling things are going to get very explosive around here—very soon." She whirled toward her coat lying on a side table.

"Oh no you don't." Angie grasped her arm. She propelled the teenager through the door and into the auditorium. "We'll go shopping together later."

CHAPTER

"It really is three wives?" Angelina asked.

Jarvis slapped his palm on Angelina's center island countertop so hard he nearly knocked himself from the stool. The idea was unbelievable. Did people actually do this sort of thing these days? Divorce was so easy—too easy as far as he was concerned—to come by. But three wives! Besides the illegality of the whole thing, how did Stone remember which house to go to at night? How did he keep all their names straight? Who controlled the checking account?

On the other hand, spouted Jarvis's devilish side, *how cool it must be to have such variety.*

Yeah, responded his dutiful side, but you're never able to truly relax.

Never bored, gloated the devil.

Always worried what stories you told to whom. Whose name you called out during sex. Which drawer your socks were in.

Jarvis shook off the debate going on in his head. Regardless of what might happen to Angelina's next performance, it was time to report this. He dished up a spoonful of soup, and opened his mouth.

"Careful. A minute ago it was boiling in the pot," she said.

"What do you think, I never ate hot food before?" He blew a second time, exaggerating the act, his breath sending drops flying off the spoon. He sucked in the entire spoonful at once.

It seared the roof of his mouth. No way would he flinch. No way he'd admit she was right.

How did Stone remember which side of the bed each woman slept on? Did he remember how they liked the dishwasher stacked? Where they kept the extra roll of toilet paper? The names of his mothers-in-law…

"This is really good," he said after taking a more careful taste of the soup.

"Thanks. I think I put in too many noodles though."

"Never can have too many noodles." Noodles didn't matter—the fact that she was learning to cook meant everything.

The oven timer beeped. As Angelina bent to take a loaf of bread from the oven he whistled at the view. She threw an embarrassed glance back at him.

He'd made a silly comment yesterday about Stone's looks—about how one person could have so much while others… He'd been talking about Stone at the time, but the same went for his lady. Angelina Nadia Farnsworth Deacon was tall and naturally blonde. She kept herself in shape with a three-mile jog at dawn every morning. At fifty-seven, there wasn't an ounce of fat on her, or a bit of sag. What she saw in him, he couldn't fathom. At fifty-nine he was balding—an unconscious hand raked through what was left of his hair—two inches shorter than her, and ten pounds overweight, although he'd lost twenty pounds in the last year.

"What's the matter?" She dumped the loaf from the pan onto a wire rack to cool.

"Nothing. Why?"

"You sighed."

He said, "No I didn't," even though he probably had. To cover, he ate another spoonful, again burning his mouth.

"Slow down there, detective, I planned the bread and the soup to be ready at the same time."

Though she'd made the bread from one of those frozen loaves rather than flour and yeast, he had to give her credit. For a person who two years ago couldn't cook at all—and admittedly didn't even want to try—she was doing a mighty fine job. He wasn't sure what prompted the change. More than likely it was her mother's constant nagging. Heaven knew Gloria showed little pride in her daughter. Jarvis was sure something from their pasts caused this, but since neither of them talked of it, chances of getting to its heart were remote. Now and then, he thought of speaking to Gloria. But he was pretty sure Angelina wouldn't like him interfering.

So, to please her mother, or more likely, to silence her, Angelina was learning to cook. Maybe something positive could come from the negative relationship. Jarvis couldn't imagine how Rickie, the toy-boy Gloria brought here a year ago, stood it. Rickie was about half Gloria's age—young enough to be Angelina's son—though Jarvis never mentioned that detail out loud. He and Angelina—like the townsfolk—originally thought Rickie put up with Gloria's moods because of her massive lottery jackpot but had soon realized the couple really doted on each other. Another thing Jarvis had trouble wrapping his mind around was why the odd couple stayed in town. Gloria disdained small town life, where there wasn't something momentous going on every second. She also disdained police work as a profession. Which made it equally odd that she allowed Rickie to take criminal justice courses to further his goal of becoming a private detective.

Rickie's confession to Jarvis about the new car would sooner or later burst the bubble they'd created around themselves. Jarvis didn't want to think about that right now. And he hoped, when Gloria and Rickie arrived, they'd managed to put the problem behind them.

"What did you say?" Angelina slid a long-bladed knife from the drawer.

"I didn't say anything."

She turned the loaf and held the knife poised above it. "Yes. Sounded like you said something was weird. What's weird about my soup? Or the bread..."

"I told you the soup is excellent. I was thinking about Stone Powers," he semi-lied.

"Speaking of that, how come you mentioned the wives to Rickie last night?"

"I did?"

"That's what he told me."

"Shit."

"And he was mad as hell about it."

Jarvis frowned.

"What's wrong?"

"I don't recall saying anything. Seems like, if he'd been angry I'd remember that."

"How many beers did you have?"

He grinned. "Not that many."

"Speaking of Rickie, they'll be here in a few minutes." The knife clattered to the counter. A dishcloth appeared in her hand.

Jarvis jumped from his chair and took hold of her arms to guide her onto the stool beside his. "Sit." He jammed a spoon into her hand and forced her fingers to close around it. "I will slice the bread." He went to work on the crusty loaf. "So Rickie and your mom are coming here, tonight, together?"

"I have no idea if both are coming. All I know is Mom said she is."

"Eat."

Angelina obediently sipped from a spoonful. "Three wives. It just can't be true."

He set a bread slice on a plate and pushed it in front of her, then did likewise for himself. "I can't believe I mentioned Stone's wives to Rickie. Bad move."

"Were you drinking something besides beer?"

He shook his head. Didn't matter what they'd been drinking. There was no excuse for talking about this to him. Jarvis was concealing information about a crime and it hadn't set well with him since the moment he decided to do it.

He'd come to a decision. Tomorrow, he'd seek out the

multi-wedded actor and have a talk. Find out the truth of the situation. Hopefully somehow—as odd and unlikely as it might be—it was all legal. And amicable.

Which he doubted like hell since the Asian woman had not only left the theater in a snit, she'd been in a discussion with Stone—er, Martin, or was that Rocky—in that parking lot. Last thing Jarvis wanted was to ruin things by filing a biga—trigamist report. Could he possibly wait till after the performance?

To sort of change the subject, he asked, "How are things going at the theater?"

"Good. Everyone acts happy with the script. Seems as though they all like each other."

"And this bothers you why?"

She set the spoon in the bowl and faced him. "The calm before the storm?"

He leaned sideways and kissed her on the tip of the nose. "See the good for what it is. Besides, you have Kiana. She's willing to take on all sorts of jobs. Let her relieve some of the pressure."

"Jarvis, she's only seventeen."

"Almost eighteen." He grinned. "I'm not suggesting you give her free rein. Keep an eye on her but let her go. See how much she can handle."

"She is great, isn't she? She came up with an awesome idea today. She suggested we do the summer performance outdoors." Angelina explained about locating the shebang at Tyson's place, named Heaven Scent by a previous owner, out on 28A. "Except for getting permits for such a huge undertaking, I think it could really work."

"Maybe you can make a whole weekend out of it," he said.

She looked up, her green eyes flashing with excitement. "You mean like Friday and Saturday night performances and a Saturday matinee?"

"Maybe just two performances—the first one Friday night. But what about some activities related to the show's theme.

Something the whole town can come to. Something to pull in people who don't usually go to the theater. Those activities could all lead up to a Sunday matinee."

"Kiana mentioned that to Blanche—costume classes or something. Blanche was excited too." She patted his arm. "We could do skits for kids. Or method acting classes. Costume making. Or face painting."

She dipped the spoon in the bowl. The doorbell rang. The spoon splashed into the bowl. While she cleaned up the splatter, Jarvis went to see how many guests had arrived.

Gloria burst inside. She carried a white cardboard box with Amilyne's Corner Market written on the top. Yes, the shop produced excellent food, but what a contradiction from the woman who put down Angelina because she didn't like to cook.

Jarvis hugged Gloria then deposited her coat in the closet. If Angelina looked anything like this in twenty years… Wow.

He shook hands with Rickie Kennedy, who had his free hand jammed in his pocket and that ridiculous fuzzy hat pulled down over his ears. His face was unlined with worry. Hopefully that meant they'd solved their differences.

"Very nice to see you two," Jarvis said.

He must've introduced a bit too much enthusiasm into his words because Gloria's lips twitched and puckered. "You having an argument? I thought I heard a discussion going on."

"We were talk— Never mind, I'll let Angelina tell you about it." He led them to the kitchen where Angelina was clearing breadcrumbs from the counter.

"Smells great in here," Rickie said.

"Angelina made soup and homemade bread," Jarvis said for Gloria's benefit and got a look from Angelina. Though he was sure she cooked because of her mother, he didn't get why she wanted it kept from Gloria. He shot his lady a sly grin. "There's some left if you want, Rickie."

"No thanks. We just ate," he said. "Brought dessert though."

Jarvis got up to put on a pot of coffee. Angelina hugged her mother around the bakery box, then took it and dished four of the half-dozen éclairs onto plates.

To keep Gloria from introducing a negative topic, and to keep Angelina from mentioning the store-bought dessert—the pressure of keeping the peace made Jarvis think of Stone and his women—he said, "Angelina's had a wonderful idea for the theater's summertime performance." As he said it, Jarvis realized the idea might not go over too well with Gloria. First, she didn't approve of Angelina's choice of career. She said it took up too much of her time. Second, she and Rickie were renting HeavenScent while he was in New York. The idea of hundreds of strangers wandering around probably wouldn't bode well, even if it were just for a weekend.

"It wasn't my idea. It was Kiana's." Angelina told about the tentative plans for the show at HeavenScent. "What do you think?"

Gloria's eyes lit up. "I love the idea. How does Tyson feel? All that traffic will really chew up his beautiful lawn."

"I haven't talked to him yet. I wanted to run it by you first."

"Knowing him, he'll love the idea," Jarvis said. "He's all for anything that promotes the theater."

"Well, he used to be anyway," Gloria said.

Outside of her negative feelings about Tyson leaving Angie in a lurch Gloria seemed positive about the plan for the show. She shot out ideas one after another. "You could bring someone in to cater a barbecue before the show. That way the public can mingle with the cast."

"Great idea," Angelina agreed, "but not a barbecue, it's too messy. What about mini-meatballs and/or steak kabobs?"

"Good idea. Finger foods that people don't have to sit down to eat. That way you won't need to worry about having enough tables and chairs."

What just happened? Gloria agreed with something her daughter said. Jarvis flicked his gaze toward Angelina. Her expression remained neutral; she wasn't surprised. What the hell was going on?

"You could rent one of those tents in case the weather's bad," Gloria offered.

"The weather wouldn't dare be bad on Angie's special weekend," Rickie said.

When the topic of the outdoor show waned, Jarvis asked Rickie how his classes were going.

The blond man finally removed his hat. He set it on the arm of Angelina's favorite chair and fluffed his professionally styled hair with his fingers before turning around. "Official classes at NHTI don't begin until fall. For now I'm taking an online introductory course. One on gaining entry to buildings, and one on evidence gathering."

Normally when the topic of Rickie becoming a private investigator came up, Gloria made a remark or a rude sound under her breath. So far she'd been quiet. Jarvis tilted his head thinking he heard the theme from the Twilight Zone playing in the background.

"That'll give you a head start for the course," Angelina said.

"They didn't have any online stuff when I went to school." Jarvis laughed. "Hardly had computers back then." He pointed a finger at each of them in turn. "No age comments."

"None coming from this side of the table." Gloria grinned.

"Did you go to New Hampshire Tech?" Rickie asked.

"No, New England College."

"That's a hike from Alton," Angelina said.

"I lived in a dorm."

"The game last night was great," Rickie said. "Too bad Stone couldn't go. Speaking of that, anything new at the theater?" he asked Angelina.

"The current production is coming along well so far. And so is the work on the second floor. My new office is looking good, all freshly painted." She aimed her fork at Rickie. "I met someone this morning. Her name is Amber Quattro—well, she's married now but she used to be a surfer—"

Rickie's blue eyes flashed. "I know Amber! She moved to

Mission Beach—she got the coaching job I wanted." Seeing Gloria's face changing color, he added, "I admit my nose was a bit out of joint at them for giving her the job. I'd been surfing there, making a name for myself, for a long time." He shrugged. "Water under the bridge. Wasn't meant to be, I guess."

"So, you say she's moved to New Hampshire?" Gloria asked.

"Angelina?" Jarvis prompted. "Did you hear your mother's question?"

"Sorry. Lost in thought. Yes, apparently Amber is Anthony Quattro's daughter. Moved back here to be closer to her husband who works in the area."

"That's nice," she said, though it was obviously a lie.

Angelina rolled her eyes at Jarvis. He knew what that meant: change the direction of the conversation. He hadn't needed to be told; it was clear Gloria had a jealous streak—gee, something they had in common, which was not something he wanted to think about—and was about to erupt like Mt. St. Helens.

CHAPTER 9

Jarvis was terrible at topic-changing. Angelina should know that much about him. He could never come up with something new—unless it was the weather or the Celtics. Neither of which would calm Gloria down.

It was clear Angelina was trying too. She said, "Oh, did I tell you my new business cards came in?"

Jarvis nearly laughed. That was almost as lame as the weather. Help came from the least likely source: Rickie. "Oh, something I forgot to tell you, Gloria. The star of the show has three wives."

Apparently this was an interesting subject because Gloria shook off whatever anger gripped her, and asked, "Oh? Is he Mormon?"

"No, a pharmaceuticals salesman," Angelina said, which made everyone laugh, and eased the brewing tension.

"Three wives?" Gloria said, the same time Rickie asked, "What's a pharmaceuticals salesman?"

"He sells medicine—drugs—to pharmacies," Angelina said. "He's on the road a lot."

Over second cups of coffee for the women and second helpings of dessert for the men, she told about the wives, in stunning detail. "Apparently he likes women with long hair, outgoing personalities and self-sufficiency."

Gloria frowned but didn't say anything until… "I've been thinking of letting my hair grow out. Like yours Angie. Maybe longer."

Jarvis nearly laughed. For some reason the idea that Gloria might want to attract Stone's attention popped into his head. Rickie scowled. "You gonna make a play to become wife number four?"

Rather than laugh as Jarvis expected, Gloria said, "I might if some things don't change."

"You're right about that. A lot of things have to change, and fast," came Rickie's response.

Gloria's face grew red. Her knuckles turned white around the fork. Angelina leaned forward. "That's enough. Whatever's going on, work it out between you—at home."

Jarvis got up from his seat and went down the hall to the bathroom. Maybe his exit would change the room's dynamics and squash whatever was developing. As he did his business, he hoped to hear the front door slam. But no...voices—not happy ones—murmured through the walls. He feared all hell was about to break loose. Private Citizen Colby Jarvis didn't want any part of it. Why couldn't people just sit down and discuss their issues? He leaned both palms against the edge of the sink. PC Jarvis had to go out there and be supportive to Angelina.

"I said take it home!" Angelina said.

That he could hear through the wall. "Damn." Jarvis hoped Private Citizen Jarvis wouldn't have to turn into Detective Jarvis. Finally, he ventured from the ceramic tiled haven. Gloria stood in the hallway—good, maybe they were leaving. Jarvis rounded the corner into the kitchen area.

Rickie and Gloria stood nose to nose. "Let's go home!" Rickie went to the closet and yanked their coats from the hangers. He grudgingly helped Gloria into hers. While she worked the buttons, Rickie turned to Jarvis. "Isn't having three wives illegal?"

"Technically, yes."

Rickie frowned, probably at Jarvis's choice of wording. "Did you report it?"

"No, not—"

"Why the hell not?"

"Sit down a sec and I'll explain."

Rickie walked over and dropped into one of the dining chairs while sliding into his jacket. His leg jostled the table. Thankfully all the cups were mostly empty.

Though he owed Rickie nothing in the way of explanation, he gave all the reasons he'd held off. "Angelina, come here. I want you to hear this too."

She stepped around the island counter and came to sit. Gloria didn't move from the hallway. "In the morning I'm going to talk to Stone. I need to hear his side—maybe there's some dumb-ass extenuating circumstance none of us have thought of. Anyway, I can't go to the captain without hearing the full story. I could end up looking like an idiot. And bring negative attention to the theater."

Rickie nodded and got to his feet. "Makes sense, I guess." He backed a few steps from the table. "If it would make things easier on you, I can report it as a private citizen and not have to have all the details. And it wouldn't reflect so much on the theater."

"I think it still would," Gloria said from the hallway.

"You could get Jarvis in trouble," Angelina said.

"How?"

"It'll come out that he already knew."

"Folks. I will take care of it in the morning," Jarvis said. "I let it go too long."

"What's the big deal about this guy anyway?" Rickie asked. "He's the only topic of anyone's conversation lately."

Angelina went to dig through the trash and came up with a copy of yesterday's newspaper. It was damp; she assured them it was from coffee grounds, opened it to the second page—the regular spot for the theater's ad—and stabbed a finger on the picture. "This is Stone Powers."

"Nice looking," Gloria said. Those two words said volumes.

"That's him?" Rickie scowled.

Jarvis refolded the paper. Rickie followed him toward the kitchen where Jarvis heaved the paper in the trash and Rickie took Gloria's arm. Good nights were said all around.

When the door shut behind them, Angelina heaved a relieved breath. Jarvis went to pour her some red wine and grabbed a beer for himself. They settled side by side on the couch.

He was baffled. Rickie acted as though this was some sort of drug deal or gunrunning. Granted, bigamy was illegal but it wasn't like... Oh hell, stop making excuses. "How did you get onto that conversation anyway?" he asked. When he'd gone to the bathroom to hide out, they'd been ready to 'discuss' Rickie and Gloria's troubles.

"We were joking that Stone seems to go for similar types of women."

"You think so?"

"Well, outside of the few physical similarities—the wives are radically different from one another. Blanche is talented and well spoken, agreeable and funny. Chia seems impatient and needs frequent boosts of confidence. Miata Lin has a quick temper and is unsure of herself anyplace outside her comfort zone, which is the medical arena. That's when Mom questioned my quick judgment of them. 'Didn't you say you only met them once?' she asked me."

"She really doesn't know you at all." Angelina could read a person as though their physical details were written on the pages of a book.

"She said it seemed like a lot of conjecture on my part. With Miata and Chia, yes, I suppose she was right. But Blanche has worked for me at the theater since we opened."

"You do have an uncanny ability to read people."

Angelina shrugged. "I just keep my eyes open. For example, Chia held Montez's hand the whole time."

"I bet your mother said something like it meant she was staking her claim, especially since she realized you already knew Montez."

"Yes, except every time Chia said something, she'd add, 'Isn't that right, Montez?'"

"That would tell me she's insecure."

"Right." Angelina took a moment to sip some wine. He took the glass and set it on the table for her.

"There is one thing I noticed the women have in common," he said. "They're all self-sufficient. Each earn their own living. Blanche does quite well as a costume designer."

"Right. She works with some of the biggest theaters in the state."

"Miata Lin is a gynecologist." Disappointment flooded through him at his next thought. "Darn, that theory doesn't work. The third wife is a librarian."

"You missed something though. She wears very expensive clothes."

"What's that mean—Montez supports her?"

"No. I can't picture him doing that for any woman. Chia used to be a model."

"Used to be?"

"Retired I guess."

"Do they have retirement plans?"

Angelina shrugged. "Could be."

He took a slug from his bottle. "Tell me something? What is it about Stone that attracts the women?"

"First of all, he's quite good looking. He's very entertaining. He's never without an interesting and funny story. He doesn't gossip. He's polite and acts like a gentleman."

"Okay, I get it. He's all the things I'm not."

Angelina stood up quickly. For a second he thought he'd pissed her off, but she picked up the glass and bottle and wiggled a finger at him. He knew what that meant.

First and foremost: she wasn't angry.

She threw the bottle into the recycle bin, and set the glass in the dishwasher.

"Maybe he just has trouble saying no," Jarvis said.

"There are people like that," she said. "Maybe he's got

wives from coast to coast."

"I've been wondering the same thing."

Angie strolled down the hallway and into the bedroom. He didn't wait for an invitation. While she turned down the bed, he put three fingers of each hand to his temples, half-closed his eyes, wobbled his head from side-to-side and said in a spooky voice, "Spirits residing in the hea...vens," he tilted his head up, "I preee...dict that Alton Bay, New Hampshire is about to experience another mur...der. Maybe several."

Angelina heaved two pillows at him.

CHAPTER 10

Friday morning, Angie sat in the front row of the theater. Today they'd do a quick run-through of the lines. This part of the show preparation was low key. Angie and Tyson believed this to be an invaluable time for the cast members to develop chemistry and build relationships that would reflect in their performances. Adlibbing and goofing off was accepted.

Angie did a mental roll call. Everyone was here except Stone. Maybe Jarvis had cornered him for their talk. Her cell phone rang. A check of the caller ID said it was her mother. She let the call go to voicemail. *Angie.* The single word sent goosebumps popping through her skin. *Rickie never came home last night. How could he not go home? They'd left her house together. He dropped me off and said he was going for a drive. And he didn't come home.*

A metallic sound out in the green room—a locker door shutting. Must be Stone had arrived. Angie dropped the phone into her pocket, stood and clapped to get everyone's attention. "Okay folks, I think we're about ready to begin. Take your places please."

Blanche suddenly slid into the seat beside Angie. Angie sat too. "Gosh, I didn't hear you coming," she said.

Blanche balanced a two-foot square cardboard folder containing sketches for costumes, across the chair arms.

"How was your special dinner last night?" Angie asked.

Blanche broke into a wide grin. "Great! And Stone finally left this morning for Chicago."

"Left? I thought I just heard him out back. He's the only one missing." Angie stood. "I guess I'd better go see who's there." She marched up the steps at stage left and whispered to Kiana standing in the wings, "Can you get things started? I have to check something."

Kiana stepped forward and called for the first scene to begin.

Angie strode into the green room. Stone stood near the long table gripping the top of a hard-back chair and leaning over it.

"Stone."

He jumped as if she'd startled him, wobbled around to face her, and stumbled.

"Stone. How did you get in here?"

He seemed confused by the question. "Aren't I supposed to be here?"

"Well, Blanche just said you left for Chicago."

"Didn't go."

She stepped closer. Even in the dim light, she could tell his blue eyes were glazed. "The second question is, how did you get in the building?"

Again, he seemed confused. "W-with everyone else." He drew out his container of hand sanitizer and used it.

"Nobody saw you. Including Blanche."

His response was a lopsided shrug.

"Okay, question number three: have you been drinking?"

"Drinking?" His brows met in a bunch over his nose. "You mean like..." He tilted back his head and mimed tipping a bottle into his mouth. The action sent him off balance and he toppled against the lockers, setting of a metallic echo. "You mean booze?" he asked once he regained his footing.

"Yes. Drinking. Alcohol."

"I don't drink."

"Well, you're sure acting like it."

He grinned. "I'm an actor, aren't I?"

Blanche ran in. "Stone. What the hell are you doing here? You're supposed— What's wrong?" She grasped his elbow.

"It looks like he's been drinking," Angie said.

"He doesn't drink. A beer now and then, but not..." Blanche shook his elbow, which nearly knocked him over. The bottle of hand sanitizer thudded to the floor and rolled under the table. "Are you all right?"

"'Course. Fine. Just feeling a little off-kilter."

"You'd better take him home. Stone, I'll see you tomorrow. Blanche, if you want to leave your designs in the office, I'll peek at them after rehearsal." Angie swung around and strode back to the stage area.

"Is Stone here?" Kiana asked.

"I sent him home. He's a bit under the weather." Hopefully this was a one-time thing. Granted, she didn't know Stone very well. And yes, she kept learning new things about him every day. But Blanche's reaction to his drunkenness was that of a concerned wife, not like someone covering up a problem.

Angie's suspicious nature couldn't help but conjure a reason for a non-drinker to suddenly over-imbibe—right after a confrontation with wife Number 3.

She took a seat in the front row to watch the actors but her mind kept shifting to the image of Blanche holding Stone's elbow and leading him down the hallway from the green room.

Oh well, for now there were more immediate issues. She'd worry about Stone tomorrow—if his situation turned into a two-time event. For the time being, they worked on scenes that didn't require his presence.

Normally Angie didn't leave the building for lunch. It had become custom for either Kiana or Jarvis to bring something. Today, she needed time away so Angie phoned him and made a date to meet at Shibley's. She arrived first, was shown to a table, and did something else out of character: ordered a glass of wine. Jarvis arrived as she was about to take the first sip. He ordered wine also. They ordered chef salads. Seemed as though they were both doing things out of character today. For Jarvis to ask for something on the more healthy side—shocking!

"I checked on Miata Lin's marriage license."

Angie sipped and set the glass on the table. "I thought you were going to talk to Stone."

"I figured he'd be busy at the theater all morning and I'd catch him later."

"Actually, he was supposed to be on a plane to Chicago."

"Supposed to be?"

She waved a hand. "Long story. Finish yours first."

"You want to know what Ms. Powers' marriage license said?"

If she left the impression she was anxious to know, he'd draw this out all afternoon with teasing and innuendoes. If she feigned disinterest, he wouldn't believe her then draw it out anyway. The answer that seemed appropriate: "If I say no, you're going to tell me anyway, aren't you?"

"Yes."

"So, get on with it."

"You take all the fun out of this stuff."

"You shouldn't be so transparent."

"You shouldn't be so damned smart." Jarvis tasted the wine and grimaced. He pushed the glass toward her and asked the waitress to bring a Sam Adams draft. She returned with the beer and the salads.

"So, what did you want to tell me?" Angelina hoped he didn't decide to give her the salad also.

He set the fork on the edge of the plate. Angie smiled inwardly. This must be good. For him to delay stuffing food in his mouth…

"I met up with your mother this morning."

Angie stifled a scowl that said she knew he was indeed going to stretch out the storytelling. "Just so you know, I only have an hour for lunch."

"That's BS. You're the boss, you can take all the time you want."

"Jarvis…"

He heaved a long-suffering sigh. "Okay, you win. Miata Lin and Martin Powers were married July 7th this past year. The marriage certificate was signed by a pastor in Boston. I phoned him. He said he did the ceremony during the 7th inning stretch at a Red Sox/Yankees game."

"She told me they first met during a game between the same two teams."

"Makes sense then."

Angie stabbed a wedge of lettuce. "There's more?"

"While I was in the records, I checked for a certificate between he and Blanche. They were married July 12, 2011."

"Almost four years ago."

"Right."

"There's no mention of a divorce, is there?"

"What do you mean?"

"Well, it's possible he and Blanche were married, then divorced but are now back together, though not remarried."

"And you're suggesting that in the meantime he could've married Miata Lin."

She shrugged.

"I admit, I didn't look for anything like that because even if there was a divorce, it doesn't explain his marriage under the name Leland Powers to Chia Mariachi in 2012."

No, it didn't.

"I want to say there's no solid evidence saying Stone, Martin and Leland are the same person, except we know they are."

He inhaled, exhaled and sipped the beer. "I looked for other possible marriages over the past five years. There were quite a few under the name of Powers. Not knowing what first names might've used, I don't have anything to go on… I have to talk to him."

"God, Jarvis, what am I going to do if I have to replace him?"

"You do have an understudy, right?"

"Yes, but…"

"But just so we're on the same page, you don't want me to check for divorces?"

"What do you think?"

"I think I should cover all the bases. What time does he get out of rehearsal?"

She explained how Blanche had taken him home early. Very early.

"Makes things easy then. I'll go see him as soon as I'm done eating."

"Okay. So…you said you saw my mother?"

"Yes, she and Rickie were at the country store. Arguing."

"I guess she found him." Angie told him about her mother's voicemail. "Must be she went out looking for him."

Jarvis tapped the back of her hand. "You know something."

"I know nussing, nussing," she mimicked the Hogan's Heroes character from her youth. She checked her watch. "I have to go to work." She wrapped both arms around him and kissed him enough to last till they were together again.

Back at the theater, the last of the crew and builders had gone. Mr. Quattro had said the painting crew and another crew who'd install ductwork for the kitchen would be here in the morning. The restaurant was coming together. Right now, the building was eerily quiet. Angie stood, arms crossed, in her new office, gazing at the bay. A lone fisherman holding a fishing pole stood over a hole in the ice, head ducked against the perpetual wind that whistled into this vee-shaped area at the southern end of Lake Winnipesaukee.

Angie's painter had finished her office. It now sported a fresh coat of pumpkin color paint. He'd hung her painting of Kratos—even though he said it was the ugliest thing he'd seen in a long time. She hadn't bothered explaining its significance.

Thinking of Tyson made her want to talk to him. She punched the number 2 in her auto-dial. He answered on the second ring. "Hey, pretty lady. How're things going in Prince & Pauper land?"

"Normal. Only a few glitches."

"Glitches in the theater business! How can that be?"

She didn't let out the laugh he expected. "Let's see, there's my mother trying to set me up with the restaurant guy, Montez is working in the theater, my mother and Rickie are having sexual troubles, the leading man has three wives and a nasal condition."

Tyson laughed. She pictured the handsome young man throwing back his head the way he always did, and letting it rip. Tyson loved to laugh. He and Stone would've gotten along so well. Angie realized she had a death grip on the phone. From letting the troubles become verbal, or missing—needing—her partner? Probably some of both.

"Yup. Sounds like things are running same as usual."

"So, how is the big city?"

"Going good. I got the part."

"The lead?" Her voice came out as a high-pitched squeak. A dream come true. Angie was glad for him, but had to admit, a small part of her had wished he'd miss out and come back to Alton, to Prince & Pauper.

"Yes. We start rehearsals in three days."

"I bet you can hardly contain your excitement."

"I'll manage."

She heard the grin in his voice.

"How's my replacement doing?"

"Kiana's awesome. I wish you were here to see her enthusiasm and emotional development." She told how she'd been gradually expanding Kiana's responsibilities. "Speaking of Kiana, she had a great idea. What if we present our summer performance outdoors?"

"That's a great idea. Where could... Hey wait, what if we do it at HeavenScent?"

"Tyson."

"Oh wait, that won't work. Your mother will never agree to anything that intrusive…"

"Tyson."

"No matter, I'm sure we can find someplace—"

"Tyson!"

"Huh? Sorry. I got carried away. What did you say?"

"Mother loved the idea."

Silence. Then, "You're kidding."

"Nope." Angie outlined some of the ideas they'd come up with so far.

"Is she on drugs or something?"

Angie laughed.

"Not much time to get something so huge together."

"You don't know Kiana. I swear she could have this thing ready by next week." Angie told about the plans for the staging and transportation.

"Hey, I have an idea. Rehearsals here don't start for three days. I'll come help out."

"You don't have to do that. Rest up. Learn your lines." Please come. Please come.

"I'll hire a private plane. Can you send someone to pick me up? I'll let you know what time."

"Of course."

"And reserve me a motel room?"

"You can stay at the condo. Can't wait to see you." She hung up.

A soft knock sounded. Kiana stepped through the open doorway.

"I thought everyone had gone home."

"I was out front finishing some stuff. I thought you might want to go shopping for fire extinguishers."

With a grin, Angie nodded. She took out her phone and dialed Jarvis.

"Hi," he answered. "What's up?"

"Kiana and I are headed to Concord to look for dresses for opening night, is there anything you need?"

"I have a suit for that shindig but could use a new tie. Pick out anything."

Angie didn't try to stifle the sigh. Men! "What color is the suit?"

"Blue."

She put a hand over the receiver and whispered to Kiana, "His suit is blue." Kiana gave a high-pitched cackle. She covered her mouth and whirled out of the room. "Jarvis, what kind of blue: royal…baby? Cerulean, indigo, midnight—"

"All right, I get your point. It's navy blue."

Kiana, back under control, returned.

"What color shirt are you wearing?" Angie asked.

This time Jarvis was the one who sighed. "Light blue or maybe white. Do you also want to know what color underwear?"

"That I already know."

"What time will you be back?"

"Probably late."

"Okay. Red and I will stay home and clean the house."

Good idea. She didn't say that part out loud. "Oh yes. I just talked to Tyson," she said. Kiana's eyes lit up. "First off, he got the lead in that Broadway show."

"Fantastic," Jarvis said.

Kiana raised two thumbs up.

"And he loves the idea for the summer performance."

"How did he feel about doing it at HeavenScent?"

"Believe it or not, before I got the whole thing out of my mouth, he suggested it. Also, he's got a few days off before rehearsals begin. He's on the way to Alton. I wouldn't be surprised he'll be here by morning."

CHAPTER 11

As Angie and Kiana locked the building, Angie had an idea. "Kiana, would you mind if I brought my mom? She's had some stuff going on and might need the distraction."

"It'll be fun having her along."

Angie hugged her. "You're just being polite." She phoned Gloria and posed the invitation. Her mother was happy for the diversion. "We'll pick you up in ten minutes."

An hour later, the three stood in the dressing room of a women's shop in Meredith. Kiana had slid into a pink gown and stood turning one way and the other in front of a mirror. Gloria hung an identical one in red on the top of the door. "They both set off your dark coloring to perfection."

Mom was right; the red, with its empire waist would accentuate Kiana's high, round breasts while the pink's strapless design would show off her smooth shoulders.

"If you get the pink," Angie said, "I have a sapphire pendant you could borrow."

"And I have a sapphire star you could wear in your hair," Gloria said.

"Consider it sold," Kiana told the saleslady, who hung the dress near the dressing room door.

Kiana grasped Angie's arm. "Now, we'll find yours."

"I saw an emerald green A-line that would look awesome on you." Gloria led Angie to the left and found the dress in question.

Kiana fingered the flowing fabric. "It's so soft."

"Well, hello," said a voice from behind.

Angie, Gloria, and Kiana turned as one to see the Chia pet a white gown with a beaded bodice draped over one arm.

Gloria's brows raised in question—she hadn't met Chia Powers.

"Very pretty." Kiana indicated the gown, though not sounding particularly interested. "Going to a formal or just window shopping?"

"This is for Rocky's opening night performance."

The comment perked up both Kiana and Angie, and elicited another brow-raise from Gloria who, by now, must be feeling quite out of the loop.

Angie couldn't have heard right. Had Chia just said she was going to Stone's opening night? Kiana flashed an uh-oh glance in Angie's direction. Angie hoped Kiana's thoughts didn't spew forth the way they'd done with Miata Lin.

Best option: remain neutral. "It's a very pretty dress. It sets off your dark skin."

"Thanks." She held the dress against herself and turned toward the mirror. "I think I'll try it on." She left.

Kiana pushed the emerald dress into Angie's hands. "I think you should try it on." Though preferring to make a rush to the exit, Angie took the dress and shuffled toward the dressing room.

She liked the color but wasn't sure about the style. It was a little lower cut than she usually wore. The saleswoman whispered, "Gorgeous," before installing her in the cubicle beside Chia.

Gloria said she'd go looking for more gowns. After a minute, she draped a lemon yellow over the door.

"Oh, Mom, that'll make me look all washed out."

"You're probably right. How's the style though? They also have it in a pale blue."

Angie dragged the dress over the door and held it in front of her, peering at her reflection. It had an off-the-shoulder style, which meant she couldn't wear a bra. Angie turned sideways, evaluating the situation. "I like it." She passed the dress back.

"So, are you getting gowns for the opening night also?" Chia called from her cubicle.

"Yes," Angie replied.

"What color is yours?"

"So far, emerald green, but it doesn't sound like I'm finished yet."

"Nice," was all Chia said. "Is there a party after the show?"

How to reply? Surely Blanche intended to go with Stone. She came to all opening nights because she wanted to see how the costumes looked *in action*. A meeting between Blanche and Chia would rival the fireworks over Alton Bay on July 4th. It would be wise to change the subject until she could figure out what to say. "How does your dress look?"

"It's okay. I think I need a smaller size. How are rehearsals going?"

Man, couldn't she stick to a topic Angie *could* talk about? Rehearsals were going well *except* for Stone's side of things. Best if she remained neutral. "Things are going well."

"Could I sit in on one?"

Now this was a question she *could* answer. "No. Sorry. Rehearsals are closed to the general public."

"I'm not exactly the general public."

"Perhaps not. But we don't allow family or friends either. It's a distraction for the cast and crew."

"Seems to me they'd *like* us being there."

Angie realized she hadn't put on the dress yet. She kicked off her shoes. Then she sloughed off the jeans and sweatshirt she'd worn to work that morning and slipped into the mode of Princess Angelina. Kiana was right; the dress was exquisite.

"Have you owned the theater very long?" Chia asked.

"Going on two years."

"Looks like a lot of work."

"It is."

"You should take on a partner."

"You thinking of anyone in particular?" Angie undid the side zipper and let the dress drop. She caught it before it hit the floor.

"Me."

For some reason, Angie expected her to volunteer her husband—to keep him home more often. "You have experience running a business—especially a theater?"

"I was a famous model. My name would draw customers."

That would make Angie's job easier how? Argh! She hung the dress on the hanger and looped it over the hook on the wall. Just then a pale blue one tumbled atop the door. Angie slipped into it. The color wasn't right against her blonde hair. "Do they have this in a darker color?"

"I'll check."

"So, Chia, why aren't you modeling any more?"

"I was in a car crash. Got some serious burns. They waited till I was out of the hospital then fired my ass." Chia's tone was, understandably, bitter. "I'm suin' them but good."

"Who is them?"

She said "Harpers" as if Angie should already know. "How do you live in the meantime?"

"Huh?" The word was muffled as though she'd pulled something over her head.

"I asked how you support yourself. You said you were a librarian, but librarians are notoriously underpaid."

"Oh." Shuffling sounds. "I had a huge insurance policy on my body. All models do."

Someone entered the changing area on soft-soled shoes. "What do you think of that one?" Kiana called.

Before Angie could say she loved it, another dress—this one in royal blue—appeared over the door.

At the same moment, Chia said, "I'm damned mad, that's what."

Angie finished throwing on her clothes, grabbed the newly arrived dress, opened the door as quietly as possible, and tiptoed from the cubicle. "I'll take the green one," she whispered.

Kiana got the hint. She followed, handing the blue dress to the clerk.

"We're going to look like royalty," she said once they were clear of the dressing room.

"Let's hurry. She was asking questions about Stone. Can you find my mother while I pay for these?"

"You can't pay for mine."

"You can pay me back later. We have to hurry."

Although they practically ran, Chia caught up to them in the parking lot. "Hey!"

Angie didn't want to stop but it would set a bad example for the impressionable teen, so she turned and waited for the longhaired black woman to catch up.

"So, did you think about what I said?"

Which thing was that? Oh yes. She wanted to be Angie's partner. "About you sitting in on a rehearsal?" she said.

"Yeah. Did you think about it?"

"No need to think about it. We only allow outsiders at dress rehearsal the night before the opening performance."

"I thought you might make an exception."

"If I did it for you, I'd have to do it when Craig's mom is in town or Jacoby's daughter has just landed a part in her kindergarten play and he wants to show her how it all works. I'm sorry."

The Chia pet flared her nostrils and stepped up so close her breath was hot on Angie's face. "I knew it."

"Knew what?"

"You don't want me around because you're putting the make on Rocky."

"Oh, for gosh-golly sake."

Kiana, who stood by the open door of the car, laughed. Actually it was more of a belly laugh—complete with head thrown back and arms wrapped around the stomach. "You'd better not say that in front of her boyfriend—the cop."

Gloria came to stand beside Angie, who gave Chia a

deliberate eye-roll and whirled away. Before things could get totally out of control she urged her mother toward the passenger door. They'd taken no more than two steps when Angie's sleeve was grasped and she was spun around.

"I *will* be at those rehearsals. And you *will* stay away from Rocky."

Gloria inserted herself between them. Angie stepped around her mother. Last thing she needed was the seventy-one year old getting punched. "I've been holding my tongue, but I'm going to let it out. If your husband is so damned special to you, what were you doing hanging all over Montez Clarke the other day?"

A punch launched at Angie. It glanced off her left ear. She was about to retaliate when a dark-skinned fist flashed past her other ear and popped Chia in the mouth. Blood spurted. Chia squeaked.

Kiana took hold of Angie and Gloria's sleeves and yanked. "Come on, before somebody calls the cops."

"I was about to," Angie said with a chuckle.

"I can see Jarvis's face when he comes to *this* dispute," Gloria laughed.

Angie hung the dresses in the backseat and climbed in. Gloria got in front. The door was barely shut before Kiana jammed her foot on the gas. If the tires on the small car could've laid rubber, they would have.

She zipped into traffic. "Where do you want to go for dinner?"

How could the girl sound so poised and calm? Angie's insides were thumping like bass drums.

"You struck that woman," Gloria said.

"She hit Angie."

"She pretty much missed," Angie said.

Kiana giggled. "I didn't know that." She flipped on the right turn signal. "Doesn't matter anyway, she tried to hit you. In law school they call it *intent*."

"Riiiight." Why was a girl majoring in theater management

talking in law-speak?

"Kiana, you hit that woman," Gloria said.

"Sometimes you gotta do what you gotta do."

"Yes, but you were proactive. Most girls would stand there and screech or pull hair, wait for a man to come help. Good going!"

"She's right," Angie said. "These days we women have to take care of ourselves."

"There's something confusing me," Kiana said. "Actually two things."

"What's that?" Angie asked.

"First, what makes her think you're interested in Stone? You haven't flirted with him one bit. You barely even laugh at his stories. And you never talk to him in any way other than businesslike." Kiana went silent a moment, but Angie could see the wheels turning in her heard. Finally she said, "Second… didn't she come to the theater with Montez yesterday?"

"The answer to the first question is, because she's insecure. She'd suspect anyone who spoke to him. To the second question, yes."

"I guess I have a lot to learn about life and relationships."

No reply seemed needed.

They watched behind them all the way to the restaurant and then home. They didn't see Chia's black Audi. But Angie knew they would, and soon.

Kiana turned into the theater parking lot so Angie could pick up her car. "I had fun tonight."

Angie laughed. "Most of it was. Careful going down this hill, it looks slippery."

"Hey, what's Stone's car doing here?"

"Blanche took him home today because he was…sick."

"He was drunk, wasn't he?"

"Yes. What made you think that?"

"I saw them going out the door. Besides, the cast was talking about it."

"Drunk?" asked Gloria.

Angie explained the events of the day.

"That's just rude—to you as his boss, to his co-workers. What're you going to do about it?"

"Have a talk with him in the morning."

"Good. Don't let it go too long," Gloria said. "Angie… question: if Tyson was here, would you pass the job on to him?"

"In this case, yes. I think guy-to-guy, it would go better."

"So, why not ask Jarvis?"

"Because this is my problem. I ordered a case of big-girl panties today. Amazon must've felt sorry for me, they sent them with free shipping. You have any trouble with him, Kiana, let me know and you can borrow a pair."

A laughing Kiana made a U-turn at the bottom of the lot. "My brother always said I should grow a pair."

Angie shook off a chuckle. "Jarvis is planning to talk to him today. What Stone's doing is illegal. Unless there's extenuating circumstances. If not, Jarvis needs to report it."

"He needs to get them all in one room," Gloria said.

"And start World War III."

She stopped near Angie's Lexus. "Man, I just thought of something!" Kiana said. "We forgot to get those fire extinguishers."

Their laughter was cut off as Kiana's headlights shone on Stone's silver BMW. The entire right side of the car, from bumper to bumper, had been sideswiped. "Wow. Will you look at that!"

"That's one of the reasons not to drink and drive. Good thing he wasn't hurt."

"I'll see you in the morning," Kiana said. "Thanks for buying dinner. I'll pay you for the dress tomorrow."

"No problem. I'll double check that the back door's locked and the alarm is on," Angie said.

"I'll go around and check the front," Kiana said.

"Angie," said Gloria, "give me the keys, I'll warm up your car."

"Push the blue button, I have a car starter."

"Ooh, I need one of those." Kiana waved bye then drove up to the front of the building.

Gloria hung the gowns in the backseat of the Lexus.

Treading carefully on the slick pavement, Angie checked the theater's back door. The builders had finished the flooring for the restaurant's outdoor eating deck. From underneath, the thing looked huge. She was glad Mr. Quattro had extended it to include her office. It'd be a great place to sit and read scripts, while boaters and jet skiers whizzed around the bay.

As she maneuvered the car past Stone's vehicle she wondered if the crash had been reported. It was only nine o'clock. Jarvis should still be awake. She'd wait to call him after dropping her mother off at HeavenScent.

"I took your advice and talked to Rickie about our problem," Gloria said. "He didn't take it well."

Angie laughed. "Sorry to laugh, but...Mom, by any chance, did you try to talk to him while you were in the country store?"

"You said do it when he's calm."

"Yes, but not in public."

"That probably explains his reaction."

What world did her mother live in where she hadn't learned any common sense?

Ten minutes later, Angie pulled the car into the long, wide driveway. Snowbanks lined each side.

"I hope he's home by now," Gloria said.

"He wasn't there when you left?"

"No. He said he was going for a drive."

"Did you leave him a note?"

"No. I figured it'd be good for him to wonder. It's what I've been sitting around doing all the time."

Though it wasn't the right way to handle a problem, Angie probably would've done the same thing.

"I'll talk to you tomorrow. Love you," Gloria said.

"I love you too, Mom."

As Angie left the driveway, she checked the messages on

her phone. Tyson had called to say he would arrive at the small, local airport in the morning. She texted, *I'll meet you.*

She phoned Jarvis. "How'd the evening go?" he asked.

"Mostly good. We all found great gowns for opening night. I forgot your tie. I'll explain later."

"Now *that* I want to hear about."

"Dinner was awesome."

"Good. Tyson call yet?"

"Yes. I'm picking him up at seven. Oh yes, the reason I phoned—well, really there were two reasons. Did you talk to Stone?"

"Nobody was home. Don't worry, I'll catch up to him. Soon. Very soon. What was the second thing?"

"Did you have any reports of Stone's car being in a crash?" She described the vehicle's condition.

There was a moment of silence. Was he checking or simply surprised? He finally said, "I didn't hear anything. I'll swing by to look at it in a few minutes. Want to meet at the diner for breakfast?"

"Sounds good. How about eight-ish, Tyson and I should be back by then."

"I'll go early and get a table."

"Good. Oh, the reason I didn't buy the tie. The Chia pet was at the dress shop." She talked through his "uh-oh". She was buying a gown to wear to opening night."

Another "Uh-oh."

She detailed their confrontation. "Jarvis, you won't believe it, Kiana punched her."

Another few seconds of silence. "Why?"

"Because she swung at me."

"Are you hurt?"

"No, it was a glancing blow. Mrs. Chia pet Powers will probably have a black eye though."

He was quiet again, probably wishing he'd been there. The cute black woman would be lounging in a cell right now, unable to throw punches at anyone but cinder block.

"Mom went with us."

"Your idea or hers?"

"Mine." Angie stopped in front of her condo. "I thought it would help get her mind off the troubles with Rickie."

"Did she behave herself?"

"She was awesome. She joked around and even congratulated Kiana for whacking Chia. She said we women need to stand up for ourselves."

"Better watch out. If you're not careful, you might end up with a normal mother/daughter relationship."

CHAPTER 12

Saturday

Tyson and Angelina entered the diner chatting like lifelong friends. The two were different as night and day and yet it was odd what a rapport they had almost from the beginning. Most people who met under the umbrella of a murder would go their own way when all was said and done glad to be back to their real lives. But Angelina and Tyson had become partners in the theater, each assuming responsibilities where they could excel. They'd made money from the outset, and for two years, things only improved. Then, just before Christmas, Tyson dropped the bomb—he'd been approached by a famous Broadway producer and was leaving for the neon lights. Though Angelina must've hated the situation, she jumped without complaint into the job as owner/director/producer/troubleshooter. Far as Jarvis could see, except for a few bumps in the road she was doing great.

He stood and shook hands with Tyson. The man hadn't changed much in the weeks he'd been gone—from his expertly styled sandy blond hair to his GQ wardrobe and ready smile. Jarvis's first impression of Tyson Goodwell had been that of a womanizing wuss who'd never worked a day in his life. Never had he been so wrong about someone—except for the woman-thing—they flocked to him like flies to sugar. He should get along great with Stone.

The server came and hugged Tyson, holding the coffeepot out to the side. Tyson and Angelina settled into the booth as the waitress poured coffee then took everyone's breakfast orders.

"So, what's been going on with you?" Tyson asked Jarvis.

"Same old same old. Work, sleep, repeat. You?"

"Life's been an absolute zoo. My parents are having some health problems so I've been keeping an eye on them. The theater has me working on rewrites for their play."

"I remember it was pretty poorly written," Angelina said.

"It's tons better now. Other than that, I've been studying lines."

"You and Angelina must have a lot of catching up to do," Jarvis said.

"We text almost every day. She's doing a great job."

"Kiana's been a big help," Angelina said. "In discussions about this new play, we've come up with a few ideas. Ways to promote community interest in the theater. What do you think about putting together a five- or six-person troupe of actors that'll travel around to different venues doing one-hour skits? We could do high schools, fairs, farmers markets—anyplace a lot of people gather."

"I love the idea."

"I like it too," Jarvis volunteered. "Only one thing bothers me about it. Angelina's already got a ton of responsibility on her plate."

"Right, and I have an idea about that too," she said. "This won't be something that comes together quickly. We'll need money to buy a van or small bus, signage, advertising. I just wanted to run the idea past you. We thought of a name for it though: *One for the Road*."

"Love it," Tyson said.

"Any ideas where to get a bus?" she asked.

He and Jarvis both grinned. "I'm sure you'll find one."

They spent an enjoyable breakfast catching up on news.

In the parking lot, they were saying their goodbyes. "Hey," Tyson said, "what if I take you all out for dinner tonight—your mom and Rickie too."

Jarvis caught Angelina's eye in a non-verbal question

whether she had anything planned. She nodded to Tyson. "Sounds great. I'll see if Mom and Rickie are free."

"I can do it if you want, I'm heading to HeavenScent to pick up some clothes."

"If you drop me at the theater, you can take my car. The condo key is on the ring."

"Great. Thanks." Tyson left.

"What did he mean about picking up clothes?" Jarvis asked.

"Oh, forgot to tell you, he's staying with me."

"Good thing you told me. I would've been shocked meeting up with him in the bathroom in the morning."

Jarvis kissed Angelina goodbye and got in his Jeep. He called headquarters to let them know where he'd be for the next half hour or so. Jarvis wanted to take some pictures of Stone's damaged car. After Angelina's call last night, he'd checked with dispatch and learned that there had been no reports of either hit-and-runs or crashes of any kind in the past two days. Of course, Stone might've smashed the car before that. Or maybe the crash didn't involve another vehicle. Or maybe he hadn't been driving. Either way, last night it had been too dark to get the pictures.

He parked ten feet from the vehicle, got out and skirted the perimeter of Stone's car. About an inch of snow had fallen during the night. No footprints or tire treads marked the surface. He wondered why Angelina wasn't here. She'd left before him and it was less than a half-mile from the diner.

Jarvis walked around Stone's car a second time, this time closer up. He crouched and examined the car-length damage that graduated from a slight scrape at each end to a large dent behind the passenger door. He wrote down the facts, and some theories, in his notebook. Then he snapped a few pictures, paying particular attention to the black paint lodged in the dent. He was posting the pictures to his computer at the station when Angelina's Lexus appeared over the rise.

She gestured through the windshield, asking if it was all right to park there. He nodded so she pulled in next to the

BMW.

She and Tyson got out and came toward him. Jarvis's driver's side window was down. Red had squeezed herself between the headrest and the window frame, and managed to get her head out. Her tongue made lapping motions toward Angelina who went over and gave the big hairy dog an arm's length pat on the head. Then she kissed Jarvis.

"What took you two so long to get here?"

Tyson patted Red also. "We met up with some people I hadn't seen since before I left."

"What's going on here?" Angie asked.

"Making a report. There's black paint in the scrape. Go check. See if it looks familiar."

"You want me to see if paint looks familiar?"

"What I want is your opinion about the dent."

It wasn't three seconds before she said, "He didn't hit anyone. Somebody hit him."

Jarvis nodded. "Looks like it."

They followed Angelina to the dented side of Stone's car. She bent and gave Jarvis a good view at her perfect backside. He refrained from looking at Tyson who had the exact same perspective.

"Lots of people have black cars, but I'll keep my eyes open for one with damage. It should be extensive." Angelina stopped. And grinned. "The Chia pet has a black Audi."

"Is that right? I'll add it to my report." He waved the notebook in the air, ducked into the car, and stashed it in a folder on the front seat. Red, who'd been lavishing under Tyson's attention, tried to get to Jarvis wiggling so hard she knocked herself off the seat. Jarvis gave her a biscuit from his coat pocket and the dog settled to crunching.

"What have you two got going on today?" he asked.

"We began rehearsals yesterday. That's when Stone um... got sick and had to go home. So, we'll start at the beginning today. I'd like Tyson to stand in and make sure I haven't missed anything."

"Gladly," Tyson said, softly.

"Did you have a reason for asking?" Angelina asked Jarvis.

"Only that I wondered if you wanted to ride to Meredith this afternoon. I have to pick up some paperwork at the courthouse."

"Sounds good. Call me first though to make sure nothing's happened to change things."

"Don't worry about it," Tyson said. "I'll take care of whatever comes up."

"I can't ask you to do that. You didn't come back here to work."

"Angie, shut up." Tyson laughed.

So did Jarvis. "Guess he told you."

"Don't get any ideas about ordering me around," Angie said.

Jarvis threw an arm around her and kissed her soundly. They got too close to the Jeep though and Red stuck her tongue in Angelina's ear.

Angie gagged. Jarvis laughed. Tyson handed over a handkerchief and she swiped off the dog slobber. "I have to go to work."

"Me too." Jarvis urged the dog into the backseat and got in the car. "See ya."

CHAPTER 13

Angie and Tyson walked toward the back door of the theater. The carpenters were hard at work on the long deck. "Progress on the restaurant is going forward even though it's the dead of winter," Tyson noted.

"I have the idea that with Mr. Quattro, things get done. Seasons don't matter."

"That was the impression I had when I met him." Tyson took hold of her left hand and held it in front of her face. "So, eight weeks have passed since I left for the city and you're still not wearing an engagement ring."

"Could say the same thing to you. You're not getting any younger, you know."

"You sound like my mother."

Angie laughed. "I'll take that as an insult. The times I've spoken to your mother—well, let's just say I hope I never sound like her."

"I think she is realizing her age, and the chances of her seeing grandchildren, especially since I'm an only child. So... what about you?"

"I don't want to get married."

"So, he's asked?"

"Yes, though not for a while. Probably he changed his mind."

"Or got tired of being shot down?" Tyson laughed. "Maybe he doesn't want to be married to a workaholic."

"Are you heading to HeavenScent now?" she asked.

"Changing the subject, huh? Okay, have it your way." He held the door so she could pass. "I thought I'd pop in here first. It's only ten-thirty, your mom's probably not up and around yet."

"Probably not."

"What did you mean when you said Stone got sick?" Tyson lowered his voice halfway through the sentence as it echoed up the stairwell.

Angie reluctantly told him about Stone's drinking problem. This was all on her shoulders; she didn't want to make it his responsibility. "I'm going to speak with him today. I'm not putting up with any nonsense."

"No need to. There are plenty of actors willing to step into his shoes. Tell him that."

"Besides, if I let one person get out of line, I'll end up with anarchy."

"Who's his understudy?"

"Jacoby."

"Jacoby Meyers would be perfect," Tyson said. "You are giving Stone another chance though, right?"

"Of course. But he'll be on a short leash."

"Good. You did exactly as I would've done."

"Thanks for saying so. That makes me feel better."

Angie showed Tyson around the second floor. A lot had been done while he'd been gone. They ended the tour in her new office.

"Nice choice of colors."

"I coordinated it with Kratos."

Tyson walked close to the painting. He laughed. "Ugly dude, ain't he?"

"Yup." She laughed. "You should've heard the painter when I gave him the color scheme."

Tyson laughed. "I was sure you'd hide him in a closet."

"Why would I hide a painter in the closet?" She giggled. "Believe it or not, Krato is my inspiration."

"I love the office though. Great view." He stood watching the same fisherman who'd caught her interest yesterday.

"I'd hoped to move in here today but Mr. Quattro's man is installing French doors to the deck."

"Deck? You're getting a deck?"

Tyson went to look as she told him how their tenant had taken things in-hand. "Like you said, he gets things done. I gave him hell though." She lowered her voice for effect. "Though secretly, I'm glad to have it. I don't have an outdoor place at the condo so it'll be a great place to sit and read scripts."

"And escape your mother."

"That goes without saying." She sighed. Was it being a bad daughter to wish Momma would find her own town to live in? "I planned to have the carpenters put an identical one outside your office in the spring."

He assumed a pouty expression. "Does that mean you expect me to bomb on Broadway?"

"Don't be ridiculous. I envision your name in ten foot tall letters."

They walked down to the first floor, Tyson's wistful expression said he'd missed the place.

The phone was ringing in her closet-office. He patted her arm. "You have things to do. I'm going to walk around and get re-acclimated."

Angie settled at her desk. She let the machine answer the phone. It was most always a salesperson. She checked messages, paid bills, and proofed some ad copy.

Thumping in the hallway had her going out to check on the commotion. She found Montez on hands and knees—at least that rear end looked familiar—attaching cable wire to the wall studs. He must've sensed her standing there because she didn't think she'd made a sound. He glanced up and back, then sat on the floor and wiped the back of a hand across his sweaty forehead.

"Like the view?"

"Yeah." Damn, she should think before letting things pop

from her mouth. Before she could stick her foot further into her maw, Angie asked how things were going with Chia.

"Dunno. Haven't seen her. She's called and texted a few times but I'm done with that BS." He shot her that legendary Chiclet grin. The one that sent trickles of shivers all the way to her toenails.

"I heard something." He glanced up and down the hallway. Lowered his voice, "Heard this Powers guy got more than one Chia hanging around."

Angie didn't answer right away. She wasn't sure how much to divulge.

Montez nodded. "Figured you knew."

She smiled. How could he always tell what she was thinking?

"Not gonna end well, you know."

"I know. Jarvis is on it."

"Good." Montez hiked himself back onto his knees. Before going back to work, he said, "You be careful. No good can come of this." He lifted the cable wire, but lowered it and looked up. "I don't wanna have to rescue you again." He chuckled and went back to work.

Angie, wishing she *had* gotten those fire extinguishers yesterday, returned to her office, this time closing the door. Outside of Montez's continued snide chuckles, the place was dead silent. For the moment, she would enjoy it because sure as the sun rose in the east, it would only last another—

The back door banged open. Thumps releasing slush from boots, and the shuffle of those boots approached. Seconds later, the set designer stepped through the doorway. Fred Saunders, wearing his trademark bib overalls and a coating of sawdust, knocked on the frame. "I wondered if you'd like to come check out the sets."

She guessed that was one of Tyson's regular duties though she didn't recall it being on the list he'd left. Angie rose. "Of course." She followed Fred to the other side of the building, hoping to meet up with Tyson so he could look too.

In Fred's workshop, piles of lumber graced the wall near

a loading dock. On the other side of the room, used sets were suspended from runners along the ceiling. They could be turned like giant pages. He gestured to the third in line. "We'll use this one: a basic office, and the fifth: a storage room."

In the center of the room was what Fred had been prepping for this show: a landscape of a construction site. Since this play took place mostly 'on the site' this set would be used more than any of the others.

"This is great, Fred. I especially like the realism of the bulldozer." She made a clicking sound with her tongue. "You boys and your toys. Great work. I wonder…can you possibly add a couple stacks of building supplies?" She pointed behind the dozer.

"Sure, good idea, miss."

"Angie. I'm Angie."

Thankfully, he hadn't acted as though the request was anything unusual. Tyson was a perfectionist; surely he requested a lot more than that. Angie reminded herself to ask him. She told Fred, "You do very nice work," and went back to the green room.

"Well done," came Tyson's voice behind her.

"What?"

"What you said to Fred."

"You were spying?"

"Of course not. I was on my way to say hi to him."

"Would you have asked him to make other changes than what I did?" she asked.

"Might've asked for a more detailed background—a highway, cars, people."

"I didn't think of that."

"You can't think of everything. I'll mention it later."

The cast had arrived; the multiple clomp of feet rattled the floors of the old building.

"Come on. Let's go see the cast."

She stood back and let him go into the green room alone. The cast turned, expecting to see her. They stood open-mouthed as Tyson rushed forward to hug them all—even the newcomers.

Craig Evert, one of the six regular cast members, grew somber. "Does this mean you bombed on Broadway?"

"No. I got the part." Above the catcalls and cheers, he said, "I had a few days off and came to visit."

Everyone took off their heavy coats and either dumped them on the table or hung them in lockers.

"Ready to get to work?" Angie asked. "Scene one actors, on stage. The rest of you in the pit."

They filed past. Everyone was here, including Stone. With the crowd surrounding Tyson, Angie hadn't seen him long enough to assess his condition. Were the others avoiding him or was it coincidence? Did he keep his head turned away on purpose? She understood if he was embarrassed.

Angie followed them through the hallway. Stone appeared to be walking straight and steady.

He was playing the part of the construction company owner. Craig Evert was the crew foreman and Vic Jason would be one of the construction crew. They turned left and stopped just off-stage to don hard hats—the only 'costume' they'd use for the time being. Then they headed onto the stage. Angie, Tyson, and the rest of the cast filed down the stairs. She took up her usual spot in the center of the first row. Tyson settled beside her.

She pointed to Kiana, who took charge. They waited for Stone to dose his nasal condition, then he nodded that he was ready.

Craig stepped up to Vic and took off his hard hat. He ran a hand through his tousled hair—a good adlib, Angie thought. "What's the boss gonna say when he finds out those tools are missing from the shed?" he said.

Vic shrugged. "Somebody's in some deep crap. Any idea who did it?"

Craig shook his head. "No clue."

"You know I'll have to tell him I saw you arguing with Brad

yesterday," Vic said.

"Don't you dare."

Angie stole a look at Tyson. He was leaned forward in his chair, elbows on knees, focused on the stage. She wondered if he wished he'd stayed. Sure, acting on Broadway had been a lifelong dream, but so had owning a theater. His enthusiasm for it was the only reason she'd remained here after the divorce. But she hadn't regretted a moment. What a learning experience it had been to go from an ER nurse to half-ownership in a community theater.

On stage, Vic said, "Here comes the boss now."

Craig shook a fist at him. "You say anything and you'll be sorry."

Stone arrived from stage right carrying a clipboard, the strap of a hardhat dangling from a baby finger. Vic stepped forward, his gaze avoiding Craig. He explained the problem.

Stone nodded. "Was the shed locked? I—" He stopped and visibly swallowed, his adam's apple making up and down movements. What was with that? No way he could be nervous. It was only a rehearsal. And he wasn't adlibbing; it didn't fit the scene.

Stone's face went white. The hardhat and clipboard clattered to the floor as he spewed vomit all over the other two men. The cast seated around Angie grunted as if someone had held up a big sign. Instead of APPLAUSE it said GROAN. Craig and Vic stood in stunned silence, looking first at Stone then their clothing.

Stone sagged like a burst balloon and dropped into his own mess.

"Call an ambulance!" Kiana shouted.

Tyson raced up on stage. Craig and Vic rolled Stone over. "He's breathing," Craig said in obvious relief—probably that he didn't have to perform CPR.

"No amb—" Stone shouted on a groan. He clutched his middle.

"But—" said Kiana.

"No."

Angie hurried up the steps to stoop beside the ailing man who was struggling to sit up, grasping his stomach and moaning. "Is there anything we can do for you?" she asked.

Stone rolled his head from side to side once. "Home."

"I don't think that's a—" Tyson said.

"N-no—" Stone threw up again, specks getting on Angie's sneakers. She took a half-step backward.

The cast stood at the front of the stage looking scared but ready to help if needed.

"No hospital." Stone swiped the back of a hand across his mouth.

"Somebody bring him to my office, please," Angie said.

Vic and Craig guided Stone to his feet, and, one on each side, shuffled him down the hallway.

"Somebody get him a pail," Angie said. "Do I have a volunteer to clean this up?"

"I got it." Fred hustled in from the wings with a mop and pail.

"Thanks."

She waited in her office doorway till Stone was made comfortable on the shabby sofa, a plastic pail on the floor beside him, which Stone used almost instantly. Angie turned away. She wanted to barf herself.

Tyson plucked a handful of tissues from the box on the desk and shoved them at Stone. "Do you want us to call anyone?" he asked.

"Blanche."

Angie dialed. While she waited for her designer to pick up, Kiana entered. "Is there anything I can do?"

"Can you keep the rehearsal going? Keep things as normal as possible."

"Sure." She tilted her head toward Stone, which Angie took to mean *what do I do about his part?*

"One minute." It looked like she had to use her first understudy. Thankfully he was in the building. "Stone, there's no answer at Blanche's. Would you mind if I call my mother to take you home?"

"If you think...she wouldn't...mind."

"Don't worry. If she can't, I will," Tyson said.

Gloria answered on the second ring and agreed without argument to help out. "I'll be there in ten minutes."

Angie hung up. Now that the emergency was over, her anger blossomed. And grew. How dare he come to work in that condition? She stepped from the office so she wouldn't say anything for which she'd later be sorry. Angie understood how the pressures of his living situation could drive him into a bottle, but there was nothing ruder than bringing it to work, subjecting other people to his troubles, making a disgusting mess in front of his co-workers.

Kiana came back in the office. "Uh, there's a problem out front."

Must be a doozy if 1-Kiana couldn't handle it herself, and, 2-she couldn't talk about it in front of Stone.

"Hang tight, Stone. I'll be right back."

"I'll stay with him," Tyson said.

As they cleared the green room, Kiana whispered, "The Chia pet is here. She insists on sitting in on the rehearsal. I didn't think you'd want me to hit her again."

Angie patted Kiana on the shoulder. "Hang around, I might need your right hook." Usually Angie liked proactive people, but didn't like ones who wouldn't take no for an answer. "Where is she?"

Kiana raised her hand to point toward the foyer, but angry voices near the stage made her drop it and turn. Not only was the woman stubborn, she was also bold.

"Tell me now!" Chia shouted. "Where is Rocky? Where is my husband!"

Thankfully, the crew had no idea who she meant. Their open-mouthed stares were genuine.

Angie marched toward her. Not in the mood for games, and, if she were to be honest, desperate to keep Stone's condition a secret, she took hold of Chia's coat sleeve and tugged. The woman dug in her boot heels but the model-turned-librarian was no match for an irate Angelina Farnsworth Deacon.

Amid cheers from the cast and crew, Angie hauled Chia up the aisle, through the double-doors, and out into the foyer.

"Okay people," Kiana said, "show's over. Let's get back to work."

Angie spun Chia around and got in her face. "You're not a stupid woman but you're really acting like one. I know you understood when I said no general public allowed—"

"And I told you I was keeping an eye on you and my husband. Where is he? I noticed neither of you were on stage."

"A number of people aren't on stage. Oh, why am I explaining anything to you? I don't owe you crap. Now, unless you'd like a ride in a police car, I suggest you leave. Now." She grasped the woman's arm again and thrust her toward the door.

Chia shook off Angie's grip, gave her a shove against the wall, moved around her, and started back into the auditorium. Angie caught up to her partway down the aisle. Craig and Vic leaped from the stage and had Chia in-hand before Angie could make contact again.

"Where do you want her?" Craig asked.

"Off the property."

Chia wrestled and kicked but she was no match for the men who'd been chosen for their roles as construction workers because of their brawn. "God, you two smell awful," she said.

Finally Angie had something to laugh about.

CHAPTER 14

As they manhandled Chia through the doors, the remaining cast cheered.

Angie waited till they grappled the woman into her car. Vic and Craig returned to the building but remained in the entrance, arms folded. Montez had joined them. He alone could've filled the doorway. No doubt about it, Chia Powers was not getting back in the building today.

With a sigh, Angie slipped between the three men, her arm brushing Montez's as she did. He didn't move one inch. She hurried back to her office, goosebumps popping like corn in a movie theater. Tyson was leaned against her desk, arms crossed, eyes on Stone.

Kiana returned. "I brought his jacket." Then she added, "And, your mother's here," in a won't this day ever end tone.

Tyson rolled his eyes. Angie smiled. "Mom's here to drive Stone home."

She and Tyson fed Stone's arms into his sleeves, then each took an elbow and guided him through the auditorium—where everyone wished him well—then out into Gloria's new Mercedes. Kiana took one look at the car, and said, "I'll go get the pail."

Angie gave her mother Blanche's address to plug into the GPS unit. "Thanks, Mom."

Finally Stone was on his way. Angie, shivering, went back inside. She felt bad for asking this of her mother. It had to bring back a lot of negative memories. How many times had Gloria run the same rescue mission for Angie's father?

"Man, when you said there was never a dull moment, you meant it! What's next?" Tyson asked.

"Gotta get the understudy." She sought out Jacoby Meyers. Hired as a gopher/janitor last year, he'd made himself invaluable around the theater. At one point, he'd tried out for a part and surprised them all. His voice was deep with a natural resonation that went to the back of the auditorium.

She found him backstage helping Fred paint the requested details on the set wall. Jacoby's dark hair was cut short. His closely trimmed beard outlined a strong chin. "Jacoby, when you get done here, could you come to my office?"

"Sure. Just let me wash my hands."

He was of similar build to Stone, but didn't possess the confidence or charisma, though he doled out humorous lines equally as well.

In less than five minutes, he stood in the office doorway. Angie got up from her chair, though she much would've preferred staying there, and waved Jacoby toward the couch where Stone had just been. Once he got comfortable, she leaned against the front edge of the desk. By now everyone had to know of Stone's problem so she got right to the point. "Starting tomorrow, I *might* need you to fill in for Stone."

Jacoby grinned wide and nodded hard. Then he sobered. "Would it be too forward to admit I've memorized his lines—and Craig's too—just in case? I'm ready to go anytime you need me."

"A good understudy is always ready to assume the job." She was glad Tyson had hired this man. "Hoping for a big chance, huh?"

He gave a wistful raise to his eyebrows. "Reviewers don't notice minor characters."

"They do, but you're right, it happens a lot less often. So, you'd like larger parts?"

"Someday I'd like to star on Broadway." He shook his

head. "I will get there...like Tyson."

"I'll keep your request in mind, but there's something else. I've got an idea—two ideas, actually—brewing in the back of my head." She waved her hand. "Don't look so frightened."

She explained her idea for the One for the Road group. "They'll put on one-hour performances at small venues like schools, nursing homes, outdoor events."

Jacoby broke into a toothy smile. "Are you saying you want me as one of that group?"

"As I said, it's just a germ of an idea right now. My thought was for you to lead up that troupe." She held up her hand as his grin widened. "If it happens. The idea is to promote interest in community-theater in general, and particularly in Prince & Pauper... But at the same time it'll give you actors—whether on the road or here—wider exposure. The second idea..." Tyson entered the room. When he hesitated, she gestured that he wasn't intruding. "The second idea is that we're going to start giving acting classes," Angie finished. "For all age groups."

"I'd love to be involved in either thing," Jacoby said. "Wherever you think I'd be a better fit. I don't know what sort of transportation you'll use when the troupe is on the road, but I have a current CDL license."

Angie thought that meant he could drive a truck.

Tyson broke into a wide grin. "I love the idea of acting lessons. We'd have to hire an instructor."

"Yes. This is just a germ of an idea, so I'll have to be looking around."

"You might contact the theater association. Surely, they'd know someone." Tyson pointed a finger at Angie and then Jacoby. "I was thinking about the troupe. Why not see if the town will add it as part of their Old Home festivities in August. If you want, I can talk to the town manager and get his thoughts."

"Would you mind?"

"I offered, didn't I?"

"Those are all good ways to promote," Jacoby said. "Especially if you take that to schools and places where there are a lot of young folks. If the troupe performs, it could draw people to the acting lessons."

"Exactly. Anyway, there have been a few delays around here that are, in part, keeping the ideas from germinating properly."

"I've noticed."

Angie smiled and leaned away from the desk, a sign their meeting was ending.

He stood and shook her hand then shook Tyson's. "Thanks. It's nice to see you again, Tyson. And I appreciate the opportunity to take over for Stone, even if it's temporary. I won't let you guys down." He started for the door, stopped and turned back.

"Thanks. Jacoby, would you tell Kiana that when rehearsal's over I'd like to see her?"

"Sure." He shut the door.

Tyson leaned against her desk, arms crossed. "Jeez, it's dark. How could you stand it here while I was in the bright, sunny office?"

"Wasn't easy sometimes," she laughed. "Good thing I'm not claustrophobic."

He didn't laugh. "Jarvis is worried you're stretching yourself too thin."

"These are only ideas we've been tossing around. I'm thinking about hiring a general manager."

"Might be a good idea. I could come back now and then too."

"No, you have enough on your hands in New York. Especially now with your parents not doing so well."

He feigned a pout. "A guy could get the idea you didn't want him here."

She threw a pillow from the sofa at him.

"I assume you're thinking of promoting Kiana." He replaced the pillow, plumping it into a corner.

"No." She told him her idea for paying for Kiana to go to college.

Tyson nodded. "Good idea. I'm headed back to HeavenScent for a while. I want to check the logistics for the summer show."

The idea for the acting classes had popped into her head just a millisecond before the words left her lips. In spite of that, it seemed like a great idea. Angie also had another thought—jeez, ideas were sprouting faster than weeds in a garden.

She was deep in thought and started when Kiana knocked on the doorframe. Angie stood and went around to lean in her usual spot on the front of the desk.

"I don't get this thing with Stone," Kiana whispered. "I know I'm just a kid, but I never had a clue there was a problem."

Angie shrugged. "Don't feel bad. Neither did I." And she should have. God knew she'd had enough experience dealing with an alcoholic father. She'd thought there wasn't much that could get past her in that department.

"Do we give him another chance?"

"I need to talk with him—though he's a big boy and shouldn't need the *or else* discussion."

"I'm sure he's gotten it from Blanche."

"What are your thoughts?" Angie asked.

"Three strikes you're out?"

Angie nodded. Stone should have one more chance. "I'm doing it mostly because of Blanche. If he pulls this again, he's out for good. Blanche will either have to understand or…"

"Or not."

"I'd hate to lose her. Do you have anything special on your schedule this afternoon? I'd like to take a few hours off."

"For now everything's under control." Kiana shrugged hair back from her face with a grin.

"Famous last words."

"Going to buy those fire extinguishers we forgot the other day?"

Angie laughed but hoped the joking wasn't foreshadowing.

CHAPTER 14

Friday

Jarvis arrived at one o'clock to pick up Angelina. He stood in the double doorway of the auditorium peering down the aisle. She stood on the stage beside a round red-haired man. They were in serious discussion. Had to be about sets because several times they each pointed to a wall-size picture of a construction site.

She looked frazzled—kept raking a hand through her hair. Must've been a hell of a morning.

"She outta get more rest," said a voice from the shadows to Jarvis's right.

Montez popped up from behind the ticket booth counter.

Damn, what was he doing here? It was none of this man's business how tired she either looked or didn't look. Jarvis's logical side told him to play nice. "Not sure you know that eight weeks ago Tyson left to star on Broadway."

"He didn't seem like the type to desert her."

"He had an offer that was hard to refuse. She didn't want him to miss out on what could be the opportunity of a lifetime."

"Still...left her with a lot."

Jarvis smiled. "That's the truth. She seems to be handling things pretty well."

"Till today," Montez said. "I don't know what happened, I had my head buried under here, but about an hour ago there was a lot of commotion. And then..." Montez showed a mouthful of bright white teeth. "You would've been proud of her. She hauled my ex lady out of here. Handled her like she was a bag of horse feed." Montez laughed out loud now. "Told her not to come back. But she did. She shoved right around Angie, but a second later a couple of blokes practically carried the lady out to the car." He dropped a crimping tool on the counter. "And then her mother came."

Jarvis gave a strangled sound that made Montez laugh.

"Knew that'd getcha." He reached for a coil of co-ax cable from the floor. "Well, gotta get back to work. Keep an eye that she doesn't spread herself too thin. She's not the type to ask for help."

Actually, Angelina was learning her limitations. She'd asked for help on more than one occasion. But Jarvis wasn't telling any of this to Montez Clarke, a man he was sure Angelina had feelings for. Though neither Angelina nor the Jamaican had flirted outright, a look—something sexual—frequently passed between them. Jarvis had never known what to make of it.

He changed the subject, hoping to get some insight into one of Stone's wives.

"What's up with the woman I saw you with the other day?"

Montez laughed. "She's the one they hauled out of here. Seems like I keep finding the unavailable ones."

Was he referring to Angelina? Jarvis wouldn't let himself think about that. "Apparently she and Angelina had a bit of a to-do last night in Concord."

Montez frowned. "What's Chia want with Angie?" He grew thoughtful. Then he nodded. "Chia's got a bad jealous streak that goes from here to China. I bet she thinks Rocky—oh yeah, you guys know him as Stone. Bet she thinks he's messing with somebody in the cast—probably Angie."

The double doors to the auditorium whooshed open. Nearly whacked him in the backside. Angelina entered. She spotted both men and smiled, which sent a rush of emotion through him and made him feel guilty for his thoughts about her and Montez.

"You ready to go?" Jarvis asked.

She went to the broom closet and took her coat from a hanger. "I am." He helped her put it on. "Montez, if you need anything, Kiana will be here and about."

"Sounds good."

Jarvis held the door for Angelina, keeping a possessive hand on her waist. "Brr." She jammed her hands in her pockets. The air had grown colder; he wouldn't be surprised if more snow was in the forecast. "You don't mind leaving Montez alone with Kiana?" he asked once the door was closed.

"Not at all."

Jarvis let the topic rest. He wasn't sure why he'd asked the question. Since the murder investigation, Montez had been nothing but a prosperous, upstanding citizen. "He told me Chia was here."

"We had to bodily remove her from the place. Don't tell anyone I said this: it was kind of fun."

He held the Jeep door. She climbed in, buckled then leaned the passenger seat back a couple of notches. He had lots of questions but they could wait. He drove to Shibley's. While she went to the ladies room, Jarvis ordered a beer and, in a burst of male initiative, an apple martini.

She returned the same time the server was delivering the drinks. Angelina raised her eyebrows at the drink. "Trying to get me drunk?"

"Nope. I thought it might help you relax."

She patted his hand. "Thanks." She slouched back in the booth and gazed unseeing at the hockey game stats running across the television screen over the bar.

He wondered if he should try and get her talking or wait till she was ready on her own. She made the decision for him. "I had a hang-up phone call after you left last night."

"What was the number on the caller ID?"

"There was nothing."

"Wouldn't matter, I guess. People who make crank phone calls don't do it from a traceable number. Something makes me think you suspect it was Chia Powers."

"I did at first, but I don't know how she would've got my number. Nobody but you, Mom, Kiana, Tyson, and my brother have it."

The thought flashed through his head that Montez might also be one of the recipients. "Any reason to think it's her besides the run-in with her at the dress shop?"

"She seems a little…for lack of a better word: unbalanced." Angelina tasted the drink, swallowed then licked her lips. "Good."

Jarvis relaxed. "Why did she come to the theater today?" he asked.

"She planned to sit in on rehearsals—that's what our discussion was about last night. I told her we don't allow it. She wasn't taking no for an answer so Vic and Craig escorted her out."

"I heard you did the escorting."

Angelina smiled. "Tried. She got around me."

"You should've called me. I would've been happy to heave her ass into the slush."

She laughed. "I think Vic and Craig were thinking the same thing."

The server arrived and they ordered lunches.

"Next time, will you promise to call me?"

"Yes, but once she hears Stone—er, Rocky is out of the show, she'll give up coming."

"He was drunk again?"

She sipped and set the glass on the table. "Weirdest thing I ever saw. One minute, he seemed perfectly normal. Then, not ten minutes later, he came out on stage, said one line then barfed all over the guys."

Jarvis couldn't help flinching; vomit always made him queasy. He didn't know what he ever would've done if he'd had children because dirty diapers probably would've produced an even more extreme reaction. "Where is Stone now?"

"Mom took him to Blanche's. I'll give him one more chance tomorrow, then that's it, Jacoby will take over his part permanently."

Their meals arrived: chicken croquettes for Jarvis and a chef salad for Angelina. "That was fast," Jarvis told the server.

"We aren't too busy," he said, "but on top of that, I figured you two were in a hurry to get back to work."

"Thanks. Today we're taking it easy."

After he left, Angelina changed the topic of conversation. "Remember I mentioned doing the summer performance outdoors?"

"At Tyson's place. Right."

Her phone rang. She checked the caller ID and answered with a happy, "Hi, Mom."

What was up with that? She usually grimaced when her mom called.

"Thanks. He's okay though?...All right. Thanks again... Yes, he did. You two can make it?...Great, then we'll see you tonight." She punched the Off button and laid the phone on the table. "Where were we?"

"The summer performance at Tyson's."

"Oh yes. What do you think if I ask my mother to handle everything that's not production-related?"

"I'll answer that in a minute—after I ask this: Are you the same Angelina I knew a few days ago, or has some alien taken over her body?"

She laughed. "There's been a sort of shift in our relationship over the past few days. I'm trying to do what you told me— go with the flow. She's all for having the outdoor production at HeavenScent, so I thought she might enjoy...I don't know, arranging the menu or something. She could rent the tents, get permits, print tickets. Lots of things that would keep her—"

"Busy and out of your hair," he said around a mouthful of mashed potatoes. Angelina laughed. She didn't laugh enough lately. Jarvis gave himself a mental pat on the back for urging her away from the theater. "Getting your mom's help is a good idea. I think."

"But you're not committing yourself. Afraid I'll blame you

if things go up in smoke?"

"No." He forked up another serving of chicken but held it in the air while he said, "My thoughts about your mother: I think she's a very organized and detail-oriented person. I think she could run the event perfectly."

"Do I smell a *but* in there someplace?"

He shoved the fork in his mouth and replied with a shrug. Once he'd swallowed, he said, "It's her moodiness."

Her own mouth full, Angelina simply nodded.

"I wonder if she's got an *in* with the weather gods."

"Trust me," Angelina said, "if the weather knows what's good for it, no way would it consider raining on what will be called 'my mother's weekend'."

"I guess my question would be, can you work with her in an ongoing situation such as this?"

"She'd mostly be working with Kiana who'd be organizing the show side of things. With her, Mom would behave herself."

"Mom was there when she clobbered the Chia pet, right?"

Angelina laughed. "Right, that's why I know she'll stay in line. Besides, I was just doing what you told me—delegating responsibility."

Though she was joking, it was good that she knew how much work was up coming. Good that he didn't have to remind her. Volunteering that sort of information, even when needed, didn't go over well with a workaholic. They usually tried to do it all. He'd mull over the reason for choosing Gloria when he had some spare time. A lot of spare time.

Once they were back in the Jeep and heading north along Route 11, he asked, "So, how's your brother, heard from him lately?"

"About a week ago. Robin's band is on the road in the Midwest all month. Then they're headed to someplace in California. Some small town whose name I can't remember."

Jarvis pulled into the courthouse parking lot. "You want to come in?"

"No, I think I'll wait here."

"I shouldn't be long."

"Famous last words."

He stretched across the seat and kissed her cheek. "If you get bored, there's a coffee shop around the corner. If you're not here, I'll know where to look."

As Jarvis shut the door, Angelina leaned her head against the window and closed her eyes, her left hand fondling the long hair on the dog's ears.

She was still in that position when he returned forty minutes later. She woke with a start, pushed one hand through her hair; the other knuckling an eye. They chatted about unimportant things and took the long way back to the theater. Jarvis wanted to keep her here; she seemed so relaxed.

But she had to get back to work. Truth be told, so did he. At ten past four, he stopped the Jeep behind the theater. "The deck looks great," he said. "I love the crisscross pattern on the railing. Can't believe the guys can work in this cold."

"Did I tell you Mr. Quattro extended it to include my office? His contractor—" she stepped back to give him a better look—"installed a set of French doors today."

"I think that guy likes you."

"I think he likes anything with..."

Jarvis ran around to open her door, not because he was being particularly polite; he wanted to touch her, to hold her. "I'm making spaghetti for dinner," he said. "Want to come when you're through here?"

"Did you forget? We're supposed to go out with Tyson, Mom, and Rickie."

"Oh, right. I'll do spaghetti tomorrow then."

"Sounds good." She grinned. "I know going out with them isn't your favorite thing. You're very brave to do this without complaining."

"It's easy right now because I'm distracted thinking about talking to Stone. I'm headed there now."

He waited till she was safely in the building, then opened his car door, hooked on Red's leash and walked along the edge of the snowbank. Then he helped her up into the car.

The back door of the building opened. Jarvis waited to make sure it wasn't Angelina before moving the Jeep. But it was Anthony Quattro who exited. The Ricardo Montalban lookalike stepped carefully in his expensive Italian loafers. Jarvis let down the window; it wouldn't pay to be rude to the guy.

"Good evening. Now I see where our Angie has been," said the smiling restaurateur.

Like it was any of his business.

"Nice she's got a little time off."

"She has a lot on her shoulders." Jarvis didn't know why he was defending her to him.

"It wasn't very considerate of her partner to take off the way he did."

"The term take off implies something negative. It was mutually agreed upon."

"Still, he left her with more than she can handle."

Jarvis smiled. "She's doing just fine." Not that it was any of his business.

"My daughter's facing the same thing right now. She's just gotten a position in the trauma center of Lakes Region General. Being the low woman on the totem pole, so to speak, they're deluging her with work."

"Angelina used to have that job. After that—this is a cake walk."

Quattro rolled his eyes. "A woman like her should be taken care of."

What the hell was he insinuating?

Jarvis closed the window and gunned the car up the hill. He wound the heat to high and headed for Blanche and Stone's home. He had time to have sobered up by now.

CHAPTER 15

Later that night, the Manchester restaurant was busy. Angelina, Jarvis, Gloria and Rickie, Tyson, who'd found a date—sat around a long table at the back of the room. The table had a great view of downtown though Jarvis and Angelina had their backs to it. The chatter was amicable for the most part. Every now and then Jarvis sensed a tension between Gloria and Rickie. Wasn't good to let that car thing hang between them so long. Another in a long list of things that were none of his business.

He had his own tension-thing going on. Neither Stone nor Blanche had been home when he arrived in Pittsfield. Everything locked up tight; no cars in the yard. Had Stone's car still been at the theater this morning? Yes, it hadn't been moved since he examined the scratch. Which made him wonder how Stone had gotten to work that morning. Too bad really; he'd planned to charge the guy with drunk driving.

While he'd been lost in thought, the conversation had turned to the play. Jarvis didn't know anything about it except that it was a comedy and took place at a construction site, so his attention wandered as they touted the acting talents of the understudy. A loud male voice across the room had the whole group turning in that direction. A woman—it was hard to see her features from here—stood up. When she shook her fist at the man, Jarvis felt sorry for him. Bad enough to argue, but in public...

"I can't believe you'd do this to me!" the woman screeched. She launched away from their table and rushed toward Jarvis's group. Closer now, he realized several things: 1-she was tall and gorgeous, 2-she was heading their way and 3-she was the Chia pet—Stone Powers' wife.

As the black woman hung a right, Jarvis nudged Angelina with an elbow. She broke off a conversation with Tyson, excused herself and followed Chia into the ladies room.

Jarvis couldn't see the man at the table from here. Was it Montez? Or Stone? Or maybe someone else altogether? The curious side of Jarvis had to know. He excused himself and went to the table, feeling the eyes of everyone in his group burning into his back. The chatter would have something to do with not being able to mind their own business. And they'd be right. After all, he was off duty.

Soon it was clear her date was none other than her husband. Stone had his head down and was doodling in his mashed potatoes with a butter knife. Jarvis eased into a chair.

Stone dropped the fork and looked up. His blue eyes were glazed. His head wobbled as if it was too much work for his neck to hold it up. "Wazzup Mr. Cop?" he asked.

Jarvis started to say he'd seen them arguing but figured that would set off the wrong emotions, so he said, "I noticed Chia crying."

"Chia?" Stone's face scrunched as if her name were foreign, then he nodded. "Yes. She's pissed off. Says I'm drunk." He shook his head and winced. "Not."

"I thought you were supposed to be in Chicago."

"Chic—" He nodded and winced again. "Oh yes, work. Didn't go."

"I can see that. Why not?"

"Sick. Where is, um…Chia?"

"She went to the ladies room."

Stone hobbled to his feet. His left hand gripped the edge of the table. "Tell her I went home—sick." He pulled in a breath and swallowed. "I'm getting darned tired of people saying I'm drunk. Don't drink." He looked Jarvis right in the eye. "I. Do. Not. Drink."

"Then you ought to get yourself to a doctor because there's something seriously wrong."

"I will. Def-inite-ly." Stone threw some bills on the table and yanked a set of keys from his pocket.

"You can't be driving in your condition."

"Not drunk."

"Still, you're in no condition to be behind the wheel."

Stone held up a hand for Jarvis to stop. "I won't drive. I will sit out there and wait for Chia. Is that good enough?" When Jarvis hesitated, Stone held up a hand and crossed two fingers. "Promise."

"Yes, but I think I'll wait with you till Chia returns. Just to make sure you're all right."

"I can do it myself." He dropped the keys on the table. "See, this proves I'll wait for her." He stumbled to his feet. Jarvis helped him put on his parka.

"Okay, I'll tell Chia where you are."

He went to the ladies room and called Angelina's name. She opened the door a crack. "Stone wants Chia to take him home."

"Okay, I'll tell her. She's pretty upset."

"Tell her he's not drunk, he's sick. She needs to take him to the hospital."

Jarvis gestured to Angelina's family that he'd be right back. He ran to the door. It was snowing again. Wind whipped sharp flakes at his face and ears. Jeez this wasn't what he'd wanted to do tonight. At least Stone had remained true to his word. He'd settled himself in the passenger seat.

Hopefully he didn't freeze to death before Angelina convinced Chia to come out.

***

Angie leaned against the sink, waiting for Chia's sobs, in the last stall, to subside. So far, Angie hadn't spoken, afraid to anger the woman even more.

Finally, the metal latch clinked and the door opened. Seeing Angie, Chia started. "What are you doing here?"

"Having dinner with my family."

"No, I mean, why are you here? In this place. At the same time I'm here. I'm sure you can see, it looks like you're following me," she said.

"I just said I'm out with family and friends. But I couldn't help seeing you were crying."

Chia's face grew red, her eyes squinty. "You been after my man. Well, far as I'm concerned, you can have the damned drunk. I can't believe, we've been married two years and I didn't know that side of him."

There were many, many things Chia didn't know about her husband.

"He always said he didn't drink. He specifically asked me when we started dating—apparently his parents drank too much or something—and he didn't want to marry a woman who did."

"And you don't?"

She shook her head. "Not that he knows. I have something on occasion—with the girls. You know? But never while I'm with Rocky. I don't even keep anything in the house."

"So, you're being as deceptive as him."

Chia slapped a palm on the sink and gazed at her reflection while she spoke. "He was concerned about having a drunk for a wife. He doesn't have one." She turned to Angie. "Get it?"

"Got it. So, where do you two live?"

"A townhouse here in Manchester. Why?"

"Just curious."

The ladies room door opened. In stepped Mr. Quattro's daughter Amber. Her eyebrows raised seeing Angie there but she continued past and into a stall.

Chia didn't bother lowering her voice. "I know about you

and your so-called curiosity. Montez told me all about it. You're a nosy busybody."

Angie couldn't picture Montez saying anything like that. Would he?

Whatever. There didn't seem to be anything else worth responding so, Angie held the door for Chia to pass.

Jarvis was standing beside Stone and Chia's table. Angie parted ways with Chia and returned to her table, bypassing Tyson and his date on the dance floor.

Jarvis and Chia spoke softly for a moment. He helped put on her coat. Jarvis shoved something into her hand—looked like a business card. She snatched keys from the table and left.

Jarvis made his way back to their table looking worried. He took his seat beside Rickie, noticed Tyson and his date dancing up a storm and frowned. Angie nearly laughed—he and dancing were not compatible. He claimed his feet got all tangled up. He turned his attention to the exit.

He was worried about Stone. So was Angie. Something was seriously wrong with the man. Jarvis's "uh-oh" had her looking now too.

Chia was storming toward them. "Where is he?" Chia screeched.

"I escorted him outside," Jarvis said. "Left him in the passenger seat waiting for you."

"He's gone. Where is he?" By now, the attention of the entire restaurant was on them. The hostess started in their direction.

At that moment, Amber also appeared at tableside. She spotted Rickie and broke into a wide grin. Wearing the same gorgeous boots as the other morning, she clip-clopped to the around to him. Rickie stood. The couple embraced.

"It's nice to see you."

Rickie made introductions. As he got to Gloria, Amber's eyebrows shot up. "Oh my God! I finally get to meet your mother!" She grasped a very shocked Gloria's hand and shook it.

Angie could barely keep her emotions hidden. She felt sorry for her mother, but at the same time this kind of thing must happen all the time.

"I've heard a lot about you from my father," Amber said to Gloria. To Rickie, she said, "It's so nice you got back to the east coast. It's important that family be together. That's what I did," Amber continued. "I moved to be nearer to Allen."

"Is he here?" Angie asked. He would make a good buffer for the darts of rage shooting from every one of her mother's pores right now. Funny. Amber didn't seem to notice them. But Rickie did. He shuffled from one foot to the other.

"No," Amber said, "he's out of town. Back tomorrow though! Can't wait! I'm having dinner with my father." She pointed to a private alcove at the back of the restaurant. "I'll get back to him before he comes over and disrupts your evening. Nice to see you again Rickie. Nice to meet you, Mrs. Kennedy. Maybe we can all get together when Allen's back."

Gloria didn't speak. Something seemed stuck in her throat.

Jarvis stood took Chia by the elbow. He said over his shoulder to Angie, "Can you manage to get home?"

"Of course. Do you need help?" Please.

"No. You enjoy the time out, I'll call you later."

Damn. She really wanted—needed—out of here. Her mother was close to an eruption.

Chia fought Jarvis a little but he got her outside without too much more noise. Once the door closed on them, Angie was forced to focus back to the table. Tyson and his date had returned. Rickie sat, red-faced, located his glass from amongst the clutter on the table, and finished it in one drag.

Tyson nodded toward the exit. "So, I see Jarvis left you for another woman."

Angie grinned. "He escorted the Chia pet to the parking lot. She promised she'd take Stone to the hospital. I feel bad for thinking he was drunk."

"What does that do for your show?" Gloria ignored Rickie. He might as well drop her at HeavenScent later and keep on driving.

"Not sure. I guess we have to wait and see what the doctor says."

Gloria excused herself to use the ladies room. Which happened to take a route past Amber's table.

"You all right?" Angie asked Rickie. "You look a little tense."

"More than enough of that going on around here tonight."

"Yes, Mother looked a bit surprised."

"You always know that age thing is going to be mentioned. It's just weird when it is."

"Were you surprised to meet up with Amber? From one coast to another. Such a small world."

"I already met her at the theater the other day. Remember when I brought your mail?"

She did recall. They'd stopped at the top of the rise and spoken through the open windows." Angie put a hand on Rickie's. "I think you two have a lot to get out in the open."

He frowned. "There's nothing between me and Amber."

"That's not what I meant."

He took a long drag from his glass. "I know."

"Do you want to talk?" Angie prayed for him to say no.

For a second, Rickie looked confused, probably wondering if he should open up to her. They hadn't exactly been bosom buddies. "Your mother's pressing me to get married."

Wow, that wasn't how she'd heard it. But, there are two sides to every story.

"Tell me what to do," Rickie said.

God, she hated when people demanded advice. She was a theater owner—a divorced one, so clearly she didn't have marital-quality answers—but she could listen. "Do you want to get married?"

"Yes. And no."

Angie let raised eyebrows ask the next question.

Rickie tapped his glass on the table. The server raced over. "Could I have another please? Make it a double." He glanced at Gloria's place setting and saw her glass was more than half empty. "Another for the lady too." The server left. Rickie said, "I did something."

Somehow she managed not to let all sorts of uninvited thoughts about sex—or the lack of it if her mother's interpretation was to be believed—invade her brain. Finally, when he didn't elaborate, she managed, "I find the best thing on most occasions is to be honest. Talk to Mom." Angie didn't say what people usually say in these situations: "she'll understand," because there was a good chance Gloria would do no such thing.

Rickie nodded. "I know. That's what Jarvis said too."

"Then you already have your answer."

No more could be said, thank goodness, because all the others arrived back at the table. Angie didn't feel like partying any more but she wouldn't ruin Tyson's happy-to-be-home celebration by asking him to take her home.

The topic of conversation between Rickie, Tyson, and even his date, turned to sports—namely the Celtics, who were playing a team in bright blue uniforms on the wide screen over the bar.

Angie shrugged at her mom and amused herself by people watching. To the right, a white-haired couple gazed at each other with loving eyes. Celebrating an anniversary? Beside them, another couple ate without speaking or looking at each other. There didn't seem to be tension, just apathy—another day to get through.

Angie couldn't see Mr. Sheldrake from here. He sat in deep shadow in the circular booth. Not that she wanted to capture his attention. That might open a whole other can of tuna.

At the bar, a man shifted his attention from the Celtics on the widescreen, to the exit. All Angie could see was the back of his head. His silhouette and posture looked way-too familiar. It didn't take long to realize it was Montez Clarke.

What was he doing here? Coincidence—or had he followed Chia and Stone? Angie needed to know. She got up.

"Where you going?" asked Gloria.

"Be right back. I have to check on something."

"Need help?" Rickie asked, hopeful.

Angie said, "No thanks," knowing he'd popped into his detective wannabe mode.

She heard her mother ask, "Can't any of you leave the police stuff at home?"

Angie went to the exit and peered outside. Jarvis and Chia stood in the parking lot. Both seemed calm so she returned inside, then pretended to notice Montez at the bar. "Well, fancy meeting you here."

He tilted the beer toward her in greeting. "Your cop run out on you?"

Angie grinned. "You've been here long enough to know what happened."

"What's wrong with the actor guy?"

"What—you can't even say his name?"

Montez gave a shrug of those wide shoulders. "Don't know it."

"You didn't by any chance follow Chia here?"

He gave a deep laugh that pushed that familiar sensation through her pores. "Told you, I wasn't that into her. You know I don't lie."

She frowned. Why would he think she'd know anything like that? "Well," she said, "it's been nice seeing you."

"See you tomorrow."

Exactly what she was worried about. Would the handsome Jamaican make trouble between Stone and Chia? Or, worse, initiate meetings between he and Angie. She flashed back to a motel scene that awful night she'd been mugged. She'd nearly done something way out of character for her.

But those had been desperate, emotional times. Best left in the past.

Angie returned to the table and finished the last of her apple martini—since lunchtime she'd decided they were pretty good.

Something besides the multiple-marriage thing nagged her about Chia and Stone Powers. She squeezed her eyes shut and rubbed her temples with her knuckles. What? What on earth could it be?

"I think it's time to get Angie home." Tyson tapped her on the shoulder. "Come on, woman, I'll drive you."

That's when Angie realized what had been bothering her… there had been no alcohol on Stone's table: only two glasses of ice water and two what looked like colas. The man had been telling the truth. Suddenly long-forgotten memories—of classes from nursing school—rushed back. Stone's symptoms, dizziness, stomach pain, and nausea could represent poisoning of some kind.

CHAPTER 16

In the restaurant parking lot Jarvis dialed the Manchester police. "This is Detective Colby Jarvis of the Alton PD." He gave his badge number and explained what had transpired during the evening. "I'm at the Hanover Street Chophouse. I just had a sick man take off in his car. He's in no condition to be behind the wheel. Hold on a sec." He said to Chia, "What's the make and model of your car?"

"Audi A4, black." She recited the license plate number and her home address, which Jarvis repeated to the dispatcher. "No idea which way he went...Okay. You're welcome." He ended the call then asked Chia if she wanted a ride home.

"No, I'll call a cab." A phone appeared in her hand and she made the call.

Once that was done he asked if she wanted to climb in the Jeep to get warm.

"No. I'll stand out near the street, maybe I'll see him drive by."

"Where did he get keys?"

"Under the bumper, on a magnet."

He waited with her, thinking how stupid he was to have left Stone alone. He never expected the man to have—or be able to recall—an extra set of keys.

"You can go," she said. At least she'd calmed down.

He didn't have to argue with her. The cab swung into the lot. She got in the back. No *goodbye*, no *thanks for the help*. Surely she wasn't blaming him for Stone's actions—though he was, in part, blaming himself.

Jarvis stowed the phone in his pocket and got into his Jeep. He went off in search of the missing black Audi, praying he didn't find it wrapped around a tree. And he particularly wanted to check and see if it had any damage because someone with a black car had sideswiped Stone's car.

He drove up and down Hanover Street, then checked the address Chia had given the police, but the driveway was empty. There were lights on in the apartment so she must've gotten home all right.

An hour later, not spotting Stone's vehicle anywhere—the local cops would take care of that anyway—he headed up Route 28 toward Alton. Maybe Stone had gone to Blanche's.

The black Audi wasn't in her driveway.

Jarvis phoned Angelina. She answered sounding sleepy. Damn, he'd wakened her. "Sorry to get you up. Do you know where Stone lives? I mean, when he's not with Blanche?"

"No...wait. When I signed him onto the cast, he filled out a form—for insurance purposes, you know?" He heard the sound of bedding rustling. She was getting up. "I'll meet you at the theater in ten minutes."

"No—"

"Yes, I'll never get back to sleep without knowing anyway."

"Okay, meet you there."

Jarvis had no sooner hung up the phone when it rang again. He assumed it was Angelina—maybe she'd found the address at her condo. But it was the Manchester police dispatcher relaying a message that the officers had been unable to locate Stone Powers. "Okay, thanks for letting me know. I've driven home to check a few places he sometimes frequents, but found nothing."

Jarvis headed back out into the cold. The Jeep had already cooled off.

"Our officers will keep looking throughout the night."

"Okay, thanks for letting me know."

"If it's any comfort, there were no reports of crashes, nor was anyone admitted to the hospitals."

"Thanks." He shut off the phone and dropped it in his lap.

He stopped at the fast-food joint on the way by for two cups of coffee, one gallon-sized and one regular. At the theater, he handed the smaller one to Angelina. She hadn't bothered to dress; her nightgown poked between the folds of her coat. Her hair was a tumbled mess. She looked amazing; it was a compliment he figured she wouldn't want to hear.

They went in through the front door. It was cold since they always shut the heat down when the last person left. She shivered and strode down the aisle and up the trio of steps to her office. From the top drawer of the file cabinet, she drew out a manila folder. God, she was so organized.

She set the file on the desk and shuffled through to find Stone Powers' signed application. "Damn, he gave Blanche's address as his place of residence.

"I already checked there. Just her car in the yard."

"Jarvis, you don't think he's going to bring Chia's car to Blanche's house, do you?"

He hadn't thought of that. "Think he's at a motel?"

"I hope he's at the hospital."

"Do you think he might've called Blanche?" he asked.

"I suppose I could call..." They left her office and walked back toward the front of the building. "But last time I talked to her, she said he was on his way to Chicago. If only her car was in the driveway and no lights on in the house, then I'd be pretty sure he's not there."

"Your mom brought him to Blanche's today, right?"

Angie locked the door and set the alarm. They walked to the idling Jeep in silence. "Yes, Mom took him to Blanche's" she said after sipping some coffee, "but Blanche couldn't have been home." She set the cup in the holder.

"What makes you think that?"

"Because he turned up in Manchester with Chia. Blanche wouldn't have let him out of the house in his condition."

"Do you think she would have driven him to the airport?"

"That I don't know. It was important to him, but being so sick, even if she did—they probably wouldn't let him through security." She clasped her hands between her knees, leaned forward and spoke softly. "I don't have a good feeling about any of this."

"Something's bothering you besides what happened tonight."

She looked up. "After you left the restaurant, I realized something. There was no alcohol on his table."

Jarvis dug through his mental image of Chia and Stone's table—and realized she was right. "And yet he's been acting drunk for a couple of days."

"Right."

"He kept stressing that he doesn't drink. I didn't believe him. Nobody did. Not even Chia. But now I'm thinking he really is sick."

"Expand."

"Maybe like some kind of brain tumor."

He started backing out of the space. When she said, "Or poison," he slammed on the brakes.

CHAPTER 17

Jarvis arrived home, took the dog outside. When she picked up a stick and wanted to play he threw it once then hurried her along. It was freezing and he'd had enough of this day. Something told him that although Stone said he would see a doctor, he didn't. Could they force him to be checked out?

As he stepped into the house and cleaned the dog's feet, a thought jumped into his head and bopped around like a Mexican jumping bean. What about drugs? Could they account for his behavior in some way?

Afterward, warm in a flannel shirt thrown over his dress shirt, he settled on the couch with the rest of his coffee and the remote control. Though it was well after midnight, no way he could sleep. Angelina's words spun like whirlpools in his brain about Stone having a tumor, or maybe his symptoms pointed to poison. Tumor, drugs, or poison—why hadn't he thought of them?

If it was something besides a tumor, it was sure Stone didn't take poison or drugs on purpose; Angelina said he was a health buff, and a germophobe. Besides, he was too baffled over what was happening. Which meant someone was giving them to him.

But who, and why? And what? There were too many possibilities, and they vaulted into the whirling mass of thoughts in his head.

The phone rang at 3:58. He shut off the paid advertisement with Chuck Norris touting some kind of exercise equipment and answered. The dispatcher wasted no time on preliminaries. "Jarvis, we got an attempted robbery at the convenience store."

The stuff clogging his brain evaporated. He checked that his gun was loaded and raced out to the Jeep. His headlights speared the winter darkness as he sped toward the trouble. The attending patrol car blocked one entrance. A state police car stood guard at the other. He showed his badge to an officer wearing a state police uniform

"Since you were notified, the situation has escalated. Looks like the robbery is now a homicide."

"Is the perp on-scene?"

"No. Gone."

Jarvis parked, heart pounding, gun back in the holster, camera and notebook in-hand. God, he hated cases like this. Of late, there'd been way too many both locally and in-state.

A group of people he assumed was customers and employees, hopefully all eyewitnesses, stood outside the entrance. He bypassed them even though all eyes had turned toward him—probably hoping he'd be the one to shoo them all home—and stepped inside.

At first, the place looked empty. Then he saw the body about halfway down the aspirin and canned food aisle. He stopped at the head of the aisle to visually examine the scene. The rest of the store was empty except for two state police: a man and a woman; and the local on-duty officer, a rookie. All stood near the beer cooler, watching his entry. Right now he was a god to all these people. He was the one to sort out this mess. The one with the power to send them all home to bed. Or back to nice calm patrols up and down deserted highways.

To Jarvis's right was the checkout counter—two registers, both closed up tight. There was a heap of junk food near one of them, probably belonged to a customer who took off when this whole thing—whatever it was—went down. Nothing else immediately remarkable about the room.

He took a step into the aisle, watching the floor for evidence. The victim lay half on his side, in a semi-fetal position, the top of his head facing Jarvis. It was a male with longish light brown hair. Hard to tell height, but he guessed about six feet tall. The guy had on blue jeans—the Levis label showed on the back pocket—and a royal blue parka. Jarvis had seen that jacket someplace before. For a moment he tried to remember where but quickly gave up and went to work.

He approached the victim, eyes darting everywhere, taking in everything…on the floor, the shelves, and under their front edges. The floor was dirty, dried slush and mess from outdoors. Just everyday dirt. He snapped pictures of everything even though the forensics team would arrive any minute.

No weapon was visible. Jarvis knelt beside the man and put two fingers to his carotid artery. Nothing. He watched the cheeks and corners of the man's nose. Not breathing. But the lips weren't blue. "Anyone call 911?" he shouted.

"Is he still alive?" someone called back.

"Call." Even if the man was dead, Jarvis wasn't qualified to declare him dead.

The man lay on his right side, facing away from him. Both arms were splayed as if he'd tried to break his fall. Jarvis tugged on the jacket; the man rolled so he lay flat on his back. He needed to perform CPR just in case. He gestured to one of the officers near the beer cooler. "Come help me."

A tall state cop came. They began CPR.

While Jarvis performed fast chest pumps, he asked, "Anyone find the weapon?"

"Weapon?" the officer said between breaths into the man's mouth, over which he'd placed a plastic separator. "No, sir."

"Anyone find the weapon?" he shouted.

"No," someone called.

"Find it!"

Jarvis evaluated the situation as he performed chest compressions. No blood. No obvious wounds. But vomit had made a trail down the right side of the man's face. Not much was on the floor—most had been absorbed down the front of his parka. Which meant he'd vomited while on his feet. The throw-up explained the gurgling sound witnesses heard. Man, he hated doing CPR, especially if this was indeed a corpse. Glad he had seniority and could choose which end to be at. "Shit."

"Yes, sir?" The rookie officer said from over his shoulder.

"What?" Four... Five. God this was tiring.

"You said something."

Jarvis gave a nervous chuckle. "Cursing. Know this guy." Stone Powers had never gone to the hospital. He'd somehow driven from Manchester back to Alton, a distance of forty-odd miles.

Three excruciating minutes later, the EMTs relieved Jarvis and his partner.

Working around them, Jarvis stooped and got shots from each angle near the victim's head. The body took up most of the space between the aisles so he walked all the way around, past the long row of junk food and came up from the other end. He made notes about the victim's position and shoes—white Nikes with black stripes. The soles were worn. The cuffs of the jeans weren't. There was no blood, no visible cause of death.

He leaned against a shelf containing Pepto Bismol and aspirin and focused on the head and as much of Stone's face that was showing. Wait. He lowered the camera. Stone had come here to buy something to settle his stomach.

"We got a pulse!" shouted one of the EMTs.

Jarvis hurried around to where they were inserting an IV into Stone's arm. In a flash, they had him on a gurney and were shooting toward the exit.

Jarvis hurried to the bathroom to wash up. The state cop was just exiting. "Man, I hate doing that."

An officer was waiting just outside the door.

"Did you find a weapon?" Jarvis asked.

"No sir."

He grunted and began his own search. The officer followed, probably feeling as useless as an umbrella in a hurricane. They peered under every inch of shelving. On every shelf. Behind every box and can.

Jarvis instructed the others to spread out. "Find that weapon." While they searched, Jarvis scribbled more details and snapped pictures—the crime scene guys would arrive soon, but he wasn't wasting any time.

The rookie returned. "We can't find a weapon anywhere, sir. Not unless you count the baseball bat under the cash register."

Jarvis shouted, "One of you go check with the clerks. Find out if it was theirs." Then lowered his voice, "What was the initial call? I was told it was a robbery."

"That's how the alarm came in. The clerk said there was a commotion near the back of the store between two people, a man and a woman. He assumed it was a decoy for the person who'd just come to the register." He pointed to the junk food on the counter. "He'd had it happen before where people staged a fight so the third could rip off the place. The clerk said he shouted at the ones arguing to take it outside. The customer at the counter ran out. The female in the dispute ran out. The man she'd been arguing with moved toward the front as if he was leaving, but suddenly started having trouble breathing. He was staggering and gurgling. Then he dropped to the floor. That's when the clerk panicked and pressed the alarm. He said he thought the guy was having a heart attack."

So it hadn't been a robbery. Stone had come in to make a purchase. But what *had* happened? What did the woman have to do with this? When Jarvis first arrived, he assumed Stone had been stabbed. That would account for the clerk's version of Stone staggering and gurgling. But the staggering, gurgling, and vomit—he shivered—weren't related to anything the woman did.

"So, who is it?" asked the state cop who'd helped with the CPR.

"Name's Stone Powers. He's a—" What was he anyway?

A salesman or an actor? "He's a pharmaceuticals salesman. Home based locally." Someplace.

Though he'd expected something like this to happen, the reality still came as a shock.

"Get me a description of the woman he was arguing with," he called to the rookie, who raced off.

He took more pictures. Forensics guys would do the same thing. As a matter of fact, their vehicle had just maneuvered into the parking lot. Jarvis stood, a hand on his lower back. He shoved the camera in his pocket then made a bunch more notes.

The rookie returned. He stood waiting for Jarvis to finish writing. "The woman was tallish, about five nine. She was wearing a big heavy coat. Anyway, she had long blonde hair held back with some kind of glittery barrette. She had blues eyes and kind of pointy nose—pretty lady. She'd been crying, her makeup was smudged."

"Thanks. Find out if there's a security camera here. If so, get the tape and have it sent to the station. The Aubuchon Hardware across the street has one. Not sure if McDonald's camera would pick up anything down here. Please check."

"The state cops are on it."

Jarvis wondered why they hadn't installed themselves into the case already. Technically a murder fell more into their jurisdiction. Probably they were waiting for his team to do the preliminary work.

Jarvis felt a solid ram of disappointment at the description of the woman who'd been with Stone. He'd expected her to match one of his wives: a redhead, an Asian or a tall, thin model. He'd had his finger poised over the phone to dial and get a warrant issued for whichever one matched the description.

Of course, nothing could be that easy.

Jarvis spent the next two hours dealing with the coroner, taping off the crime scene, and interviewing witnesses. He was exhausted. He should call Angelina; she needed to know about Stone. Hopefully he'd make it. The EMTs didn't seem too positive. But miracles had been known to happen.

He huffed, wishing for a cup of coffee. It was two hours past the usual time he either called or brought one to Angelina. Jarvis took out the phone but before he could hit a button, the captain called with a direct order to come to the station.

Jarvis waited a moment in the Jeep, for the heat to start flowing. He wished that, rather than stop here for temporary medicine, that Stone had gone to the hospital. Perhaps they could've stopped him going into a coma. Were comas reversible? Sure, they must be—sometimes.

He developed a theory: the woman saw his car here—or came in for something, then spotted him. Either way, the clerk said she'd confronted him.

Funny there was so much activity in the place; it had been well after midnight. From his nights as beat cop years ago, he knew this town to be very quiet after 11 p.m. this time of year.

Jarvis pulled into the driveway at the station. Captain Folsom stood outside the front door smoking a cigar. He squished the butt under a heel and held the door for Jarvis. Together they tromped down the hall to the captain's office. Jarvis envied his boss; he was six years older yet still had all his hair.

"While you were en route," Captain Folsom said, "hospital called. Stone didn't make it."

"Shit."

"You got that right."

"Can't say I'm surprised."

The captain shook his head.

Jarvis flopped in a chair and told the robbery story start to finish. He downloaded the photos from his camera to the captain's computer and then sent them to his own. There didn't seem anything else to talk about so the captain dismissed him.

In his office, he was just about to phone Angelina to let her know the news about Stone when a knock came on the doorframe. Jarvis stifled a grunt of frustration. One of the state cops from the scene held up a clear plastic bag containing videotapes from the convenience store and the hardware store.

The men notified the captain. All three tromped to the viewing room where they sat staring at the fuzzy black and white images. Jarvis fast-forwarded through hours of useless footage, occasionally chuckling at the attire or behavior of customers. Finally, Stone stepped into the store…alone.

"Is that him?" the captain asked.

"Yes. "The name is Stone Powers—well, one of his names. He is—was—the star of Angelina's new play." Which reminded Jarvis that she still didn't know of his death. Though she'd been involved in several murder investigations around the area, this would hit her hard.

On the video screen, Stone staggered toward the aisle containing aspirin and the Pepto.

"Looks like he's been there before," said the captain. "He didn't even check to see what aisle he was in. Can't help wondering why one of my officers didn't pull him over for drunk driving." He shot Jarvis an accusatory look.

Jarvis shook his head but didn't elaborate.

The angle of the camera showed just the top of Stone's head at this point but it was easy to see he'd picked up a bottle of the pink medication—and turned toward the checkout. He just stood there though. Looked like he was breathing heavy. He seemed to be contemplating whether to open the bottle right there in the aisle.

A woman with long blonde hair—the sides pulled back from her face—entered. She stood in the doorway, a large dark colored purse slung over the shoulder of a long white fur coat. A set of keys dangled from her hands. She spotted Stone's head over the top shelf and marched on spiky-heeled boots toward him. She was pretty, with high cheekbones and a perky nose.

She must've called to Stone because he looked up. He tilted his head and leaned down as if putting the bottle back on the shelf. Then he straightened and squinted in her direction.

She came close; he backed a few paces, stopping when

his butt hit the beer cooler. Now the camera showed his face, and the back of her head—and the glittery hair clip the clerk had mentioned. Clearly she was giving him hell. Stone merely stood against the refrigerator, cheeks looking pinched. Every now and then he'd swallow. Knowing what he knew about the vomit on his parka, Jarvis assumed he was trying to hold it in.

Stone shook his head—said something. Trying to lip read, Jarvis thought he said, "Can't deal with this right now." Stone waved a hand and attempted to step around her. She held him back with a long-red painted index finger to his chest. Stone drew something from his pocket.

"What is that?" the captain asked, suspicious.

"Looks like a cell phone."

That's when the clerk must've spoken to them because the woman peered over her shoulder, giving Jarvis a clear, though grainy look at her expression: angry. A woman who was probably quite pretty when she smiled. Jarvis didn't recognize her. He wished Angelina were here; she might.

The blonde turned back to Stone and said one more thing—probably something like, *you haven't heard the last of this*—snatched the item from his hand, and hurried from the store.

"Look at that! She took the phone," the captain said.

Stone lurched after her, but suddenly gasped for breath. Both arms wrapped around his middle, then one hand reached up to tug on his collar as though it was too tight. He gasped again. Suddenly he vomited, then tumbled over right into it. The scene made Jarvis queasy. He leaned back in the chair, swallowing hard, rubbing his burning eyes. The time stamp on the tape said 3:37 a.m.

CHAPTER 18

Angie hadn't been able to go back to sleep after returning from the theater. And it wasn't because of the coffee. She lay there, her thoughts bouncing from Stone, his wives, Gloria and Rickie, to the summer show.

The show was a fabulous idea. They'd introduce the acting classes by having some practice ones first. Maybe they could do a costume shop—with dress-up for the youngsters.

Gloria would make sure the food was prime. But the pièce de résistance of the weekend would be the two performances.

At 4:30, she gave up trying to sleep and went for an early run, north up Route 11. The weather was what Jarvis would call *brisk*. So long as she didn't breathe through her mouth—which froze her lungs—she was comfortable, though it wasn't easy dodging slushy spots.

By 6:30, Angie was seated behind her new desk—in her new office—into which Vic, Craig, and Fred had moved the furniture. She'd had them set the desk so she could look out over Alton Bay. Right now, wind was forcing snow up the bay and slamming it into the building. She cupped her chin in her hands and thought about Stone Powers. The change in his personality had been too abrupt. No doubt in her mind he'd been drugged or poisoned. The possibility of a tumor was remote because his personality had changed so fast.

He swore he didn't drink. Though she hadn't known him well or very long, he hadn't impressed her as a liar. She chuckled. He hadn't impressed her as a trigamist either. The fact that there had been no alcohol in front of either he or Chia at the restaurant last night was a very significant clue.

For now—or at least until Stone showed up for work this morning—she'd table the topic in favor of more immediate events.

Yesterday Kiana had proudly brought the rejections she'd written for the two of the three scripts she'd taken to read. The rejections were nicely done—pointed out the best elements of the plays and made notes where improvements could be made, but specified that even if changes were made, they wouldn't fit the format of their community theater. Angie fit the script and rejection note into the envelope Kiana had supplied, complete with the author's address. The second script was, as Kiana said, not right for them, but Scene Three had possibilities for the On the Road Again series. She made a copy of the script, then attached a PS to Kiana's note to the script writer.

The third script lay open in front of Angie beside a cup of congealing coffee. She checked the clock. Jarvis had usually popped in with coffee by now. Probably he'd overslept. The idea of getting up and making a fresh cup got lost as she read that third script. A number of Kiana's red marks decorated the margins but stapled to the top corner was a note that said she thought this might be perfect for the summer production. Kiana was right; it was great. Angie made a note to phone the author for either an in-person or Skype meeting.

She'd also come to a disturbing decision. She and Tyson had discussed it at length before retiring last night. They'd decided that whether or not Stone was incapacitated today, they should replace him. He'd lost the respect of both management and the cast. Tyson had offered to do the dirty deed but Angie said she would—after donning a new pair of big-girl panties. Maybe she should order another case of the things.

At 7:05, Kiana clomped down the hall in heavy boots. She plopped a steaming cup of coffee on the desk.

"Ooh, thank you! You're a doll."

Kiana looked around the office as she unbuttoned her big furry—fake, she always made sure to tell people—coat. "I hope you don't miss that other office too much."

"Isn't this view awesome?" Angie went to the window. A man dressed in a bright blue one-piece winter outfit, was trudging across the bay toward a tall, rectangular bob house. It had a pipe sticking out the roof, which meant it at least had heat. Angie shivered. She couldn't imagine spending a day inside one of them hoping to pull a fish through a hole in the ice.

"By the way," Kiana stood beside her, "the guys didn't waste any time. They're discussing the best layout for our new kitchenette."

"Great. I'm so excited to be here, with this view, that I've just about forgotten the windowless cubicle I was in for two years. NOT."

Kiana drew out her phone, hit a few buttons and showed pictures she'd taken of it. I thought I'd put them in an album for you."

Angie giggled then arched her spine to crack out the sitting too long knots. "C'mere. I want to show you something." She took Kiana by the elbow and guided her into the hallway.

To the left and taking up most of the length of the waterside of the building was Quattro's restaurant. The hallway was crowded with building supplies right now. The street side just opposite the restaurant held the four shops. They would have wide, walls of windows so passersby in the hallway could see inside.

Directly in front of Angie's office door was an open area, about 20' x 40' that ended at the green room. Doors opened off the left of this area: dressing rooms, storage, and Angie's old office. Angie pointed to the 20 x 40 area. "If it's okay with you, once the guys are done with the kitchen. I'm going to have them enclose part of this space as an office for you."

Kiana literally leaped in the air. "My own office! Woo hoo!" She grabbed Angie, lifted her off the floor, and spun in a couple of circles.

Once back on her feet, Angie gestured to the window overlooking some of the bay and what in spring would be a great grassy park. "At least your first office will have a view.

Kiana wrapped Angie in another hug. "OMG, that's the greatest news. I love you, love you." She released Angie and danced up and down the space. Fred came from the ex-office slash kitchen to see what the commotion was about.

Angie explained his next duty. "An office for Kiana, then another space beyond that for storing smaller props like weapons, shoes, jewelry. It seems like they're always being misplaced among the wardrobe items."

He paced it off with a grin. "I think we can build you a good-sized office, my dear."

Kiana whooped again and head off to work with a bouncier—if that was possible—step.

At 7:15, the slamming of doors and thump of feet indicated the cast had arrived.

Fred approached. He lowered his voice. "Did you hear the news? There was a robbery at the convenience store across from Aubuchon last night. I heard there was a shooting. Somebody died."

Angie shook her head in dismay. "The world seems to get worse every day. Any idea who it was?"

"No, nothing being released yet."

Angie went back to her office. The new developments did explain why she hadn't heard from Jarvis though.

Angie let Kiana handle the rehearsal and went back to her office to read more of script number three. By ten-thirty, the echo of Kiana's voice giving everyone a twenty-minute break came down the hallway.

Kiana knocked on the office doorframe and came in. She shut the door because the cast had congregated in the green room and the noise floated into the room. She flopped on the brand new cocoa-colored microfiber sofa.

Angie pushed aside the checkbook and bills. "Things go all

right? Did Stone get here yet?"

"No but I didn't expect him."

"Neither did I." She told Kiana about meeting up with he and Chia the night before.

"Weren't you worried the Chia pet was going to punch you or something?"

Angie grinned. "It crossed my mind. I had my fingers on the buttons ready to call you to the rescue but got a brainstorm." She grasped the strap to her handbag with both hands and mimed swinging it. "Works as good as a right hook."

"Probably makes less of a mark too."

"I'll have to remember that."

"Jacoby took over for Stone. We did a quick read-through without any issues. I was impressed how well he'd prepared. I think things will move forward from now on." Kiana got up and started for the door. "There are a few things with the dialogue that don't feel right." She tossed a copy of the script on the desk.

Angie thumbed through it. Kiana had penciled in a number of comments and suggested changes. They discussed them and Angie gave her okay.

"Maybe you'd like to come listen in person."

She was sure Kiana's suggestions were sound, but the girl wanted validation so Angie followed her out front. As they passed, the cast followed.

Angie took a front row seat and watched them run through the proposed changes.

She guessed Stone not showing up was a good thing. It made the decision to fire him easier. Angie called to Jacoby. His Reeboks made thumping sounds on the steps. He flopped into the seat beside Angie.

Kiana said she'd be right back and followed the cast out back—probably to give Angie and Jacoby time alone.

"Nice job today," Angie told him. "You've earned the part. Congratulations."

"Thanks. I promise to make you proud." They shook

hands. Jacoby strode up the trio of steps and down the hallway to the noisy green room.

Angie stayed where she was, glad the way things were working out, but also wondering how Stone was feeling. "Kiana!" she called.

"Yeah?" came the return shout. The teen appeared at stage-left.

"Do you have Stone's cell number?"

"Hold on, I'll check." She returned a moment later with the corner off a newspaper.

"Thanks." She dialed the number. There was no answer.

Kiana sat beside Angie. "What did you think of the changes?"

"Perfect. Except for the scene where the two workers have a beer after work. Their joking was a little stilted." She wrote a few notes in the margin. "What do you think of these?"

Kiana read them and laughed out loud. "Love it! Should I let everyone go home now?"

"Yes. I had a text from Blanche. A few costumes are ready. Can you have Craig, Vic, and…" The cast clomped in from out back. "I guess I'll tell them myself." Angie stood. "You can all head home for the day. See you at nine a.m.? Except Craig, Vic and Caroline—Blanche has your costumes ready. Can you come a half hour early for a fitting?"

Everyone said yes and voiced their *goodbye, see you tomorrows*.

Kiana hugged her. "Thanks for everything."

"Before you go." Angie gestured for Kiana to sit beside her. "There's something I wanted to ask you. Since you'll be working so closely with the summer show, I wondered how you'd feel about my mother handling some of the side stuff—" Angie put up a hand before Kiana could speak. "I mean, things not related to the production, like food, printing tickets, renting tents and furniture. And…before you answer, this is my mother I'm talking about. We all know what a… strong personality she can have, so don't be your usual polite self. I want you to be totally honest. If you think it's—"

Kiana broke into a wide white smile. "I think it's a great idea. Your mother is a go-getter. I love that she doesn't take crap from anybody."

"Diplomatically said." Angie laughed. "You ought to go into politics. No—forget that—stay with us. Anyway, take some time to think about it. I won't hold it against you if you change your mind."

"I'll think about it but I doubt it'll make any difference. I don't like how your mother treats you, and"—she smiled wider—"that relationship with Rickie Kennedy is a bit weird, but otherwise she seems like a good person. Someday we'll talk about why she acts the way she does toward you. And why you take it."

"The other day you were a law student and now you're a psychiatrist?"

Kiana laughed and hugged her again. "Everyone has reasons for behaving the way they do, even if they're not aware of them. Would you mind if I took the rest of the day off? My old drama class needs help with their script."

"Of course. Go on."

"Do you have anything you want done first?"

As far as Angie knew there was only one thing to do—put on her big girl panties, get on the phone, and fire Stone Powers. It would be her first firing. And it should be done in person, but under the circumstances, it seemed prudent not to have him back in the building. And she sure as heck didn't want to do it at his house with Blanche there. Maybe a little strategy was in order. First, find out where Blanche was.

Angie went to her new office and Blanche's cell. She answered on the third ring.

"I called to see how Stone is doing."

"Stone?"

"Yes, that tall George Clooney lookalike you're married to."

Chuckle. "I know who he is. I assume he's fine. I haven't seen him since Thursday."

"Thursday?" Uh-oh. That was two days ago.

"I brought him back here from the theater and put him to bed. God, he was sick. I had to go to Portsmouth to deliver some designs. When I got home about six-thirty, he was gone. I assumed he'd finally left for Chicago."

But on Friday, Gloria had taken him home. To Blanche's house.

CHAPTER 19

"Replay that, will you?" the state cop said to Jarvis.

Jarvis punched a few buttons, listened to the whir as the tape rewound, then hit Play. They watched the scene unfold again.

"If she killed him, she did it without touching him," the captain noted. "What a drunken fool."

"I don't think he was drunk. Angelina and I are pretty sure he'd been drugged," Jarvis said.

"You mean *on* drugs?" the state cop asked.

"No. Drugged. With something. The past two days at the theater, he'd been exhibiting signs of a heavy drinker but he swore up and down he didn't drink. He was a health food nut and a germophobe."

"You're saying you believed what he said? asked the other state cop.

"Not at first, but I learned that the week prior, he'd been fine. Laughing and joking with everyone. Flirting with the ladies. Tonight, we had dinner in Manchester. He was there with one of his wives."

When the captain's nose wrinkled, Jarvis diverted to explain about the trio of long-haired beauties. One state cop gave no reaction; the other chuckled; the captain frowned. Jarvis related how Stone got away from them at the restaurant, then the subsequent search for him. "That's why I was so late getting back to town. Cops couldn't find him around the restaurant or the home of the wife he had dinner with—so I drove everyplace I thought he might go. Finally I came home."

"So, he'd been acting drunk but swore he didn't drink," said a state cop.

"Right. And, a big point of interest: there was no alcohol on his table. Two glasses of water, and two sodas. This was verified by the waitress. I have a copy of their check from that night. Also, the no-drinking fact has been corroborated by his other two wives."

The cop who'd laughed at the mention of three wives laughed again and received a scowl from Captain Folsom.

"Tell me more about them." This from the captain.

They retired to the kitchenette area where Jarvis made some fresh coffee. While the machine gurgled and spit he described Blanche, Miata Lin, and the Chia pet. Angelina's name for the third wife made Captain Folsom chuckle.

The state cops sucked down the coffees in a couple of gulps and took their leave. The captain watched them clomp off down the hall. "That's weird. Usually they insinuate themselves into our cases."

Jarvis laughed. "It's like five in the morning. They've been up all night. Like Arnold Schwarzenegger, they'll be back." He let a few seconds pass then added, "Once we've had time to do all the legwork."

They refilled their coffees and wandered back to the viewing room where Jarvis nudged the second convenience store video into the machine. This tape gave a view of the parking lot. Jarvis scrolled to the 3:33 time stamp and let the machine play at real-time. It was quiet in the wee hours. As couple of cars passed on the main road but the only one to come in was at 3:35 when Chia's black Audi entered the lot from the roundabout from the south, which meant he came directly from Manchester.

The car jerked to a stop straddling the parking lines near the door. Stone got out and lurched into the building.

A minute later, a small two-door car entered the lot from the direction of town. It stopped near the entrance to the pizza shop—on the other side of the building. All that showed clearly of the car on the tape was a pair of taillights. They had a slightly better image of it on the version from the hardware store.

"Any clue what kind of car that is?" Jarvis asked.

Captain Folsom leaned forward, squinting. He shook his head.

"Taillights can be as telling as a name brand," Jarvis said. "I'm not up on things like that. But I know someone who is: Detective José Rodriguez."

"He that cop you worked with in Nashua last summer?"

"Yeah. José knows cars inside and out. He can recite models and even the size of tire that's standard on each one." Jarvis got him on the line. While they caught up on the past seven months, Jarvis forwarded him a picture of the car's rear end.

José laughed. "Jeez Jarvis, I expected you had a tough one on your hands. That's a 2011 Toyota Prius."

Jarvis thanked José and promised keep in touch.

"Send that image to the lab," the captain said, "to enlarge the license plate."

Jarvis had an idea. He rushed to his office and dug out his notes on the three wives. Surely one of them owned a Prius.

None did.

"Have the wives picked up," the captain said.

"Sir, it's the crack of dawn."

"All the better. Make sure they don't see each other coming in and put them in separate interrogation rooms."

"Do we have that many?" Jarvis joked.

Captain Folsom flashed him an *another time and place and I would've laughed* look. "I want to find out what, if anything, they know about each other."

CHAPTER 20

Angie set the cell phone to conference call and laid it on the desk. "You didn't hear what happened yesterday?" She got up and went to the big new window, watched the fisherman lock his bob-house, then haul his catch strung on a line, back to shore. "He got sick again. I couldn't reach you so I had my mother bring him home."

"But..." There was a short silence from Blanche. "But Angie, like I already said, Stone was in Chicago yesterday."

"Not unless he has a twin." Or a triplet. "He was here at the theater."

Another silence. Angie pulled her hair into a ponytail and secured it with a scrunchy from around her wrist.

"What time was this?" Blanche asked.

"About lunchtime."

After another silence, during which Angie heard the sewing machine running, Blanche said, "I got home about one-thirty yesterday. Angie, he wasn't here. It didn't look as if he'd been here." She laughed. "You can always tell when Stone's home: shoes near the door, jacket on the arm of the sofa; socks in front of the armchair; remote lost down the crease of the chair. Angie, I'm confused."

"So, you last saw him on Thursday—two days ago. When was the last time you actually spoke to him?"

"I texted him Thursday night asking how he was feeling but didn't hear back until yesterday morning." Which was Friday.

"Is that unusual?"

"Not under the circumstances. If he's with a client he doesn't respond to phone calls or texts. He says it's rude. Anyway, he thanked me for being patient. Said he still felt like shit and had gone to bed right after meeting with the client. I texted back saying it was his own fault, and how dare he go to my place of work and embarrass me like that? He swore—actually cursed at me, which is something he rarely does—that he was not drunk. Angie, don't get mad at me, but I believe him. I know you can't see it, but have my hand over my heart. I swear to you, I've been with him over four years and never known him to be a drinker. Once during summer, if it's really hot, he might, but he never even finishes it."

How to respond? She didn't want to bring up talk of drugs or poisoning yet. "I don't know how to tell you this, Blanche, but yesterday he was staggering around, couldn't organize his thoughts. Then…" She shivered. "He barfed on the stage—well, actually on two of the actors—during rehearsal."

Blanche was quiet a moment. Then she sighed. When she said, "I don't know what could've happened," Angie felt better because it was clear Blanche was weighing the evidence. Of course Blanche was confused; she was learning new things about her husband of four years.

And Angie had just learned he was a liar because he said he was texting from Chicago but he'd never left New Hampshire. No way he could have.

After this, Angie would call her mother and find out what happened. Blanche said he hadn't been there, so perhaps he'd talked her mother into dropping him someplace else.

"I'm sure he got his act together and left for the airport. Work's been a zoo lately. Three theaters are prepping productions right now. I've been running in a hundred directions at once. Maybe I was so busy I didn't notice he'd been here. I suppose it's possible he didn't make a mess." She laughed. "First time for everything, right?"

"It would explain why he didn't show up at the theater

today."

"You knew he was leaving town, right?"

"Yes. When I hired him we talked at length about his schedule. He assured me he could work around it, that he might only miss a few rehearsals."

Blanche sighed. "His schedule is flexible but I've rarely seen him deviate from it. All this is so out of character. He's usually the most responsible person." She laughed. "Sloppy but responsible. Angie, I'm really sorry for all this. Since I brought him to you I feel accountable."

"I won't hold his behavior against you. So long as you don't hold it against me when I have to fire him."

"Fire him?"

"I'm sorry. My reputation's on the line."

The sewing machine stopped. A giant sigh oozed through the phone. "I understand. I'll be in touch." The call went dead.

Angie hung up thinking that Stone's behavior might be normal for a man with three wives whose lives had suddenly converged at one small town community theater. Angie liked Blanche; she wanted to be there for her when the inevitable bomb exploded.

For now, life had to go on. She took a copy of the script out to meet with the staging crew. They spent a few minutes going over the changes Tyson suggested to the scenery. Gosh, she'd missed having him around.

The theater building was silent. Angie went out the back door. As she stood on the step wrestling with the frozen lock, her cell phone rang. She considered hurrying to the car that'd been warming for several minutes, but the phone had already rung three times. Voice mail would pick up soon. The call was from Kiana.

"Hi Angie. I wanted to let you know I've had time to think and I'd really like to work with your mom."

Angie somehow refrained from saying, "Are you absolutely, positively, without a doubt, sure?" and just said, "Great. I'm going to see her this afternoon. Text me some ideas you have and I'll add them to a list I've made."

"Let me know what she says."

"I will. Talk to you Monday."

Angie disconnected the call.

She'd worked many years in the ER but she faced mainly emergencies. Sure, a few drug overdoses, but those were hardcore things. Whatever was being given to Stone was nothing like that. Especially if it was a poison—she knew nothing about them at all.

She dialed a number she knew by heart—the main desk of the ER at Lakes Region General Hospital—and asked to speak with Zoë Pappas. She and Zoë had run the ER department for many years. After some lengthy salutations and apologies for not keeping in touch, Angie got to the point. "What do you know about poisons?" She explained her star's recent behaviors.

"Look, hon, as you well know, we deal with the effects here in the ER. We hardly ever see the causes. What I suggest is talking to Doctor Morton. Chris does all our toxicology tests. I'll put you through."

"Thanks. You free on Tuesday?"

"Sure, let's get together. It's been too long. I'll tell you about the new man in my life."

The call to Dr. Chris Morton connected. It turned out the doctor was a woman with a high, squeaky voice that made Angie wince. She went through a long explanation about Stone's abrupt personality change, and the ensuing symptoms: acting drunk, stomach pains."

"It does sound like you're dealing with some sort of poison. Something administered in small doses over a period of time."

"I was hoping you'd say something like a brain aneurism."

"No. Sorry."

"Over how long of a period of time might you think?"

"You're asking a lot here. Putting a timeline to something we don't even know..." She was quiet a moment, asked a couple of questions related to his symptoms, then said, "Depends on the strength and frequency of the dosage, but since the symptoms seemed to escalate this quickly, I'd guess it's most likely just a few days. And in fairly large doses."

"Any thoughts on what it might be?"

"Off the top of my head: some steroids, or acrylamide—a soluble chemical compound generally used in water treatment facilities. Then there's cassava found in yucca and sweet potato plants. Ethyl alcohol, isopropanol, chloral hydrate, and PCP, to name a few. How did his eyes look?"

"Dilated."

"That leans me more toward the alcohols or cassava—but there are dozens and dozens of other possibilities. Without testing…"

"Can tests determine what it is?"

"They can narrow down our search. We do extensive blood workups. It's much easier if we have an idea what we're looking for of course. As you know, there are thousands of things both chemical and natural that can be used as poison." She sighed. "It would sound gruesome to a layman, but I know you'll understand when I say I'd love to get my hands on this case. Either way, I suggest you get him in here asap. Sounds like he's in the later stages. Time is of the essence."

"I will. Thanks." Angie hung up the phone feeling awful. She'd not only misjudged Stone's situation, but she, as a nurse, should've realized much sooner that something serious was in the works. Angie dropped the phone in her pocket. She wanted to call Blanche to find out if she knew where Stone was staying. She also wanted to notify Jarvis. But not till she was in the warmth of the car with hot air blowing in her face. Shivering, she hit the unlock button on the car remote.

Before she could get the door open, a blue car zoomed up beside her. Miata Lin got out. She was smiling, which didn't bode well since during their last meeting she was ripping mad.

"I forgot to pick up a schedule the other day when I was here."

She also hadn't completed the process for paying for the

season tickets, but right now Angie wasn't about to remind her. "I don't suppose we could delay this a day or so, I have an emergency I have to tend to."

"Can you do it while I finish making out the membership card?"

"Actually, could we finish payment on Monday, please? As for the schedule, I think I have a box of them here in the car." Angie circled to the passenger side. When she opened the door she was hit with a blast of nice, warm air. Would it be rude to climb in and finish the conversation through the open window? Angie retrieved one of the tri-fold brochures. "Did you tell er, Martin about the tickets yet?"

"No, he's out of town. Right now he's in Chicago."

Angie drew her phone from her pocket hoping to give Miata Lin a hint. "So, you haven't talked to him?"

She shook her head. "He always calls around seven in the morning. My fault this time, I had to leave at six so I missed him. I texted him a few times during the night—to tell him things that happened during the day—that's the stuff we always talk about in the mornings. But I didn't hear back." She shrugged. "He hasn't been feeling well lately so he probably sacked out early."

Angie rubbed her freezing fingers together. "Well, I hope you catch up with him soon. I know he'll be excited about the tickets. Do you have far to travel for the shows?"

"Not too far. We live in Canterbury. I'm thinking it'd be fun to make a night of it. Have dinner. See the show. Get a motel. You know."

Angie nodded and started to get in the car. She was freezing. It was snowing again. And she needed to talk to Stone asap.

Finally Miata retraced her steps to the blue Cooper. Angie dialed Stone's cell while watching the woman execute a U-turn and gun it up the hill.

Stone's voice mail answered. "Stone. I am worried about you. Please get yourself to the hospital as soon as you can. It's very important."

Stone's voice mail beeped, ending the message. Where on earth was he? Should she call Chia? One of his wives had to have heard from him.

She considered phoning Jarvis but he had to be up to his ears in that robbery and murder at the store. Again she wondered who it could be. Like whenever a fire truck passed, she hoped it wasn't racing toward someone she knew.

Angie wound the heat full-blast and then did call Jarvis. No answer. She hadn't expected him to answer. She didn't bother leaving a message. Next she called her mother who sounded like she'd just gotten out of bed. It was nearly noon. "You busy? I thought I'd come visit for a few minutes," Angie said.

"Sure. Come over. I'm alone."

Argh. Suddenly a visit didn't seem like such a good idea. Angie made the five-minute drive to HeavenScent thinking about how her mother had changed. When she was sad or lonely, Gloria usually grew clingy and obnoxious. She'd practically driven Angie crazy when she first came to town. Was this lack of those qualities a bad thing, meaning her mother was especially depressed? Or did it mean she was maturing, had learned to accept things as they were? It was one of those things to which Angie didn't want to know the answer.

HeavenScent was a grand place that Tyson's parents had leased two years ago while they visited Alton Bay for the summer. Tyson took over the lease when they went *back to civilization*. Then when he left, Gloria and Rickie assumed the lease.

The expansive lawns would be perfect for the summer show—a wide flat area overlooking the lake would hold the biggest of the tents. Another spot for a smaller food tent, and a lot of grassy space for the other events. The three-car garage could house the props and sets. Angie grew excited as she approached the front door.

Gloria had it open before Angie reached the stoop.

Inside, Angie followed her mother to the back of the house, where a long kitchen wall of windows looked out over

Lake Winnipesaukee.

"The show is what I wanted to talk to you about. Kiana and I had an idea—a brilliant idea, if I do say so myself."

"Coffee?"

"Thanks." Angie slid into a somewhat familiar chair. She'd sat in this kitchen once listening to a tirade from Tyson's mother, about how she was a gold digger and should be ashamed for chasing after her precious son.

"What are you smiling about?" Gloria poured coffee into heavy ceramic mugs. Angie related the story of her first meeting with Agnes Goodwell and Tyson's handsome, long-suffering father.

"She was sure I had designs on her son. She couldn't get over that we were just partners."

"God, even Jarvis, the most jealous man in the world, knows that." Gloria dropped into a chair at the other end of the thick, highly polished oak table. "So, what's the brilliant idea you and Kiana came up with?"

"We thought you'd like to work with us on the show committee."

"I don't know anything about theater—except as a spectator, which I assume wouldn't help you much."

"We'd like you to handle things not show-related, things like caterers, advertising, scheduling, renting the tents and furniture."

Gloria Farnsworth's blue eyes grew wide. Small crinkles appeared at the outer corners. "Now that I could do! We'll use Lindquist Caterers. They're the company we used when—"

Angie snatched an envelope from a pile of mail on the corner of the table. She produced a pen from underneath. "Write."

She stood and walked to the windows, sipping the expensive brew of coffee as her mother gushed ideas, intermittently stopping to scribble on the envelope. It was nice to see Gloria excited about something. Angie hadn't seen her this way since she appeared on Angie's doorstep toting a thirty-something boyfriend. She chuckled to herself remembering how she'd originally deemed him under thirty.

She wondered where Rickie had gone but would not ask. Nothing should spoil Mom's mood right now.

Suddenly Angie was hit with a dreadful sensation that buckled her knees and made her lightheaded. Something had happened to Jarvis. She set the cup in the sink with a clank. "I have to go."

Good that her mother was distracted. It kept her from asking questions for which Angie had no answers. All she said was, "I'll call you later." Angie kissed the top of her mother's head and hurried out to the Lexus, that dire, almost disabling feeling still gripping her. She dialed Jarvis's number.

"Hi." In that one word Angie read bad news.

"What happened?"

"How did you— Oh, never mind. I'll just spit it out. Stone Powers is dead."

CHAPTER 21

Angelina didn't speak. Stone's death shouldn't have been unexpected. Hadn't they joked about it yesterday? With three wives—once they learned about each other, a hurricane the likes of which Alton Bay had never seen would roll in.

Most likely her silence was her brain working through which of the wives did it because no way would she think it was anything but murder. Right now though, Stone's cause of death was unknown. From alcohol poisoning to brain tumor, to whether the Prius owner had inflicted a killing blow not visible on the videos—they just weren't sure.

"What happened?" Angelina's voice came out so softly he almost didn't hear.

He described the events inside the convenience store.

"I heard something happened there. None of us had any idea Stone was involved. What an awful thing. How did it happen?"

"Not sure yet. It wasn't gunshot or knife, or anything you could see with the naked eye. From the videotapes it looks like he had a heart attack or something." He described the scene on the video. "Then he threw up and keeled over. We're waiting for drug tests and all that to come back."

"Did you ask them to check for poisons?"

She never failed to surprise him. "I'm sure that's part of the autopsy, but as you know, poisons are nearly impossible to detect unless you have an idea what to look for. Did you have any particular ones in mind?"

"I talked to Doctor Morton at the hospital."

Dammit, she was always at least a step ahead of the cops.

"She suggested several things, which you might pass along." Angelina named them. He scribbled the words in his notebook but could hardly keep up. "Mind if I just put the coroner's office in touch with her?"

"I know she'd be happy to help. I urged some information from her. Mind you, none of it is official but she thought possibly, from the way the symptoms manifested—that he'd only been given the dosage for a matter of days."

Which brought the wives to the forefront as suspects. As far as he knew they were all converging in this area over that period of time. Chances were good they knew about one another.

Angelina had been quiet for several moments. From past experience, Jarvis wouldn't be surprised to learn she'd already formulated an idea of the killer's identity. Just in case she was constructing the jigsaw pieces in her head, he didn't interrupt.

The silence went on so long he wondered if they'd lost the cell connection. So he said, "A woman was seen arguing with him just before it happened."

"Interesting."

"What's so interesting about that?" Stone was always surrounded by women.

"You didn't mention anyone's name. So, that tells me you don't know her identity."

This woman was a marvel!

"The captain and I went over the videotapes looking for a sign that she murdered him but the only physical contact they had was when she took something—looked like his cell phone—from him."

"That explains why he didn't answer."

"Come again?"

"Doctor Morton suggested I get him to the hospital as

quickly as possible. I called several times and left messages but there was no answer." A few more seconds of silence, then. "So she never touched him…"

"Other than what appeared to be her snatching the cell phone, it didn't look like she touched him in any way." He laughed. "And it was clear she wanted to! You can look at the video. As a matter of fact, we'd appreciate your input."

"Now?"

"Sooner the better."

"I'll be right there." The line went dead. He laughed. She was a woman of decision, a woman who got things done.

She arrived in his office in seven and a half minutes. He gave a direct look at the wall clock as she stepped into the room. "What'd you do, walk?"

Angelina grinned. "I was at my mother's." She kissed his cheek. Her lips were cold.

"Where were we?" she asked.

"You asked if the unidentified woman could've done anything to kill him."

"You said to come."

"Do you always do what you're told?"

"Not usually."

He threw back his head and laughed. Together they walked to the viewing room.

"Describe the woman," Angelina said.

"You're going to see her in a few minutes."

"I want your impression."

Jarvis recited the details he'd picked up from the videos and the clerk. "She drives a Prius, is about your height, has long light-colored hair. Man, can she holler—" Angelina laughed, but that didn't deter him. "She was wearing a long, white fur coat and high-heeled boots."

When Angelina didn't speak, he asked, "Wasn't that what you wanted to know?"

She nodded. "Did she wave her arms around a lot? Did she get in his face and shout?"

He felt a frown crease his brow. "Where is your mind heading?"

"What I was thinking is that if one of the wives planned to kill him, knowing there'd be witnesses in spite of the early hour—she might have worn a disguise. It would cover her physical attributes, but her personality might come through. For example, when Miata Lin got angry that day at the theater, she waved her arms a lot. When Chia was angry she got right in my face." Angelina showed him by moving just inches from his nose. He took the moment to steal a kiss. "I've never seen Blanche get riled about anything but the point is, you said the woman was mad at Stone. How exactly did she act?"

He thought hard and let his mind replay the footage. "She did all those things." He shrugged. "Come watch the video."

They sat side-by-side as the convenience store's tape played. The captain entered and took a seat beside Jarvis. They were silent until the woman entered. Though the sides of her hair were pulled back, not much of her face was visible because of the collar of the big coat.

"What kind of fur is that?" Captain Folsom asked.

"Expensive. Real," was all Angelina said. She leaned forward, elbows on her thighs, chin cupped in her hands. "It can't be Miata Lin. She's too short."

"Maybe she wore special heels."

"I doubt they could help enough. Can you back up the tape to where she comes in the door?"

"Sure."

The woman entered. The clerk, not five feet away, greeted her—the clerk Jarvis had met, who was about five foot seven. This woman towered over him.

"Okay, you're right," he said. "It can't be Miata Lin. Blanche is tall. Could it be her?"

Angelina tilted her head. "Can you move it forward slowly?" Before the woman reached Stone, Angelina was shaking her head. "You can do lots of things with disguises, and this woman has a similar bone structure to Blanche but she doesn't walk like Blanche."

"Well, it's definitely not the Chia pet," Jarvis said.

The captain finally spoke up. "Why not? Didn't I read she was once a model? Aren't they always tall?"

"I guess many are, but Chia is black."

"Oh." The captain stood and faced them.

"So where does that leave us?" Jarvis asked.

"With Blanche of course," the captain said. "Have her picked up."

"It's none of my business," Angelina said, "but I wouldn't if I were you. That's not her."

The captain frowned. He tilted his head, appraising Angelina. After a moment, he nodded. "Okay. For now. Since I suspect Stone was the only target, I'll put it off for now." He stood. "But if there's one single clue…"

"Captain," Jarvis said. "Stone had women around him all the time. This one could be a girlfriend—one he hasn't married yet." They all groaned. "Or, heaven forbid, a wife we haven't learned about yet."

Another collective groan.

Angelina was still watching the video. "That's definitely his cell phone she took."

"She probably wants to check who else he's been talking to," Jarvis said.

"Do you know anyone who lip reads?" she asked.

"I'll find someone," said the captain.

When the video ended, Angelina stood and paced the width of the room.

"You know something," the captain said.

She raised an index finger to stop him from saying more.

After several minutes, Jarvis asked, "Want me to put in the other video?"

"Not yet. Will you play the first one again?"

She remained on her feet, arms crossed, her beautiful blonde hair hiding her facial reactions. Jarvis loved watching her mind work. She had an amazing ability to read people, to pick up details other people—he in particular—missed. He assumed that's why the captain agreed not to pick up Blanche yet. Jarvis hoped like hell it was the right decision. He'd been about to issue the directive too.

"Have you let them reopen the store?" she asked.

"Not yet. Why?"

"She dropped something just outside the door. Rewind the tape slowly?"

The machine clicked, the video played backwards. The woman walked into the store. As she got near the cash register, Angelina said, "Stop." She strode to the screen. "Move it slowly forward." The scene clicked into motion. "Stop." The captain hit the button; the woman froze in place. Angelina pointed with an index finger. It showed on the screen as a giant penis-shaped shadow. Jarvis shook his head to dislodge the image and managed somehow not to laugh or comment.

Now that her idea was planted in his head, he saw what the woman dropped: something small—maybe the size of a saltshaker—that was the best he could tell from the grainy image. A forensics team had been through the place. Had they taken evidence from outdoors? Dammit. He didn't know. Jarvis radioed to the rookie who'd been on duty and asked.

"Yes, sir. They picked up everything within four feet of the door.

He and Angelina went to the evidence room. The bags hadn't yet been catalogued. They had been stowed in a box in a locked closet. Jarvis got the box and removed the evidence. Most of it, as usual, was useless rubbish. Some could be days old, missed by errant janitors. He flipped through.

"Nothing." He picked up the house phone on the wall. "Sergeant Wilson, can you come here?"

Ambrose Wilson was a fellow officer but also a good friend. Jarvis and the sergeant had been on many stakeouts together. They'd shared histories, silly stories, and personal secrets. The big man in street clothes today, stepped in. Jarvis showed him the video and asked him to go do another sweep of the entire area.

"I have the feeling it's going to be a long couple of days. While we wait for the arrival of the suspects, let's get something to eat," Jarvis said.

"The suspects?"

"We're having the wives all brought in for questioning."

She made a pinch-faced look.

"What's wrong?"

"You just agreed not to bring in Blanche."

"I know, but the captain changed his mind. Besides, she's not being singled out."

Angelina nodded but he could tell she wasn't convinced.

They went to his office to retrieve his jacket. "You do think one of the wives killed him, right?" He wiggled his eyebrows at her, which made her laugh.

"Why are you doing that thing with your eyes?"

"Well, don't we have a rather limited suspect pool?"

She tilted her head at him, which meant she was about to dispute what he said. He hated when she did that. It meant he'd missed something—usually something serious. "I can think of a couple of others. Less obvious, smaller motives, but..."

"Who?"

"Well, there's Jacoby Meyers."

"You think he wanted the starring role so much he'd kill for it?"

She shrugged. "Murders have been committed for lesser reasons."

She had a point.

"And then there's Vic Jason."

"He's one of the guys Stone barfed on, right? Think he'd kill him for that? For me it'd be a pretty damned good reason."

"Stone was already— Oh, stop it."

"Anyone with a really good motive?"

"No, right now, just the wives. Nobody stands out ahead of the others. I suspect as the investigation opens up, deeper motives will come to light."

"Do you think they know about each other?"

"If we know," she said, "then there's a darned good chance at least one of them does."

They stepped into the hallway and headed for the exit. Just then the door opened. Two people entered: a state police officer with a bushy mustache. More notable was the handcuffed woman just ahead of him. She was sobbing hysterically. Jarvis didn't recognize her with her face buried in a wad of tissues.

But Angelina did. She moved toward the woman and took her in her arms. The state policeman took hold of Angelina's arm and pulled her away. "Don't touch the prisoner, ma'am."

"Prisoner?" She spun on Jarvis. "I thought you said she was being brought in for questioning."

"She is." Jarvis took Blanche's arm and steered her down the hall. "Sorry," he told the fuming Angelina. "Be right back," he said, though he wasn't sure he wanted to go back.

He returned slowly, gauging her mood. She looked calm. She stood and went toward him. "Can I sit in on the questioning?"

He shook his head and said, "Sorry. I already asked. Captain said no because you're too close to her."

"We aren't going for lunch, are we?"

He said "sorry" again.

"Okay. I'll see you later." She kissed his cheek and started to open the door.

"Wait." He went to her and whispered, "What's wrong?" expecting she was pissed at him and hiding it. But she wasn't.

"The woman in the convenience store... She looks familiar."

CHAPTER 22

Angie picked up a sandwich and went to her new office. Right now it was the best place for privacy. Except for the builders, the place was a ghost town. She blocked out the voices shouted over the loud plunking of the hydraulic nail guns.

As she'd told Jarvis, the woman at the convenience store looked familiar. But all during the ride from the station to the restaurant to the theater she tried, and failed, to recall where she'd seen her. Okay, she told herself, the best way to remember something is to not think about it. She'd go about regular daily activities, immerse herself in theater stuff and prep for the summer show. Suddenly—probably at three in the morning—it would come to her.

So. Angie checked the mail and messages on the machine. Nothing that couldn't wait until Monday. She slid the most recent copy of *American Theater Magazine* from a pile on the desk. She read it cover to cover, picking up pointers to boost their small town theater—but also looking for news about Tyson's show. Nothing in this issue.

She finished the sandwich then went to stand in front of the new sofa below the Christmas gift from Tyson, the painting of Kratos, the Greek god of strength. "I hope you have some influence inside this building. We sure can use it."

When he didn't react—for some reason, he never did when she appealed to him—she stretched out on the sofa, right arm propping her head so she could see out the new sliding door. From this angle, all that was visible was the bright blue sky and the naked branch of a maple tree, but it was comforting.

Had Stone been murdered? Or had he died from natural causes—some kind of aneurism or heart problem? The autopsy would be completed quickly and would give them some answers.

But Angie couldn't stop thinking about what Doctor Morton said: that poison was a likely being used on him. Had it killed him? If so, who was dosing him?

She ran what the meager list of suspects through her head starting with Blanche, the one Angie knew best. Had she known about the other two wives? If so, she put on a good front against it. As long as Angie had known her, she'd acted the perfect wife. She seemed to adore Stone, was always there with a smile and a home cooked meal when he returned from his business trips. Angie's mind flashed back to their meeting at the diner. They'd flown into each other's arms. The reunion bordered on embarrassing. No way that had been fake. No, they didn't spend an extraordinary amount of time together; their jobs precluded that, but they made the best of what time they had. Good marriages had been made under less positive circumstances. They'd been married four years. From Jarvis's research of Stone's marriage licenses, as far as they knew Blanche had been his first. She laughed at the assumption that Blanche was first. Who knew how many others there might've been? Maybe one while he lived in Rhode Island working at the marina? Another while he worked at the Providence theater? Or while he worked in the Portsmouth boatyard. Maybe, like the old Rickie Nelson song, he had a girl in every port. Hadn't he said he was in the Marines?

The second marriage they knew of had come under the official name of Leland Powers to Chia Mariachi in 2012, though Chia called him Rocky.

Then one to Miata Lin just last year at the Yankees/Sox game. At that time, he'd used the name Martin. If Stone had married one woman a year, the possibilities were mind-boggling.

None of this information generated an inkling of an idea in her brain. Perhaps the murder had nothing to do with his wives. What if one of these women had been married before. Maybe a vengeful ex wanted her back and had killed Stone to make her available.

Or his death could have something to do with his job. He did, after all, work for a pharmaceuticals company. Medicines, chemical compounds, potential poisons. Maybe he'd been stealing them, or bootlegging and took something by accident. Again, the possibilities were unimaginable.

She hated to consider it, but maybe Jacoby killed him to get the understudy job. No. No. No. This she would not think about.

The only person Angie was certain had nothing to do with Stone's death was that fisherman down on the bay. He was wrestling a wiggling fish through his newly chopped hole in the ice, and looking pleased as could be.

Footsteps sounded in the long hallway. They thumped from the stage through the green room. She recognized Kiana's footsteps and sighed. She really wanted to be alone. But the speed of her protégé's steps tapped out the word trouble. More than likely news of Stone's death had made the rounds.

Kiana entered the office and flew into Angie's arms, toppling them against the big glass door. Angie disengaged the teen's arms from her neck and righted herself.

"I'm so glad I found you," Kiana gushed. "I checked your house and you weren't there. I called Jarvis to ask him." She frowned. "He didn't answer. I can't believe the news about Stone."

"Jarvis is kind of wrapped up in the case right now."

Kiana flopped on the sofa. "I should've said I do believe it happened. When a person acts like Stone did, I guess bad things are going to happen. It's just that...you never expect it to actually..."

This wasn't Kiana's first brush with murder. Her drama teacher had been murdered last year. She'd managed to put the emotion behind her, took it with a mature grace and strength, and put on a tremendously successful charity show in spite of the circumstances, rumors and innuendoes bombarding the high school. Kiana was strong; she'd be fine. Hopefully it wouldn't change her attitude toward the world.

"How did he die?"

"They don't know for sure yet. They're pretty sure he was drugged though."

Kiana nodded as though the thought had occurred to her also. "Drugs like what he sells? Or drugs like cocaine?" Her dark eyes widened. "Or drugs like...poison?"

Angie didn't want to rehash what she'd been thinking. Besides, it was best to keep Kiana focused on things other than death; Angie owed that to the girl's adoptive parents. "No idea yet." She put out her hand. "Come on. Let's go to my house. I need to get out of here for a while."

Kiana clearly had a lot more questions, but she pulled her hat tighter to her head and followed Angie outdoors. They got into two cars, but as they were leaving the parking lot, Jacoby Meyers arrived. His eyes were red and sort of wild looking. He stumbled against the bumper of his car then he shot toward them.

Gosh, was he drunk? Or, heaven forbid, had he been given the same thing as Stone? Angie panicked inside at the thought that somebody might be trying to eliminate members of her cast. What sort of vendetta could there be against Prince & Pauper? Was there a killer in their midst? A killer focused on more than a trigamist?

She laid her head against the steering wheel for a second to gather herself, pulled in a breath, let it out, and lifted her head. Kiana was already out of her car and rushing toward Jacoby. Angie got out too.

Kiana touched his arm. "Jacoby. What's wrong?"

He righted himself, squaring his feet on the pavement, sniffled twice, and shook his head. "You heard about Stone?"

"Yes. Awful, isn't it?" Angie said. From the few spoken words, she hadn't been able to discern his emotional condition. "We'll have a memorial for him here on Monday. And I'm not sure what…er, Blanche has planned yet."

He nodded. His lower lip quivered. "Angie. I-I'm scared."

She hated weak men, and thought she already knew the answer but it seemed appropriate to ask, "Scared of what?"

He threw out both arms and rolled unbloodshot eyes. "Of everything." He counted on his fingers. "That someone's coming after all of us. That—"

The thought of a serial killer was nothing to sneeze at. Angie couldn't comfort him by saying it wouldn't happen because it might. So she said nothing.

"Wh-what do I d-do when the cops come?"

Cops? "Did you do something wrong? Why should the police—"

"They're gonna think I killed him."

"You killed him?" Kiana practically shouted.

"No!" He took a breath. "They're gonna think I did because I wanted that part. I wanted it so bad… And I told everyone. People saw me studying the lines."

"Understudies are supposed to know the lines." Kiana's nose was turning red in the cold.

Angie put an arm around his shoulders and turned him toward his vehicle. "Don't worry so much. Things will be just—"

Jacoby stopped so short Angie walked another two steps before realized. "What's wrong?"

"I had a fight with him a couple of days ago."

Really? She couldn't imagine Jacoby fighting with anyone. He was about the most mild-mannered person she knew. "What could you two have to fight about?"

"He heard I got his part."

"Damn. You should've come to me if he was giving you trouble."

"I told him it was because of his drinking but he shouted at me, 'Why does everyone keep accusing me of that?' Then he socked me…" Jacoby held back the hair near his left ear. "Here."

Sure enough, there was a bruise under his ear. "Where did this happen?"

"At the skating rink in Laconia. I took my girlfriend. She saw the whole thing."

Thank goodness it wasn't at the theater. Angie was embarrassed at the totally selfish thought, but Prince & Pauper didn't need any more attention.

"Stone was ice skating?" Kiana asked, frowning.

"Yes. Well, he was trying but, he kept falling down."

"Was he alone?" Angie asked.

"No." Now it was Jacoby's turn to frown. "He was with a Chinese girl." He lowered his voice. "I know it's none of my business, but isn't he married to Blanche?"

"Yes. But you're right, it's none of our business." Angie wondered why she hadn't taken her own advice and just stayed out of this.

"What should I do?" he asked.

"I think you and your girlfriend should go to headquarters and talk to Detective Jarvis."

"What if he arrests me?"

Angie laughed. "If he does, I'll come bail you out." The joke didn't even make him crack a grin, so she added, "It'll be okay. Trust me."

"B-but they'll be looking for people who didn't like him."

"You did like him though, didn't you?"

"Yes. Yes, I guess I did. Until…"

"Jacoby, I suspect Stone was sick—not drinking. The illness caused a change in his personality."

He nodded, relieved. Kiana walked him to his car. She came back, then she and Angie stood shoulder to shoulder as he drove away.

"Wow, that was unexpected," Angie said.

"Do you think he killed Stone?"

"No." Not really. Then again, perhaps he did.

"Do you think others will die?"

"No! Oh, sorry, didn't mean to shout. No, I don't think we have a serial killer on the loose."

"You don't sound too sure."

"Tell you what I'll do. I'll hire a security team to watch the place."

"Now?"

Angie shivered as a cold wind shuffled up off the bay and down her neck. "No. From home."

At the condo, Angie set some cookies on the counter and made a pot of chamomile tea. Kiana's favorite. Angie hoped it would calm the nervous teen. She made a vow to talk to Jacoby and ask him to keep his emotional outbursts under wraps from now on. She couldn't have him upsetting the entire cast and crew.

Kiana dumped a spoonful of sugar into her cup. She'd been quiet—too quiet for her normal self. After a couple of sips of tea, she finally spoke. "You really think he might've?"

"No, hon, I don't think Jacoby's got a murderous bone in his body."

"But he confessed to that fight."

"Killers usually try to hide things like conflict."

She took a bite of cookie, chewed and swallowed. "Jacoby is smarter than the average person."

Angie couldn't stop a rise to her eyebrows. "How do you know that?"

"He reads *Foreign Affairs*. Do you know it's written by actual world leaders? And one time I saw him reading *The New Criterion*."

Wow, an intellectual. That was a surprise, but Angie wasn't sure why it gave Kiana the idea he might have killer instincts. Even though it was between lunch and dinnertime, she asked,

"Want a grilled cheese?"

"Sure."

Angie went to the living room to retrieve a copy of last month's *The American Theater* and tossed it in front of Kiana. Then she went to work making sandwiches.

As Angie set a plate in front of Kiana, she laughed. "Far cry from *Foreign Affairs*, isn't it?"

Angie sat on the stool beside her, wondering if Jarvis would find time to call tonight. She smiled to herself; like a boomerang, thoughts of murder kept whirling back around.

Kiana pushed aside the magazine and picked up a sandwich half. "Do you think the cops will arrest Jacoby?"

"No."

"Are you sure?"

"No. You asked my opinion."

"Does Detective Jarvis have any real suspects yet?"

Angie tilted her head to look at Kiana. "Why are you so concerned about this? I don't recall you being so worried when your teacher died."

"I know. I guess I was in shock. Ms. Forest was practically my best friend. I couldn't imagine…" She gave a long sigh. "I can't get Stone out of my head. I feel awful for the things I was thinking about him. I mean, imagine…I might know—or work with—the person who killed him." She set down the sandwich.

"Honestly, I think his death is related to one of his wives."

"That doesn't make me feel any better—they've been all over the building lately."

Angie went to get a telephone book and laid her cell phone on the counter. "As of tomorrow, nobody will be allowed in the building without our knowledge or permission." She phoned the first security company in the yellow pages that advertised they were available 24/7. She made arrangements to meet with the owner at Shibley's for brunch the following morning.

"Which of the wives do you suspect?" Kiana asked the moment Angie hit the Off button.

"None in particular. I hope it'll ease your mind to know the cops were rounding them up for questioning."

"The ones we know about…"

Angie smiled. She said succinctly, "They're rounding up the wives *we know about* for questioning." She didn't mention Blanche's distraught condition or the fact that she was brought in wearing handcuffs. "I do think the police will have this wrapped up quickly."

A wide smile broke onto Kiana's Indian princess-like face. "So, you're not getting involved?"

"Hmm?" Angie looked up from pushing a corner of bread crust back and forth on the plate.

"Solving it. You don't seem like you're thinking about clues and suspects."

"Actually, I was," Angie said with a grin.

"And…"

The doorbell saved her from answering. Angie went to the living room, knelt on the couch, poked aside the curtains, and groaned. "It's my mother."

"One of these days you two have to talk about your problems."

Angie laughed. "Said the part-time psychologist."

CHAPTER 23

Jarvis slid the chair up to the metal table opposite Blanche Powers. She'd gotten her hysterics under control. A box of tissues sat on the table beside a bottle of water and a wad of used tissues. Blanche clutched another cluster of them in her left fist. Her right hand lay palm-down on the table. Now and then she smoothed long-nailed fingers through her hair, which was tied back in a pretty barrette with an interwoven shell pattern. She'd made eye contact the minute he came in the room and hadn't broken it yet.

As soon as his butt hit the chair, she said, "You can't possibly believe I killed Stone."

"You aren't here necessarily because someone thinks you're guilty. We're just gathering information. Besides, his death hasn't been ruled a homicide yet."

"I wouldn't be here if you thought he died of natural causes."

"You are here to help us figure out what happened. To provide information toward that end."

"Then why was I brought in handcuffs? I've never been so embarrassed in my life."

"I'm sorry about that. The officer said you resisted. Hard."

"What the heck did you expect? I was dragged out of bed and—" She stopped, dabbed at her eyes and slumped her shoulders. "It-it was a thief, wasn't it? A guy robbing the store? And Stone was killed in the crossfire. Please tell me that's what happened."

"Who told you that?"

"I heard on the police scanner that there was a robbery in progress at the store. Since Stone would never steal anything, I assumed—"

"No, Blanche." Jarvis leaned forward, trying to add an I'm still your friend stance to the cop one. "Okay, here's the thing." He had to tell her about the other wives. But how? Blurt it out? No, it should be done easy, with the right words. He wasn't a finesse sort of guy though. Angelina would know exactly what to say. But he'd be a laughing stock if he brought her in to do his dirty work.

"Blanche…"

"Detective, we've known each other too long for you to be tiptoeing around me like this. You have something bad to say, just spit it out. If Stone was robbing the place, well, I'll have trouble believing it but it is what it is. If he had the gun, which is even more unbelievable, and he was shot while it was being wrestled away from him—again, I'll have to live with it. But don't sit there and pussyfoot around me. Just say what you have to say."

He nodded. Determination soaked his cells, oozed out through his pores. "Okay, Blanche. It's like this. You aren't Stone's only wife." There, he'd said it. Just like she asked.

What was wrong with her? She was just sitting there, staring. Had he suddenly sprouted horns? He sure felt like he had. Devil horns.

Or was this one of those times when a woman asked you to do something and didn't really want you to do it? Man, was the captain gonna carve him a new one. Shit. Might as well finish twisting the knife. "There are two other wives."

Still Blanche said nothing. An identical pair of tears hatched in the corners of her eyes. They stayed there, growing like fledglings till finally they got too big and had to leave the comfort of the nest. Seemingly on its own, the hand holding the tissues blotted the length of each cheek.

Blanche blinked a couple of times and shook herself alert. "Two? Wives?"

"Yes. Apparently."

She shook her head. "Not possible. Just like it wasn't possible for him to rob that store. Or carry a gun. It's not possible he is—was—married to someone else. Especially not two of them. I would've known."

"I'm sorry, Blanche. When you thought he was on the road, he was—"

She shook her head several more times, but stopped. He waited till she gathered her thoughts. Seconds ticked by, but he was not sticking his foot back into the manure. Finally she said, "While he was away, he was staying with someone else."

"I'm sorry." He put all his sincerity into the words.

The room was dead silent except for the low hum of the tape recorder, capturing it all. Whoever listened to this later would think the thing had stopped working.

"I suppose," Blanche finally said, "that does explain a couple of things."

He said very soft and careful: "Like?"

"Usually he brings his dirty clothes home crammed in the suitcase. I undo the zipper and they pop out like an explosion. Well, one time they were all clean and folded. I joked that he'd forgotten to change his clothes while he was gone." She forced a smile. Then sobered. "Another time, he had a brand new bottle of aftershave. He is—was—a creature of habit. He used only one kind, Armani Code but once he came home with Polo. When I asked where he got it, he said he'd run out, and gone to a local shop to get more."

"Maybe they didn't have his brand."

"That's what he said, but I know Stone. He would not wear another kind. Period. And he wasn't wearing it at that time. As a matter of fact, the bottle hadn't been opened."

Jarvis waited a beat then asked, "Where were you last night between the hours of ten and three?"

"Home in bed—and don't you dare ask if anyone can

vouch for me."

A tap came on the door. A shadowy figure, visible through the wire mesh window, stood in the hallway. The door opened. Sergeant Wilson poked his head in. Jarvis got up and went to him.

Wilson whispered, "We have one of the other wives here. She's in Room 2."

"Where'd you find her?"

"At work. She's a gynecologist at Concord Hospital. I checked…she'd been there all night. All night. Oh yeah, another thing. We found this"—he held up an evidence bag containing a shell-encrusted barrette—"under some snow outside the store."

"Okay, thanks." Jarvis turned back to Blanche but was still speaking to the sergeant. "Do you have someone who can drive Mrs. Powers home?"

"Of course." Wilson stepped into the room. He was a big man, but his size was unintimidating—probably because of his infectious smile. Infectious was the way Angelina had described it. She said couldn't help smiling back at him each time she saw him.

He shined that smile on Blanche, but she didn't return it. And it did nothing to ease the tension in the room. "Come on." Wilson sounded like a dad taking his kids to the park. "Let's get you out of this place."

Blanche stood. The chair scraped hard on the tile floor. Jarvis and Wilson flinched. She didn't. She stepped past Jarvis. He braced himself for another blow to his ego, but she stopped. "I don't blame you. I know you think you're doing your job. And I won't take it out on Angie. Is that tape still running?" She glanced over his shoulder, but they both knew it was still turned on. "I want you to know one thing for absolute certain. I did not kill my husband."

Wilson escorted her out. Jarvis collapsed back in his chair feeling like he'd just stomped on a little kid's puppy. He shut off the tape recorder, slipped out the cassette, labeled it with name, date, and time of interview, then clicked a blank one labeled with Miata Lin's information into place. Then he stood and shuffled to Interrogation Room 2. Outside the door, he pulled in air until both lungs were full, let it expel slowly through his teeth, opened the door, and prepared to bleed out the rest of the way.

This interview should go easier, should suck less energy, because he had no personal relationship with this woman, no preconceived ideas, no worries how it would affect his relationship with Angelina.

Though short and a bit on the plump side, Miata Lin Powers was very pretty. The sides of her long black hair were held back by a hairclip. It hung to her waist in the back. She wore a little makeup—just enough to accent those dark almond-shaped eyes and high cheekbones. She was dressed in black slacks, a pink top of some sort poked out of the white doctor's smock with the blue nametag that said Dr. Miata Powers, MD, DO. A half empty cup of coffee sat on the table before her.

Jarvis set the tape recorder on the table. "Could I get you some more coffee before we begin?"

She shook her head. "What I want to know is why I'm here."

Was it possible she didn't know of her husband's death? He'd been told next of kin had been notified, but whoever the task fell to might not've known how many people to call. Probably they'd just spoken to Blanche. Okay, he had to tread lightly.

"Mrs. Powers. I-I'm not sure how to say this. I thought you were aware already. Stone—er, Martin died early this morning."

There was no doubt the information came as a surprise. The big dark eyes went round, then squinty, then glassy. He hoped she wasn't going to faint. Or throw up—he'd had more than enough of that lately.

She managed to squeak out two words. "When? How?" Before he was able to format a reply, she added, "Was there some sort of car crash? A mugger?"

The word mugger triggered a realization. She thought he was on the road. Or at least wanted Jarvis to think so. He shook his head. "It was very early this morning. Right here in town."

Her lips flattened into a straight line that popped tiny dimples into each cheek. "Not in Chicago?"

"No." That's when Jarvis realized the flat-lined lips meant she was angry. Very angry. He couldn't wait to find out why. For the moment, he had to go in another direction with the questioning. "You know he hasn't been feeling well lately?"

"Yes, he had a stomach bug."

"When did you see him last?"

She didn't hesitate before saying. "Thursday night. We went ice-skating in Laconia. After that, we went for sodas and some appetizers at Burrito Me. Then we went home."

"Where's home?"

She gave an address in Canterbury. About 45 minutes from Alton. Twenty minutes from the ice rink in Laconia. "How was he feeling?"

"Awful. We'd been planning the ice-skating for about a week. We usually do something special before he leaves town… Wait, was he that sick? Is that what killed him?"

"We believe so. Of course, the autopsy will tell us everything." Her lips had unclenched, but her face had gone quite pale. So far there had been no tears. Shock or apathy? His impression right now was shock. "Are you all right? Could I get you something?"

She shook her head. "Let's get this over with because I think I'm going to have a massive meltdown pretty soon." She gave a slow sip from the coffee, another slow motion of setting it on the table. This was a strong woman, he decided, biding time to gain strength. A quality shared also by Blanche Powers.

"I suggested changing our plans because he was feeling so bad. Besides, he had to leave for Chicago first thing in the morning." Miata Lin shrugged. "I don't know why he insisted on going. Denial, I guess. He wasn't wimpy about being sick, he usually fought through it."

"Did you examine him?"

"Yes. Before we left. He said he'd been feeling a little dizzy. He said, with some disdain, I have to say, that everyone at the theater kept accusing him of being drunk. He was upset they didn't believe when he said he doesn't drink."

"Does he?"

"No."

"Never?"

She smiled. "We are avid baseball fans. As a matter of fact, we were married last summer at Fenway Park. Anyway, he always has a hotdog and a beer at the games. He says it's a Fenway rule that you have to. Otherwise, no, never. But, to get back to the examination, his blood pressure was a little low, his skin was pale. He said he'd been having some stomach cramps. I assumed he had a stomach bug. We see them all the time in the hospital."

"In the gynecology department?" Jarvis couldn't help asking.

She smiled. "Don't be obtuse, detective. It doesn't become you. I am also"—she thumped her nametag—"an MD." She waved off the comment. "I recommended he see a doctor who specializes in stomach ailments. Martin insisted he was fine. If you knew my husband, you'd know not to argue once he's made up his mind."

Jarvis thought he'd gotten all there was to know from this line of questioning. Time to tackle the one that might just provoke the meltdown she predicted. Best to blurt it out with this one rather than softly like with Blanche. "Mrs. Powers, are you aware of Stone—Martin's two other wives?"

The meltdown did not occur. As a matter of fact, she reacted much the same way as Blanche. Dead silence. Also, as with Blanche, several emotions passed over her face before logic brought them all together in one blast of realization that this information might just be true.

Jarvis wanted to evoke some emotion, so he did what all cops do, he lied. "I see this comes as no surprise to you."

The knuckles of Miata Lin's hands, which had been clasped on the table, went white. Her lips tightened so much they were almost invisible. "Let's just say that it makes a lot of the questions I've had in the past months seem a bit more logical. A few times I thought my mind might be faulty. He'd tell me one thing and do something else. If I questioned him about it, he inferred I hadn't been paying attention. So, I started writing things down. About two weeks ago, I confronted him with one of the discrepancies."

"Let me guess, he got angry."

"Yes. It resulted in our very first argument." She shook her head and frowned. "Two other wives?"

"As far as we've been able to determine."

"You mean there might be more?"

Jarvis leaned forward. How much to divulge? Tough to know when she acted naïve to the whole thing. "Well, here's the thing. He's used a different name with each one."

"One name is Stone, isn't it?"

"Yes, how did you know?"

"Well, you said it earlier, but a week ago, I went to the Prince & Pauper Theater to buy us season tickets. Martin loves community theater. The young woman who was making out the paperwork mentioned their leading man was named Stone Powers. Of course, I knew that couldn't be my husband because his name is—was—Martin. But then she said he was a pharmaceuticals salesman—just like Martin."

She was quiet for so long after that comment that Jarvis prodded her with, "What happened after that?"

"I'm afraid I got angry. I think I said some pretty nasty things to those two women, and I ran out. But after I had time to think about it, I assumed it was just a huge coincidence. I went back the other day to complete the purchase of the tickets."

Jarvis went to the door and asked the nearest officer to get him a copy of the local newspaper. He waited by the door and the officer returned within seconds. As Jarvis walked toward the table where Miata Lin sat, he located the P&P ad that was always on page 2. It featured a good picture of Stone Powers. He set the paper in front of Miata Lin. "Is this Martin?"

Her hands unclenched. They picked up the paper. Her eyes read the ad. She set the paper on the table. "Yes."

"Can you see where I might be having trouble believing your story? This ad runs on the second page of every issue. I can't believe you haven't seen it. Or one of your friends hasn't mentioned it."

"Detective. I work sixty plus hours per week. When Martin is out of town, I'm generally sleeping. I have no social life. When I'm at work, I'm working. When he's home we're doing things together, not sitting around reading the newspaper. Besides…" She tapped the title at the top of the page. "This paper's circulation doesn't reach Canterbury."

She might have a point there. Jarvis would have to check. It was possible she hadn't been aware of Stone/Martin's dual identity."

He stood up, groped for and found one of his business cards. He set it before her. "In case you think of anything we should know. Thank you for your cooperation. I'll have someone drive you home, or to work. Wherever you need to go."

He turned her over to an officer and went to his office, shouting for Wilson, whose voice was coming from the kitchenette. Jarvis sagged into his desk chair and spun it toward the window where he had a view of the back parking lot. Nothing much to look at today except snowbanks and grey skies. Spring might force a change to his mood but he didn't think there'd be much improvement in it till his relationship with Angelina was solidified. Until he knew where they stood. Should they get married? He'd asked several times. She'd refused citing a need for time to get over the divorce from Will. Seemed like two years was enough. Maybe they didn't have to go through the official ceremony. Maybe she'd agree to move in with him; he'd been gradually updating and modernizing the house. Nothing had been done on it since Liz's death eleven years ago.

The office door opened. Wilson lumbered in carrying a mug of coffee, which he plopped in front of Jarvis.

"Thanks."

"Wife number three is here. How did it go with Mrs. Powers the second?"

Jarvis sipped while he shrugged. Some of the hot brew sloshed on the blotter. He didn't bother wiping it up. "I don't think she knew about the other wives. She and wife number one reacted pretty much the same way—shocked. Then, after the shock sank in, they both named things—discrepancies in his behaviors they'd been wondering about. She knew he was ill but diagnosed it as a stomach bug."

"Diagnosed?"

"She's a doctor."

"From what I hear he was pretty sick."

"Apparently he was in denial. Figured if he treated the symptoms it would go away on its own."

"Like most of us," Wilson said. "You hate to be running to the doctor for every ache or pain."

"Right." Jarvis sucked down half the coffee in his next gulp. He stood up, keeping hold of the cup. "Where is the Chia pet?"

Wilson stood too, chuckling at the nickname they'd dubbed wife number three. "Room 1. Better be careful not call her that to her face." They laughed together recalling a time they'd done that to a visiting captain with an enormous nose.

"I bet I wouldn't be the first to call her that." Jarvis stepped into the hallway.

"Prob'ly not. If there's anything you need, I'll be out on patrol for a while."

"Will you see if you can find the clerk who was on duty at the store this morning? See if you can jog any more information from him. He was in quite a state over the whole event. Now that he's had time to calm down and for the scene to cycle through his head a few thousand times..."

"Doubt he was able to get any sleep."

Jarvis doubted it also. That sort of event had a habit of sticking in the brain cells. "With any luck, maybe he's recalled a few more details."

CHAPTER 24

Angie peered through the slats of the miniblinds. Why did Mom have to show up now? Sure as heck she wanted to gripe about Rickie. Angie's single wish for this afternoon had been for a little peace and quiet. And a hot bubble bath with a glass of wine.

Oh well, Kiana's arrival at the theater had blown the plan to bits anyway.

"Did you tell your mother about the summer show?" Kiana asked from the kitchen.

"I did. She's pleased we asked her to get involved. As a matter of fact, she was so wrapped up in making lists of things to do and people to call, she barely noticed me leave." Angie let go of the curtain and climbed off the couch. Since they'd only seen each other a few hours ago, it was strange Gloria was dropping by now. It had to mean the talk was related to Rickie. So it was great that Kiana was here; she wouldn't talk in front of the teen.

By the time Angie reached the foyer, Kiana had opened the door. Gloria shoved a pastry box into the teenager's hands. "I'm glad you're here. I was going to have my daughter telephone you to come over." When Gloria added, "Ladies, we need to talk," Angie had to stifle the urge to run out the still-open front door. Mom pushed a notebook toward Angie's arms, missed and slammed it into her chest. She whooshed past Angie and into the living room, calling over her shoulder, "Kiana, do you know how to make coffee?"

Kiana laughed. "I think it was the first thing I learned to do after I was introduced to Angie."

Gloria hung her coat in the closet while Kiana bustled about the kitchen. Angie found plates and dished up a trio of *rugelach*. She managed to stifle a groan; the cinnamon and raisin goodies were one of her favorites.

Gloria carried the plates to the dining table. "Come sit ladies. I have some things to show you."

"Before we do," Angie said, "I need to tell you some bad news." Gloria had pulled out a chair and was about to drop into it, but stopped midway. "Stone Powers, our leading man, died early this morning."

Gloria sagged into the chair as Angie related what details they knew. "Terrible thing to happen," Gloria said. "I don't mean to be insensitive, but will that hurt the theater?"

"I-I hope not. I mean, we have Jacoby who is doing a great job filling in for him, but I'm worried about the potential fallout. This isn't the first murder associated with our theater, if you recall."

Kiana leaned her elbows on the kitchen island counter. "I imagine Angie will be hot on the trail of the killer right away."

Gloria gave a long-suffering sigh. "That's why I asked. Angie dear, I think you've got to decide what's most important, solving crimes or running the theater."

Angie didn't want to admit it, but Mom was right, even though the brutal words shot a surge of anger to her bones and indignation spurting into her throat. She opened her mouth to let some of it out, but was beaten to it by Kiana. "She would never ignore her responsibilities to Prince & Pauper, Mrs. Farnsworth!"

Gloria stabbed Angie with one of her looks. Then, something closer to home dawned on her and Angie couldn't help grinning. "Rickie." This visit did indeed have to do with the toy-boy but not in the sexual sense. Gloria, as usual, was more worried about herself but this time worried Rickie would use his newly gleaned detective lessons to work on the case.

"You can't keep him from finding out about this, you know," Angie said.

"I know. And I also know I can't keep him from horning in. I see little enough of him as it is. You don't suppose you could talk Jarvis into not telling Rickie—"

"No, Mom."

Kiana went to the kitchen to pour coffees. She carried a tray with the cups and a beautiful porcelain sugar and a creamer set Gloria had given Angie for her birthday. She set the tray on the dining room table.

They spent two hours listening to, and adding to, Gloria's ideas for the summer show. They filled out the application for the permit and made plans to attend the Tuesday town meeting. Though she periodically brought Rickie's detective participation into the discussion, the topic was easily deflected. It was so nice to see her mother being pleasant and not knocking every word that came out of her mouth.

Even though the subject of Stone's murder was never mentioned outright, it was constantly in the back of Angie's mind. Who'd done this?

Finally Gloria yawned. "I guess I should head out. God, it's after eleven. Maybe Rickie's home by now."

"Where was he?" Kiana asked.

"He went to the station to talk to Jarvis."

Oh boy, Angie thought, would she hear about this later! Not that she had any control over Rickie's movements. But Jarvis would be pissed off at the intrusion—she laughed—the same way he'd been when she nosed into Nolan Little's murder. It took a long time before he admitted she was instrumental in solving the case.

After Gloria left, they cleaned up the dishes and got the coffeemaker ready for morning. They had a long day ahead of them—surely they'd be closed the next day to attend the memorial service for Stone.

Finally Kiana brushed her hands together as she surveyed

the area. "I'm heading out also. Can't believe how late it is."

Thoughts of that bubble bath tickled the back of Angie's mind. If she didn't hurry and leave, the bubble bath dream would become history because soon, Jarvis would finish with his investigation for the day and show up. He'd bring food—probably pizza—and beer. And, 1-he'd be in a rotten mood, 2-he'd want to talk about the case, 3-he'd expect her to have already determined the killer's identity.

Unfortunately, Kiana was in no hurry to leave. The biggest clue was the way she wandered into the living room and sat in Angie's favorite chair rather than haul her fake-fur coat from the hall closet. The second clue was the serious manner in which the usually bubbly girl moved. Perhaps, after their extensive girl-fest, she'd realized she didn't want to work with Gloria after all.

No. Something much more serious was at hand.

When she said, "Angie, there's something…" Angie froze halfway into the room. She hated when conversations began this way. Heaven knew enough of them began that way with her mom. Angie waited, arms dangling by her sides, feet planted in the cushy pile of the white carpet.

"Oh gosh," Kiana continued. "I don't want to carry tales. You know I don't gossip," was followed by fifteen seconds of silence broken only by the ticking of the kitchen clock and the refrigerator turning on.

"It might not even mean anything. I don't want to cause trouble for anybody. But something's been bothering me. I don't know who else to talk to about it. Except maybe Jarvis, but he's got enough troubles right now. But then I don't want to put you in the middle of anything…"

Angie crossed her arms and let her ramble till she ran out of steam, and excuses. She shot her a wide grin.

Kiana laughed. But didn't relax. Angie began to worry. To have the unflappable Kiana upset, this had to be big. Did she want to hear? No. Could she say so? Nope. A grin popped unbidden. Maybe she was just like Stone—unable to say no.

Angie sat in the corner of the white leather sofa close to Kiana, legs tucked under her. "You ready to tell me now?" she said.

Just a head shake.

"Did someone in your family die?"

She frowned and shook her head again.

"Are you pregnant?"

She burst into a wide smile. "No!"

"Are you quitting your job?"

She knitted her brows. "No!"

"Then nothing else matters. Just pretend you're yanking off a bandage. Do it all at once. It'll hurt less."

Kiana inhaled. She let the breath out with the words. "I was at the Rusty Moose on Tuesday."

"Uh-huh…"

"Rickie was there."

Angie said, "Uh-huh," then realized the problem. "He wasn't alone."

"Right."

"And he wasn't with my mother."

"Right."

Did she want to know any more than this? No. Did her mother deserve to know? Probably. Angie would've liked to know what her husband had been up to a lot sooner than she had. Was it her job to tell Gloria? Sort of. If—and that was a big if—anyone should tell her, it should be her.

Gloria would want details. Lots of them.

Angie did her own inhale/exhale and played the rest of the twenty questions game out loud. "Do I know who the woman is?"

"Sort of."

"Does Mom know her?"

"I don't think so."

"Does Jarvis know her?"

"Not sure about that. I don't think so."

"Which means it's probably someone from the theater."

"Sort of."

What the heck did that mean? Think, Angie. Someone who came to the theater but wasn't part of the cast or crew. A salesperson? Other jobs jumped to mind: snowplow guy, repairman, builder—but they were all men. God no, it couldn't be. She shook her head. For the time being, Angie ruled out a homosexual relationship.

Kiana's eyes were on her, amused watching her work through the puzzle.

"Okay. Not working in the theater."

"Right."

"But has been there. Lately."

"Right."

"So—Chia pet?"

Kiana shook her head, enjoying the game.

"Miata Lin?"

Another head shake. Left with no other options, she said, "Blanche," even though it couldn't be.

Thankfully the name got a negative response.

But now, Angie was stymied. Who else? Montez. Mr. Quattro. But again, if it'd been that sort of relationship, Kiana would've approached this conversation in a whole different way.

"Okay, I'm stuck. Who?" Angie finally asked.

"I don't know her name but I'm pretty sure she's Mr. Quattro's daughter."

Angie gave a mental head shake that actually hurt. Of course. Rickie and Amber already knew each other. Had known each other in California. From Rickie's explanation it was a very short-lived relationship because he'd left in a snit, which she could imagine him doing. They'd spoken in the parking lot the day he brought Angie's mail. The meeting might—probably—meant nothing. Angie explained this to Kiana. "So, I guess my next question should be, how were they acting?"

This question required a slight hesitation. "Friendly." She shook her head. "No, that's not right. They acted like they just happened to meet. There was a quick hug and a little conversation."

Nothing wrong with that. She'd done the same with Montez more than once.

"You think there's anything to it?"

"Damned if I know."

CHAPTER 25

Jarvis got out of his Jeep in front of Angelina's condo. It was nearly midnight. The living room light was on. Kiana's car was parked next to the Lexus. Nothing unusual or alarming. They often met late at night. Even with the age difference, they had a lot in common.

He let Red out then grabbed the six-pack and the pizza—glad he'd brought an extra large, though this time of night, Angelina rarely ate. He made the dog sit in the foyer.

Jarvis greeted the women who were lounging in the living room. They were smiling, but there was something in the air. Something that made him want to take the pizza and beer and go home. In spite of the misgivings, he set the stuff on the counter and went back to clean the gook from the dog's feet.

Once Red was free, she bounded into the living room, glanced from one woman to the other, then lunged at Angelina. After a sloppy greeting, she did the same with a giggling Kiana. By the time he got plates and napkins and set the pizza on the table, whatever that'd gripped the mood of the room when he arrived had gone.

Kiana grabbed a slice of the pizza and ate standing up. Once it was gone, the sauce wiped from her shapely lips, and her coat donned, she said, "Goodnight, call you in the morning," and was gone.

Jarvis went to pour Angelina a glass of wine. She came to drink it at the table while he ate. Red positioned herself beside him—in case a stray crumb toppled from the table.

"You look exhausted," Angelina said.

"Understatement," he said between bites. "So do you."

"Mom was here."

He smiled. No details needed.

"Any news on the case?"

"Rickie visited."

She smiled now. "I know. Are you okay?"

"Yeah. Rickie's okay. About detective work though, he's like a kid in a candy shop. Can't ask enough questions." He shook his head and finished the first beer. "We interviewed all the wives. Blanche and Miata Lin reacted in pretty much the same way learning about the other wives. Stunned silence. Miata Lin cried then got angry. Both admitted it explained a few behaviors they'd pushed to the back of their mind. One thing though, I'm pretty sure Miata Lin hadn't known he was dead."

Angelina frowned—cute little wrinkles formed at the corners of her mouth. "How could she not know?"

"Working long shifts at the hospital," he said.

She gave a slow nod. "I know how that can happen. You get so involved you don't think about anything going on outside the building. When you go home, you just want to decompress."

"We were surprised none of her fellow workers had heard."

Angelina shrugged. "I guess it could happen. Besides, what benefit would she get by denying she'd heard?"

"I guess because it wouldn't explain why she'd stayed at work. Or maybe she did it and by pretending to be unaware she'd be less of a suspect."

"What was your take on it?"

"I don't think she knew."

She drank, swallowed, then nodded. "What about Chia? Did she know about the others?"

Jarvis grinned. "Said she didn't. I think she did. She already knew he was dead. Acted all broken up about it, but I couldn't—" He gave a half-palms-up gesture. "I couldn't a-hundred percent believe it. Wish you'd been there. You read people better than I do. When I asked where she'd been all night, she said, 'Out with friends,' then refused to provide any names or places." He sighed. "Just once I'd like one of these investigations to go easily."

"What makes you think she knew about the others?"

"I don't think she knew they were wives per se, or that there was more than one. But I think she was pretty sure he was seeing someone. Without hesitation, she said there were too many things that didn't match up. He was hardly ever where he said he'd be. Like the other day, she thought he'd gone to Chicago and where was he but at the theater."

Angelina laughed. "Explains why she was seeing Montez. She thought Stone was out of town, seeing someone else—did she seem angry over it?"

"No. I'd say resigned."

"What made her think he was seeing somebody?"

"He brought gifts that were nothing like things she'd want. For example, he knew she was addicted to Lindt chocolates. But one day he brings her butterscotch drops. What are you grinning about?"

"Will never brought me the right gifts either. I always put it off as him not paying attention to hints—or even outright requests."

The statement made Jarvis stop and think. Did he bring things she wanted? No—he wasn't a gift giver as a rule. He wanted to believe he remembered her favorite foods, movies, and sexual positions. Not that he stuck to things like cement— the apple martini the other day was an example. She seemed to enjoy fluctuations from the norm.

As for this case, he had no idea what to think. If he had to choose one of the wives as the murderess, he'd pick Blanche. Not just because she seemed the least likely; she had the type of personality that wouldn't say "oh well, that's the way things go." She'd act on her problems. He could narrow things down better when the autopsy results came back because though he'd told people Stone's death could have been from natural causes, he didn't, for a second, believe it.

He stood and dumped the empty cans into the recycle bin, stowed the remainder of the pizza in the fridge, then gestured for Angelina to follow him to the bedroom. Red moved faster though. She was standing in the middle of Angelina's white down comforter when he got there. He shooed her off before Angelina could see. Too late. She frowned but said nothing.

They climbed into bed. He pulled her into spooning hug.

Suddenly was being chased by three women heaving an endless supply of cell phones at him. He was being pummeled from all directions. All were ringing; one played the theme from Shaft. Something clomped him in the back of the head and he sat up, shaking out the woozies.

"Your phone's ringing."

Jarvis groped for it on the bedside table and growled, "This better be important," even though he knew it would be. Nobody called at 2:37 a.m. unless it was dire.

"Sorry to wake you. The results of the autopsy are ready," said the coroner. "I'm sending them to your email." The line went dead.

Jarvis turned on the lamp. Red leaped to her feet, ready for the new day. Angelina groaned and sat up. "Sorry," he said, "that was Jake. He finished the autopsy."

"What did it say?"

"Nothing. He hung up. He must've stayed up all night doing this for me. Remind me to send him a dozen roses."

She laughed. "Are you getting up? I can make some coffee."

"Let's see what this says." He opened his email and clicked on the coroner's attachment. "I'd really like to get more than an hour and a half of shuteye."

"You should also get glasses."

He said nothing. They'd had the discussion before. Besides,

right now the report had his full attention. "Examination of Stone Powers showed hemorrhaging of the trachea and bronchi, swelling, and hemorrhage in the chest cavity."

"Yuck."

"I'll skip over the rest of the gobbledegook… Oh, Jake didn't stay up doing the autopsy; he was waiting for the tests to come in. Cause of death: isopropanol."

"Isn't that rubbing alcohol?"

Jarvis gave a half-nod. He thought so but science had never been his best subject. He logged into Google and started a search but stopped seeing a second attachment to Jake's email. "Isopropanol can be absorbed through the skin, inhaled as a vapor, or ingested. It causes symptoms consistent with severe alcohol intoxication, though much more acute, resulting in vomiting and abdominal pain."

"He had those."

"It can also result in trouble breathing."

"We saw that on the video." Angelina shivered. She pulled the comforter under her chin.

"Right. 'Coma usually comes on quickly.' We saw that on the video too. Suddenly he was down and out. 'There is a treatment and patients can be saved, but…'"

"He died on the way to the hospital, didn't he?"

Jarvis pounded his fist on the bed and shut off the phone.

"We should've made him go to the doctor. Maybe this could've been prevented."

He lay back down. "Maybe not. Miata Lin is a doctor. She said he was exhibiting symptoms of a stomach bug. He said he'd been feeling a little dizzy and nauseous. She said his blood pressure was a little low, his skin was pale and he was sweaty—all symptoms of flu or a bug. Nobody had any reason to suspect poison."

Angelina lay down too. She scooched her rear-end into him. He wrapped his arms around her and tugged her close. Red nudged his shoulder with her nose. "Lay down, girl, we aren't getting up yet." Surprisingly, the second he shut his eyes he was back asleep.

Morning came too soon. Jarvis turned over and stretched. The room was dark but the clock said it was after eight. The other side of the bed was empty. So was the floor; Red was gone too. The scent of fresh coffee pulled him awake.

He got up and went to the bathroom. Shower and shave could wait. Coffee first.

The kitchen was empty. Jarvis checked the shoe rack in the foyer. Angelina's running shoes were gone. So was Red's leash. He went back and poured coffee, then sat at the island counter. The Sunday paper was laid out in his place. His mind flashed back to last night when he'd thought about gift giving and whether they did right by way of each other. The answer to that was a resounding yes.

There was a rustling at the front door. He got up and went to take Red from Angelina. He cleaned the dog's feet then she rushed to her food dish. Jarvis kissed Angelina good morning.

"What's up for today?" she asked.

"As soon as I finish this coffee, I'm calling the judge to get warrants to search all three wives' homes. And Stone's vehicle. Can I have permission to search his locker at the theater?"

"Sure."

"All right, while I wait for the warrants, let's go do that."

After a leisurely breakfast and a double shower, they left for the theater, stopping at his place to drop off the dog and pick up a few things. As they entered the building, Jarvis's phone rang—Wilson saying the warrants had arrived, that he and two officers were on the way to Blanche Powers' home right away.

Just in case Stone had padlocked his locker, Jarvis had brought a bolt cutter. The door of the locker was covered in fingerprint dust. He applauded his team.

Jarvis unloaded the meager contents onto the green room table. A container of hand sanitizer, a blue baseball cap with a Red Sox logo, a copy of the script with Stone's scribbled notes in some of the margins, a gray hooded sweatshirt. Jarvis bagged only the hand sanitizer but placed the other items back inside and padlocked the door to safeguard the contents in case they needed them later.

"Now what?"

"I take you home and start searching suspects' homes."

She nodded. "I assume since you didn't ask me along, you're doing Blanche's first."

He pulled her into a tight embrace. "You are so absolutely right." He grabbed the evidence bag, marked it with date and location, then dropped his arm over Angelina's shoulder. Together they sauntered down the back stairs and to the passenger side of the Jeep.

When Jarvis arrived at Blanche Powers' home—a two story Victorian with a wide front porch containing two wicker chairs and a glass-top table, with brown leaves caked in and around the furniture. Her car, a black Intrepid, sat in the driveway. He took a walk around it looking for a scrape that might indicate she'd sideswiped Stone's car but the surface was undamaged.

Indoors, the search was already well underway. Blanche rushed to him. Her face was blotchy; tears carved streaks down her cheeks. It appeared as though every inch of her was trembling. He'd known her a long time, and wanted to draw her into a hug, but this was business. Their friendship—if you could call their relationship friendship-by-association—had to remain in the background. Today he was Detective Colby Jarvis. Seems he'd been playing alternating roles a lot lately.

Wilson and the two officers had everything torn out of the kitchen cabinets and piled on every available flat surface.

Blanche appeared beside him. "Jarvis. Since you're here, I assume you've learned what killed Stone." She flashed Wilson a glare that should've eaten right through his flesh. "He wouldn't tell me anything."

Jarvis took her aside and sat her on the sofa, an old model with flower-patterned upholstery. "He died of acute isopropanol poisoning."

"What the hell is iso…iso whatever you said?"

"Basically rubbing alcohol."

"So, what are they looking for?"

"Anything liquid or gel that would be applied to a person's skin."

"Which means you think I killed him." It wasn't said as a question.

"Blanche, you know we have to do this. You've seen enough cop shows to know how it works."

She nodded. "Yeah. You tear apart the home of every suspect."

He patted her on the arm. Before moving his hand, he gave a reassuring squeeze, praying she wouldn't take this out on Angelina.

She bent forward, head cupped in her hands. "I just don't understand." After a minute she looked up. "Why are they tearing the kitchen apart? The alcohol is in the bathroom." She started to rise.

Jarvis nudged her back into the seat. "You need to stay out of the way."

He rose and went to grab a few evidence bags from the box on the kitchen counter. So far they'd only collected two things. On the floor in a corner were two clear plastic bags—a bottle of Kaopectate and a bottle of liquid hand soap.

"You'll notice the medicine is past its shelf life," Blanche said from beside him. "It's been in that cabinet forever. I use that hand soap all the time. And I'm not sick."

"Please." He put a hand on her arm. "Go sit and wait. We'll be out of your way before you know it."

"I already know it," she called over her shoulder. She flopped on the sofa, turned on the TV, loud.

Jarvis strode to the master bedroom. Neat and clean, but like the living room, old fashioned furniture. Clearly Blanche wasn't into esthetics. Probably she was too busy to care. William Petersen's voice blared from one of the CSI shows. He wondered if Blanche was doing it on purpose.

The master bath was good-sized, done all in tans, including

the fixtures. He did a thorough search, bagging toothpaste, hand lotion, shampoo—as he told Blanche, anything that could be infused with alcohol.

From behind came Blanche's voice. "You're wasting your time in here. Stone used the guest bathroom almost all the time."

"Why's that?"

She smiled and shrugged. "Seems like we always needed to be in it at the same time."

"Okay. I hope you understand I have to bag these anyway."

"Guess I have to go shopping."

"Guess so."

He went back to work. Under the sink, he found a quart bottle of rubbing alcohol. It wouldn't have made him think twice—everyone had a bottle in the cabinet—except for the fact that this one was almost empty.

Jarvis performed the same search in the guest bathroom, smaller than the master. With pink sink, toilet and tub. Nice for a guy's private place, he chuckled to himself.

Blanche had been telling the truth; all his shaving things, personal items, were here. He tagged and bagged the evidence. One corner of the bathroom held a linen closet. A pat-search showed it had nothing liquid in it and he almost decided not to bother searching. He tried to shove a stack of towels to one side but they wouldn't move. He divested the shelf of the towels and uncovered a black box—a safe.

He turned and went to the living room. "Where are Stone's car keys?"

"I assume he had them on him, but there's an extra set hanging from a rack in the kitchen."

By the time he got there, Wilson had plucked them off and was dangling them toward him. Jarvis gestured for the sergeant to follow.

"What did you find?" Blanche jumped off the cushion.

Wilson turned, said only, "Sit," and she did.

Once they were in the privacy of the guest bathroom,

Jarvis laughed. "Red doesn't obey that fast."

He showed Wilson the safe. Thankfully, one of Stone's keys fit. They moved the box to the counter and opened it. Inside were trinkets and mementoes, probably given to him by his wives, but one thing caught Jarvis's attention and wouldn't let go—a manila envelope. He opened it and dumped the contents on the counter.

Marriage licenses.

Six of them.

CHAPTER 26

Angie took a shower then, tempted to call a cab and leave her car at the house, headed for the theater. She parked as far around the building as she could. No one driving past would see the Lexus unless they went into the lower parking lot. And she'd know if anyone came because as a vehicle came over the rise, the sound echoed off the water and back at the building.

She walked toward the back door. Snow began falling in light flakes that felt like rain on her face. She used the stairs to her new office and stood for a long time staring out the window. The fisherman, out there most every day, wasn't here. Perhaps he spent Sundays home with his family.

Right now, Jarvis was probably tearing Blanche's house apart. Blanche, strong as she was, would be standing with her arms crossed watching every move the officers made. She'd make sure they put everything back exactly where it had been. Miata Lin and Chia would react in completely different ways. Miata Lin would rant and rave. Chia would probably try to telephone Montez for help.

She left the window and went to lie on the sofa. She stared up at the ugly painting for a long time. "So, Kratos, who killed Stone Powers? Did the wives know about each other?"

If she and Jarvis had learned about them through normal everyday activities, it was possible the women knew too. If she'd found out Will had another wife, what would she have done? Sought her out perhaps. At least gotten a look at the competition.

"Would I have approached her?" she asked Kratos then shook her head. "Probably not. What would've been the point?"

But *the point* would be different for each woman. Miata Lin seemed like the type to fight for her man. She'd been indignant when Kiana suggested Martin and Stone might be twins. Angie shot into a sitting position. As a matter of fact, she'd been too indignant. Indignant enough that there was a good chance she *did* know—probably about Blanche. That's why she'd come to the theater—not to buy a season ticket, to get a look at the competition.

Angie stood and faced the painting. "In hopes of what?" She paced a couple of steps then faced Kratos again. "Meeting up with her? Gathering information?"

Angie sat again and thought back over the conversation. It had begun when she removed the credit card from her purse. A photo of her and Stone/Martin had caught Kiana's eye. Kiana mentioned how he looked exactly like their leading man. She suggested they could be twins. Miata Lin abandoned her mission to buy season tickets and left in a huff.

Angie went behind her desk—took note out the window that it was snowing heavier—sat and opened one of the manuscripts from the slush pile. A comedy. Good. She leaned back and began to read.

But thoughts of Stone's death kept interrupting. What if one of the wives hadn't killed him? Possible, but who? Outwardly, everyone here appeared to enjoy Stone's company. Sure, Jacoby might've wanted the starring role, but he wouldn't kill for it, would he? No. She couldn't make herself believe it. If not him, who?

Just then, a car whooshed over the slope and into the lower lot. She spun the chair around to see Montez Clarke's car slide to a stop near the back door. He got out. Angie heaved a sigh. Even if he didn't come to her office, it meant someone was in the building. Noise would smash the silence she'd been enjoying.

Soon, heavy footsteps came up the stairs. Funny how he also walked rather than take the elevator.

Could he have killed Stone? Sure. But why? He didn't seem that into Chia—

Angie's thoughts stopped short. She recalled their first meeting two years ago when his best friend and cohort in crime had been murdered. He'd reacted in exactly the same way, his emotions hidden behind an unrelenting mask, even during interrogation by the police.

Why would he kill Stone? Only obvious answer: to have Chia. But she was so clingy. Which, from the way he reacted, was more of an irritation than a magnet.

Angie sighed and went back to the manuscript, hardly thinking at all of the oh-so-sexy Jamaican working in the adjoining restaurant. She laughed out loud. Angie understood why Chia might've killed to have him, but not the other way around.

She immersed herself in the story and read until her grumbling stomach reminded her it was two o'clock. Might as well head home and have that bubble bath. Excitement trickled through Angie's cells as she anticipated the tingle of bath crystals bought in Boston before the Celtics game a few weeks ago.

She donned her coat, gathered keys, manuscript, and purse, and left the office. Cold air from the stairwell blasted her in the face. It was snowing harder, but that made the idea of a bubble bath all the more enticing.

"I wondered if you were in the building," came a familiar voice.

Angie jumped. The stairwell door slammed shut. "Hi. How are you?"

"Same old, same old."

Montez's standard reply. Should she bring up the latest news? If she did, he'd jump to the conclusion that she suspected him.

"Where's Detective Jarvis today?"

"Working."

"On a Sunday?"

"Cop work knows no schedule."

"Aren't you going to ask if I killed that Powers guy?"

Angie smiled. "No. The only reason you might've had to murder him would be to make Chia free. And you told me she didn't mean anything to you." Angie shrugged.

He shot her a smirk that said her sarcasm hadn't been missed. "You think she did it?"

"Got time to talk?"

"Sure."

She opened the office door and went back inside. She took up a spot leaning on the edge of the desk. Outside the doorway he made a show of stomping off the snow—even though the carpet hadn't been installed yet. He went toward the sofa but stopped seeing Kratos' ugly mug staring down at him.

"Don't ask," she said.

He rolled his eyes and dropped onto the sofa.

"Tell me about Chia."

"Anything in particular?"

"Whatever comes into your head."

"She was great in bed."

Angie laughed and hoped he didn't see the surge of desire that hit her. "TMI."

"You said anything."

"I did. Did you get any idea how she felt about her marriage?"

"I doubt she thought much about it since she never mentioned it."

"That doesn't mean she didn't care about it. It just meant she didn't want you to know."

He nodded, leaned back and crossed left ankle over right thigh. "I gotta question. How come you called him Stone and she called him Martin?"

"No idea. As far as I know, his given name is Stone."

Montez shrugged. "Stones, rocks. Same things I guess."

"Do you think she's capable of murder?"

"I think anyone is under the right situation. Even you chickee-doodle."

"Point taken."

"But to answer your question less generically, when we were together she hung all over me. Like she was afraid to not be touching me."

"I noticed. I thought it was for my benefit."

Montez dropped his foot to the floor and leaned forward. "She didn't know we knew each other."

"I didn't mean it that way. Being in the presence of another woman can bring out insecurities."

"Especially a gorgeous woman."

Angie's insides twitched. He was doing that on purpose. He knew what he did to her. "Can you keep on topic please?"

"I thought her reaction to you was the topic."

"Why was she with you that day?"

He shook his head. "Not sure what you mean."

"Did she usually accompany you on jobs?"

"No, never before."

"So why that day?"

Montez frowned and pushed a hand across his short haircut. "She showed up at the shop that morning as I was going out the door. She asked where I was going. I told her. She asked if she could come. I said she'd be bored stiff because I had to spend the day crawling on the floor and in ceilings stringing cable. She got snippy. 'You must not think much of me being able to amuse myself,' she said."

"What did you say?"

"I said, 'I took you to Scoot's house last week. There were ten people to talk to and all you did was nag me to go because you were bored.' I told her there wouldn't be anyone to talk to." He shrugged. "She said she didn't care. So, I brought her."

Angie moved away from the desk and walked around

behind it. "Do you think she had a reason for wanting to come?"

He barked out a laugh. "I think she's a stubborn bitch who wanted what she wanted, that's all." He sobered, and added, "Now that you make me think about it, yeah maybe." He pointed a finger in Angie's general direction. "Maybe she knew her husband would be here and wanted to rub me in his face. Maybe she, I don't know, somehow knew about you and me—"

Angie raised her eyebrows at him. "You and me?"

"Yeah, like you don't know how I feel about you."

Uh-oh. She sighed. "I didn't know."

He laughed. "Liar."

Man, this conversation was getting scary. "Okay, I know there's a physical thing, but I didn't know it went further than that."

"It does."

She'd started back around the desk but decided to stay where she was. Which made him laugh.

"I'm not gonna attack you or anything."

"We're really off-topic now, but I need to ask. Why didn't you ever ask me out?"

"Dunno. Maybe I have the same inferiority thing going on that Chia has. Would you have said yes?"

She gave a small smile. "Might've."

"Shit."

Quick, change the subject. "Did you know Chia attacked me the other day?"

His smiled died. "You shittin' me?"

Angie told about the dress shopping experience and how Kiana clocked Chia up-side the head. Montez roared, slapping his hands on his thighs. "Which makes you think she *could be* capable of murder."

Angie came around the desk and leaned in her place against the edge. "It does make a person wonder. Here's some news you might not know. We've been keeping it quiet but I'm sure it won't be long before it hits the news. Stone wasn't just married to Chia. There were two others."

His eyebrows rose and stayed up for several seconds. "Anyone I know?"

"One of them, yes. Blanche—my costume designer."

He pointed that big index finger again. "Maybe that's why Chia wanted to come up here. Maybe she knew about Blanche and wanted to meet her. Confront her."

"I have been wondering the same thing."

CHAPTER 27

"Woo wee!" Wilson remarked.

Jarvis shushed him so Blanche wouldn't hear out in the living room. They packed up Stone Powers' safe and bagged it in one of the black trash bags.

The officers had loaded all the evidence bags into black trash bags and were carrying them outside. Wilson kept the precious safe tucked under one arm and followed his men.

Jarvis held back, checking the kitchen to make sure they'd put Blanche's things back in their respective cabinets. Satisfied, he turned to leave. As he passed, he said, "Thanks Blanche. I'm really sorry for all this."

She got up from the couch and ran at him, pounding him on the chest. Jarvis did nothing to defend himself. There was no defense for what he'd put her through.

"I did not kill my husband!"

Wilson stopped in the doorway but Jarvis waved him on. He took hold of Blanche's wrists and held them together, folded her arms between them. "I'm just doing my job. Can you try and understand? Please."

She collapsed against him. He wrapped his arms around her, whispered, "Be patient. We'll find out who did this," picked up his hat that had been knocked off in the scuffle, and left. "Just so you know. From here we're headed to your shop."

Blanched looked as though she was about to pummel him again, but she sagged away and melted into a chair. "Do what you have to do. But I'll tell you up front, Stone hasn't been inside that building in over a year. Do you want a key or are you going to break down the door?" She waved a hand at him. "Sorry, that was uncalled for."

***

Jarvis and the search team secured the evidence in the van in front of Blanche's storefront in Nashua, leaving an officer to keep a protective eye on it while they performed their search. The snowstorm had grown worse. It lay a couple of inches deep on the roads.

The evidence gathering at the shop didn't take long. There was nothing to find amongst the fabrics, sewing machines, and racks upon racks of costumes, containers of costume jewelry, and boxes of footwear. The tiny, spotless bathroom contained only a bottle of liquid hand soap on the edge of the single-bowl sink. Blanche had said Stone never came here. There was no indication he had.

They bagged it and headed for the home of wife number 2—though with the discovery of Stone's safe, Jarvis assumed the wife numbers would be changing very soon.

The captain had called ahead to the Canterbury police and had them make sure Mrs. Miata Lin Powers was home, and remained there. Which also helped keep her from disposing of potential evidence and—if somehow the wives were in cahoots with each other—kept her from receiving a warning call from Blanche.

The Powers house was a ranch style, something like his only bigger—probably with three bedrooms instead of two. Though it was covered in snow, a blue mini Cooper was parked in the driveway. He didn't bother checking it for damage though he did see if it was unlocked—it wasn't. Inside, the house was more modern than the one Stone shared with Blanche. It wasn't as neat and clean though. Jarvis had the idea evidence collection wouldn't be so easy here.

The Canterbury police must've wakened Miata Lin. She sat slumped sideways in an armchair, legs folded, arms wrapped around them. He wasn't sure what she had on but the entire length of her left leg was exposed right to the panty line.

She spotted him and his men, but didn't move anything more than her head. While his men went to work, he strode toward her, pulled the coffee table across the carpet and sat on it facing her. She turned those dark eyes on him. Many emotions crossed her pretty face, from anger to confusion to curiosity.

"I need to tell you something," Jarvis said.

She tilted her head, brushed hair behind her ears, turned and put her feet on the floor. Now he could tell she was wearing a short, silk—he thought they were called kimonos. It was purple with golden dragons embroidered all over. He pointed at it. "Very pretty."

"Martin bought it for me in Chinatown—while he was in LA."

"Are you from China?"

"No. Two generations removed." She shrugged. "But still, it was a nice gift."

"You didn't travel with him?"

She shook her head. "No, my job… I don't get away very often."

"Do you know why my men are here?"

"I assume you think I killed him and you're looking for evidence." Her tone suggested she would've been smart enough to dispose of it by now.

"Do you know how he died?"

"No." She threw a look of disdain at the Canterbury officer standing near the front doorway. "He wouldn't tell me."

"You don't have to hang around," Jarvis told him. The officer shrugged, indicating he'd stay. Jarvis wanted to chuckle. Sunday he probably got paid double time. Standing in Miata Lin's doorway wasn't very taxing work.

"That's because he doesn't know," Jarvis said. "He was only asked here to make sure you stayed home until we arrived."

She sat up straighter. "Then how about if you tell me."

"Martin Powers died of acute isopropanol poisoning."

Her eyebrows twitched downward. Her lips flattened as reality struck. "Administered how?"

"Through the skin. We assume it was in his hand sanitizer and nose drops but we're waiting on the autopsy."

She shook off the initial burst of shock, then laughed. "And you think, with me being a doctor, I'm the one who'd know best how to do it."

Jarvis quirked his mouth at her.

For a second she looked as though she wanted to clobber him. Then she nodded. "I guess you're right there. I don't suppose you considered the idea that anyone can find out how to do it. All they have to do is Google things these days."

"I am aware you can find anything online."

"Don't you need my permission for an autopsy?"

"No."

"So, besides evidence collection, which your minions can do, why are you here specifically?"

"Where do you think I should be? Where should I start looking for his killer?" he asked. He waited for her to name Blanche or Chia, but she said nothing. "Come on, if it wasn't you, point me someplace else to look. Who disliked him enough to want him dead?"

"Easy. Walter." She glanced ceiling-ward, thinking. "I think his last name was Wheeler. Something like that. He lives in Farmington."

Jarvis wrote down the information. "I don't suppose you know his number or where he works?"

"Well, yes. Martin worked with him. Well, at the same company. That's how they met."

"They didn't get along?"

"Used to. We even went out together a few times—as a threesome. He's not married. I don't know what happened but about a month ago I heard Martin on the phone shouting at him."

"What did he say?"

"Well, Martin got off the phone as soon as he saw me standing there, but I heard him say, 'You'd better not, or else.'"

"Did you ask Martin what he was talking about?"

"Sure. But he wouldn't say."

A good lead, for sure. Jarvis had been hoping she'd blurt something about his other wives—to prove she knew about them and solidify her own motive. But no such luck. He tried a different tack. "I heard you were at the theater buying season tickets."

She smiled. "Yes, like I told you at the police station, Martin loves—loved—community theater. 'It's like minor league sports,' he'd say, 'the actors are in it for the sheer joy of acting rather than the money.'" She shrugged. "I thought it would be a fun, unique gift. He was always bringing me things."

"But you didn't actually get the membership, did you?"

Her nose twitched. "No. That little Indian bitch..." Miata Lin's fists clenched at her sides. "She took a photo of Martin right out of my handbag. Then she waved it around saying it looked just like the star of their new show. She had her hand in my purse."

"You didn't mention this during our interview."

She shrugged.

"Is that really what pissed you off?"

"She kept calling him Stone. His name is Martin. All you have to do is check his license." She glanced around as if she might have proof there in the house.

He was about to send her searching for their marriage license but didn't want the delay because he knew it was in the safe taken from Blanche's home. Instead, he softened things with, "Haven't you ever heard the saying that we all have a lookalike someplace on this earth?"

"Sure."

He shrugged and turned palms-up. "So, why couldn't Martin's—what do they call it—doppelganger be in Alton Bay?"

"Because..."

Jarvis gave her raised eyebrows to show he was waiting for a reply.

Miata Lin sighed. "All right, all right. I know what you want me to say. Because...I knew about Blanche."

He didn't waste time congratulating himself on his powers of interrogation. Angelina would've had it out of her within ten seconds.

"I went there to see her. To—"

"To scope out the competition?"

"Crudely put, but yes. But then that girl Kiana, the way she was talking was like he was there in the building too. I-I thought... Like I told you at the station, he had to be in Chicago. The trip had been planned for over a week."

"How long had you known about Blanche?"

"Since Tuesday. I saw Martin's picture in the newspaper. I called the theater and talked to some guy. I asked questions... He told me Stone was married to their costume designer."

"What were your plans when you met Blanche?"

Tears popped into her eyes. "I don't know. It sound dumb but I wanted to let her know I existed, that I wouldn't give him up without a fight. I-I"—she smiled—"was going to ask her to divorce him."

"And you thought—hoped—she'd say, 'Sure, take him, he's yours.'"

"I realized the idea was really dumb when that girl kept calling him Stone. It was like being doused with a barrel of Gatorade."

He nodded. It sure would've been. Especially if she'd come face to face with Blanche, because Blanche would not have done anything near what Miata Lin hoped.

He stood, said, "I'm very sorry for your loss," and went to help the team collect evidence.

The completion of the work at Martin Powers' house and vehicle took three hours. By that time, Jarvis's stomach was growling and he was dying for a cup of coffee. His watch said it was three o'clock. He wondered what Angelina was doing.

Hopefully something restful and productive, like figuring out who killed Stone Powers.

They loaded the black bags into the Jeep and drove it to headquarters.

As they entered the building the captain shouted to him from his office. Jarvis grabbed a mug of coffee and flopped into a chair. He dropped the deerstalker on the adjoining chair then raked the fingers of his free hand through what was left of his hair.

"What's up, Captain?"

Captain Folsom slid two pieces of paper toward Jarvis. He set his cup on the corner of the desk and read the pages. He couldn't stop a giant laugh from bursting forth.

"It's not funny," the captain said.

"Sir, it's so ridiculous it's getting funny. And not unexpected."

"You expected more wives?"

"Sure. If he got away with three, why not a whole slew of them? As a salesman he can come up with all sorts of excuses for never being home. And"—he slapped the pages back on the desk—"I'll bet money we find out these women are as equally self-sufficient as the six we've already found." Jarvis said the last sentence in a normal voice, wondering how long it would take the captain to pick up on it."

"Six?"

Four seconds. Not bad.

He explained about the safe found in Blanche's guest room linen closet. "Can I keep these?"

"Sure. You think they're copies of ones in the safe?"

Jarvis shrugged, the grin widening. "Can't wait to find out." He detailed the remaining evidence they'd found. "Nothing specific in either house except the safe. There was no indication Blanche knew anything about it."

"Okay. Why don't you guys break for lunch, then head to Chia Powers' place. Manchester police picked her up for speeding at four this morning. Jarvis nodded recalling Angie's evaluation of the videotapes from the convenience store. "They take her into custody?"

"Yes. So her apartment is clear for you. There's an officer waiting for you." The captain leaned forward. "Could she be the one at the convenience store?"

Jarvis shook his head. "Doubtful. Angelina says she doesn't walk right."

The captain laughed. "I'm not even going to ask. If you'd told me that, I would've questioned you up and down the parking lot, but—"

The captain was right. Jarvis was usually the first to admit that Angelina had a knack for reading people. If she said Chia wasn't the woman in the fur coat and blonde hair that morning, then you could bet it wasn't her.

Jarvis rose. He collected his mug and downed the rest of the contents. He turned and was about to head from the office when the door burst open. A tall woman wearing a Celtic knit sweater, skinny jeans, and fancy leather boots entered. She was sobbing. She dabbed a wad of tissues in her eyes. The words were almost incoherent, but Jarvis thought she said, "I want to report my husband missing."

Captain Folsom rose and came around the desk. He guided her to the chair Jarvis had just vacated. "Calm down, ma'am, please. How long has your husband been missing?"

It took a moment for her to pull herself together to say, "Th-three days."

"When did you see him last?"

"Why, at our apartment, of c-course. Allen was leaving on a business trip. But I just found out he never got there."

A delay while she blew her nose and got the sobbing under control. The captain was a lot more reserved than Jarvis would've been. He would've found her fresh tissues and sat beside her rather than across the desk.

"I've talked to the hotel," she said, "and the people he was supposed to meet. I've talked to the airline. He never got there. He never got on the plane!"

"Plane?"

"Yes, he was going to Chicago."

Jarvis somehow stifled the groan that spurted into the back of his mouth.

"All right. Please calm down. Let's begin at the beginning." The captain slid a sheet of paper from one of the compartments in his desk. Jarvis recognized the missing person's report. In all his years on the force, he'd never had to fill one out. "Let's start with your name."

The captain seemed to have the situation under control. Jarvis turned to head out the still-open door.

Then the woman replied, "Amber Quattro Powers."

CHAPTER 28

Jarvis thought he was getting good at stifling reactions. This time it was the "Oh shit not another one" that wanted to leap from his lips.

He glanced at Captain Folsom. Although his head was dipped over the missing person form, his features were clamped tight. Which made Jarvis smile. Obviously the same words wanted to squirt from his mouth too. How the hell many wives had Stone Powers accumulated? His next thought was to wonder if the Guinness Book of World Records had a category for this.

He got the hell out of there, gathered the rest of the team and took them to dinner at Shibley's on the town's dollar. He didn't—couldn't—share the multiple-wife information with any of them except Sergeant Wilson. They weren't detectives, were merely evidence-gatherers. Wilson, on the other hand, needed to know about Amber but it would have to be later, maybe while they were heading toward Nashua. Then again, a text or two couldn't hurt.

The first one: found another wife pinged into Wilson's phone and elicited a loud chuckle that got everyone else's attention away from the short-shirted waitress. "Sorry, Wilson said, "my wife sent me a picture." He fended off requests to see it. They assumed it was risqué and provided some teasing while Jarvis covertly typed another text.

Amber Quattro.

Wilson's frown said he didn't know her.

Jarvis clarified: *Daughter of Anthony Quattro—restaurateur.*

Wilson texted a one-letter reply. F.

"My thoughts exactly," Jarvis said out loud. To the waitress he said, "A Sam Adams and a half-pound burger, rare. With the works."

By 5:15, they were back on the road. He and Wilson sat in the back of the police van. Jarvis caught him up on the latest news. Each took time to phone home to let family know what was going on. Angelina was quiet, which he knew translated into deciphering the Stone Powers mess. Well, that's what he thought until she mentioned a bubble bath and a glass of wine.

"What's that sigh for?" Wilson asked.

"Angelina's taking a bubble bath."

Wilson chuckled and didn't ask any more questions—a characteristic of a fine gentleman.

Chia Powers' apartment was on the second floor of a very nicely renovated three family house. Her car a new black Audi A4, that he'd seen the night Stone took ill at the restaurant, wasn't in the driveway. Probably the cops impounded it when she was arrested for speeding.

Being the lead investigator, Jarvis preceded Wilson and the others up the stairs. Even though it was a beautifully updated building, it had no elevator. A bulky man, with dark, shoulder length hair drawn back with a leather strap at the base of his neck, sat in a hard metal chair in front of the apartment door. He came alert as they clomped up the stairs.

Jarvis broke into a broad grin, as did the man in the chair, who shot to his feet. They shared a man-hug.

"Dude, when you gonna ditch that damned hat?"

Jarvis speared him with a scowl.

"Not happening," Wilson said.

"My captain didn't mention you'd be leadin' this investigation."

Jarvis made introductions all around. "Guys, this is

Detective José Rodriguez. In spite of his Tony Baretta wannabe look"—he gestured at the worn jeans and lopsidedly buttoned shirt—"he's our Manchester counterpart."

The two youngest officers frowned at the mention of the television character. Nobody bothered clarifying. Detective Rodriguez opened the door and ushered them inside. As they stood in open-mouthed silence, he said, "Nice place, huh?"

Jarvis took in the leather furniture and plush room size rug in long white pile, and—was that a Matisse on the wall? Jarvis couldn't tell a piece of famous art from a movie poster, but he was pretty damn sure that's what the signature said.

"Thought you said this girl was a librarian," Wilson muttered. "Go ahead, guys, get to work. Make sure you don't get any dirt on that rug. Or anywhere else."

The men made a big production of skirting the edges of the rug in question, putting one boot in front of the other and hands out at their sides for balance. "You morons. Get to work," Jarvis told them. To Rodriguez he said, "You don't need to hang around any longer. Thanks for holding down the ship."

Rodriguez saluted with two fingers and slapped him on the back. "I'm headed to the bar around the corner for a sandwich and a beer…or four. Stop over when you're done, it'd be great to catch up."

"Can't, man. We all came in one vehicle."

"I'll take you home."

"Shit, that's an hour's ride."

"Just show up at the bar, we'll figure out something."

Although he was bone tired, and kept envisioning Angelina with bubbles up to her—Jarvis assured him he'd be there.

This apartment had only one bathroom so they confiscated every bit of liquid or gel, including a tube of K-Y Jelly in the bedside table. The only specifically isopropyl alcohol-item they found was a pint bottle under the bathroom sink. It was unopened. They took it anyway.

The team finished within an hour. Jarvis waved them away in the van and trudged around the corner to the bar. He didn't envy the guys all the hours spent cataloguing their collection. Likely it would happen in the morning; it had been a very long day.

He found the bar in question. When Rodriguez spotted Jarvis, he slid off the stool and gestured to a booth in a corner. Jarvis asked for a Sam Adams draft, waited while the bartender poured, then took it to the booth. He slid across the well-worn vinyl with a huff.

"Dude, you look beat. What time'd your first call come this morning?"

"Two thirty-seven—the coroner with autopsy results. Yesterday it was before four."

Rodriguez was well aware of the hours detectives sometimes gave to their jobs. They'd worked together once before and developed a see you once in a while friendship.

Jarvis told him the details of the case, garnering a large guffaw from the big man when he mentioned there were at least six wives.

"Can't even imagine the confusion that creates!"

Jarvis sipped the beer, set the glass in the ring of condensation on the table. "Yes, but isn't there a devilish side of you that wonders how it all works?"

"Hell, yeah, but if my wife knew I was even thinkin' such things, she'd cut it off."

Jarvis laughed.

"Which one do you make as the killer?"

He shrugged. The wives, their personalities, their moods, motives, and financial situations had swirled through his head all day. Not one stood front and center. The one that least struck him most was Blanche, but until he got some serious sleep, he wasn't voicing anything out loud.

"Haven't had a spare second to think things through. No, that's wrong, every time I start thinking about it another wife pops up. They're like frigging popcorn. Start with a few tablespoonfuls and soon you have a bucket." He sipped then made himself comfortable, leaning back and kicking an ankle onto a knee. "If you put a gun to my head and made me pick one, I'd take Chia. She's shown violent tendencies more than once." He grinned. "You'll like this: she took a swing at Angelina the other day."

Rodriguez's thick brows did and up and down dance. "You kidding?"

"No. She ducked in time but her employee—remember the teenager Kiana Smith?"

Rodriguez nodded. "Pretty Indian girl."

"She clocked Chia upside the head."

"Go girl!" They tapped glasses, then Rodriguez guzzled from his bottle.

"Granted Chia was drunk, but…still makes you think. She shows the most emotion of all of them."

Rodriguez thumped the table. "Remember the saying about still waters running deep."

"You trying to say the quiet one should be the prime suspect?"

"Can't hurt to pay her extra attention."

Which would shoot Blanche to the top of the list. He couldn't even think about that right now.

"What the hell kind of name is Chia anyway?" Rodriguez asked.

Jarvis shrugged. "It's on her birth certificate. Another thing is, she owns a black car." He explained about the sideswipe dent on Stone's car. Jarvis shrugged again. "I don't know, man. There's no concrete evidence pointing to any of them yet."

"Buddy, you're barely twelve hours into the investigation."

"I know."

"I mean, unless you're Angelina, you ain't comin' up with a solution yet."

Jarvis laughed so hard he almost spit out his beer.

"You should call and ask if she's figured it out yet," Rodriguez said.

"Talked to her about six. She didn't mention it." He thought again of the bubble bath and suddenly regretted not going straight home. What a woman she was; she never complained about the hours he put in. If he voiced those thoughts to Wilson, he would've made a snide comment, something like, "She needs time away from you, dude."

"Has it dawned on you guys that the wives might be working as a team?"

"A team?"

"Yeah, like they found out about each other and got together to off him."

Jarvis supposed stranger things had brought people together.

"I think I saw a movie like that once." Rodriguez laughed. "Picture 'em sittin' in a bar, prob'ly just like we are. They're whispering back and forth, tossing out ideas how to do him. Call themselves the Butcher the Bastard Bigamist Gang."

Jarvis couldn't help himself; he laughed. "A bigamist has two wives dufus."

"Well, how about the Snuff Out the Sixamist Sonoabitch Society."

"Say that three times fast."

"Shit. After five beers, I couldn't say beer three times slow. What the heck do they call a guy who's married six women anyway?" Rodriguez asked.

Jarvis said, "Dead," as the bartender arrived with the beers.

"Hey man," Rodriguez said to the bartender, "we're having a philo—how do you say that? A philosophical discussion. A guy who marries two women is a bigamist, right?" The bartender nodded. "Okay, so what do you call a guy who marries six of 'em at once?"

The bartender nodded at Jarvis, said, "I like his answer," and went back to the bar.

They were quiet a moment, drinking and watching a basketball game on the silent TV screen. The Celts weren't playing and with the mess going on in his head, nothing about the game registered.

"Do you know Montez Clarke?" he asked after a while.

"Computer guy from Nashua? Sure, our department uses him for all their work. He's a hot shit."

Hot shit wasn't a term Jarvis would use to describe the tall good-looking Jamaican, though he could think of a lot of other words he'd use. Unfortunately, his opinion was influenced by things not computer-related.

"What about 'im?" Rodriguez pointed the top of the bottle at Jarvis. "Wait a minute. Didn't you say he's going out with this Chia pet lady?"

"Yeah. Or he was. Apparently he didn't know till a few days ago that she was married."

"Likely story."

Jarvis shook his head. "Angelina was there when he walked in on Chia and Stone. She didn't think he knew. Turned and left right off. And, get this, the woman didn't bat an eyelash. Clung to the husband the same as she'd been doing to Clarke a few minutes before."

Rodriguez's lips wrinkled. "When was this?"

"Monday I think."

His face unwrinkled. He pointed the beer-top again as if an idea had occurred. "I saw them together, lemme think…it was Thursday night. They were all cozied up at Billy's." Seeing Jarvis's confusion, he added, "Sports bar over on Tarrytown Rd."

Jarvis drained his glass. "How were they acting?"

"Clarke was at the bar first. He'd got through a beer before she came in. She sat beside him and was leaning all over him— just like you said. I was at a table with a coupla cops after a shift."

"Did you think it looked like he was expecting her?"

Rodriguez didn't have to think long. He nodded. "But the talk was serious. Not all honey-this honey-that but serious."

"How did it end?"

He thought a minute and said, "She just got up and left. You're gonna ask me how she walked, so I'll say slow and thoughtful."

Jarvis nodded and motioned for the bartender to bring another round. Suddenly he was glad he hadn't gone home. He needed to go see Montez Clarke and find out about the discrepancy in stories. If he was still seeing her after learning about Stone, it brought him to the top of the suspect list because it means he lied. He'd told Angelina "no big loss" or something to that effect.

Jarvis dug out his cell and phoned the captain at home. "Sir, I'm gonna stay here in Manchester tonight. We finished up the search of Chia Powers' apartment but I've got a lead on Montez Clarke." He explained the situation.

"Where the hell are you?"

Jarvis laughed. "I stayed to have a couple of beers with Rodriguez."

"How did you plan on getting home?"

"Dunno. It was a non-issue at the time."

The captain laughed. "I'll send Wilson for you in the morning. Coordinate with him where to meet up."

"Thank you, sir."

"And don't pick a 5-star hotel." He hung up.

"There's another line of thought too," Rodriguez said.

"What's that?" Jarvis asked.

"Maybe it wasn't a wife at all."

He sighed. "I know." He told about the few suspects they had at this point: Montez and three guys working at the theater."

"Seems like no matter what happens, you aren't gonna be able to keep the theater out of the news."

"I know."

"So, besides Mr. Clarke are any of the others viable suspects?"

"Not yet. I have somebody checking their backgrounds. We've talked to all the wives about friends of our vic—trying to add to the suspect list, but only one guy was mentioned. A guy he worked with, and there didn't seem to be any love lost between 'em." He got a whiff of isopropanol and sniffed his left hand. How'd that get there? He'd been wearing gloves during each search. "I need a beer and some sleep before I can wrap my brain around any more crap."

CHAPTER 29

Angie lay back in the bubbles that tickled her earlobes. On the edge of the tub sat a bowl of cashews and a full glass of white wine. Beside them was the phone, that hadn't rung once all afternoon, if she didn't count the manic call from her mother saying Rickie was among the missing again. And another call later saying he'd been found at the Alton Police station trying to pry information about the case from Sergeant Wilson. Wilson knew of Rickie's detective aspirations so he would've been as helpful as time permitted. Right now she would not think of Rickie or Mom. Or Jarvis.

As if reading her mind, the phone rang. Before she could get a hand free of the bubbles, it rang a second time, almost vibrating itself into the water. Angie made sure to check the caller ID because if it was Gloria again, Angie was "at the office working hard". But it wasn't mom. "Hi Jarvis. Bet you're one exhausted man."

"You got that right."

"Where are you?" she asked, hoping, but knowing he wouldn't say he was outside the closed bathroom door.

"I think I'm in Manchester." There was a deep chuckle in the background. "Seems like I've been all over the state today. Just finished a search warrant on Chia Powers' place."

"Should've warned you to be careful, she's got one heck of a right hook."

He told how they'd started that morning at Blanche's place.

"I felt like I was betraying her friendship. Kept apologizing to her."

"She understands it's your job."

"Not sure about that. She tried to beat me to a pulp."

"Really?" Angie sat up in the tub. The cool air hit her wet skin and she ducked back down.

"It was just frustration."

"You didn't arrest her or anything, did you?"

"Of course not. We did find something of interest at her place though. Besides a nearly empty quart bottle of alcohol—"

"Jarvis, everyone has it in their homes. I even have one."

"I'll be there to search you at some point."

She couldn't *not* giggle at that. "What else did you find?"

"A safe. And it contained six marriage licenses."

"Six huh?"

He laughed. "It took the captain four seconds to process that same news. You cut his time in half."

"It wasn't entirely unexpected. Did the six include anyone else we know?"

"They're back at the station. I haven't got there to examine them yet." Another deep-throated chuckle. "Anyway, what I called about was to say I'm spending the night here in Manchester."

"Who's that in the background?"

"Rodriguez."

"Tell him I said hi."

There was a bit of murmuring. "He said hi back."

She stood from the water and grabbed a towel. "So, why are you staying overnight?"

"I had some information—Montez was seen with Chia on Thursday night. I want to talk to him—find out why he lied."

There was a moment's hesitation, so he filled it with, "Anyway, I'll see you sometime tomorrow."

"Wait a second. Is the witness reliable, and how was the meeting between he and Chia?"

"Rodriguez said Montez sat at the bar, Chia entered maybe

ten minutes later, leaning all over him. Their manner was calm. Then she left."

She was quiet again, then she asked, "You want me to pick up Red?"

"No thanks. Neighbor Patti's looking after her."

"Okay. How are you getting home?"

"Wilson's picking me up."

"Okay. Have fun. I'll see you soon."

"Oh shoot. Forgot to tell you something important. As I was leaving the station earlier, a woman came in to report her husband missing. You'll never in a million years guess who it was."

"Amber Quattro." She waited through a couple of seconds of dead air, then added. "Powers."

"How did you know?"

"I've been sitting here in the bubbles—"

"Bubbles?" He groaned. Rodriguez, in the background, laughed.

"Do you have us on speaker phone?"

"No!"

"Good. Then to answer your question, yes, deep bubbles. Hot water and a large glass of wine."

His sigh came out more like a gurgle. "How did you know about Amber?"

"One thing I've been doing while appreciating this oh so rare quiet time is thinking. The other day Mr. Quattro said his daughter had moved east to be closer to her husband's job. A job that kept him on the road all the time."

"That's not much to go on."

"Yes, but she wears a shell barrette in her hair." Angie sipped from the glass of wine.

"A what?"

"Jarvis, my dear, you're not always very observant. You should've noticed that Blanche, Chia, and Miata Lin all have the same exact one."

"Shit." The call ended.

STONE COLD SOBER

Angie laughed and dried herself. She hadn't told him her sperm of an idea about who'd killed Stone. And she wouldn't until that little sperm joined with the egg of a clue, mated and grew. Things needed to be a lot more solidified in her mind before she put it to word—to anyone. Not that she didn't value Jarvis's input, but right now, clues and people's relationships had an all-out war going on inside her head; his feedback would only complicate matters. The what, when, and where were all etched in stone. The *who* was pretty clear. But the *why*. It was tangling her brain cells in a huge jumble. *If* the *who* turned out to be right—the *why* just wouldn't germinate. Why why why?

Clearly more research was needed but based on today's events the answers would be slow coming.

Angie wrapped herself in a lavender terrycloth robe fresh from the dryer, burying her nose in the collar. She went to the living room—the clock said ten after six—and did something rare: turned on the television. As expected, the news station was running footage of the murder scene in the small town of Alton Bay. The parking lot of the convenience store overflowed with television vehicles topped with big satellite dishes, and newsmen, running around as if being chased by lava flow from a volcanic eruption. What did they expect to accomplish? The killing happened more than twelve hours ago. The body had been taken away. The night clerk surely was home in bed. Witnesses had been interviewed and left the scene early this morning. Did reporters expect some witness would suddenly jump from behind the dumpster and announce, "Come here, I saw the whole thing."?

Trouble was, even if anyone saw the confrontation with the woman, it didn't matter. She didn't kill Stone. Well, even if authorities thought she had, she hadn't done it there. The process of his murder started days ago. He would've died at that moment no matter where he'd been or who'd been there.

Even so, Angie listened to the report. And learned nothing new. She was about to turn it off when Jarvis came on the screen. The interview had been taped that morning—she knew for a fact because he still wore the clothes he'd thrown on when the robbery call came. He'd donned his cop face, said the right cop words, like a politician telling what happened but giving no information.

Angie shut off the television and turned on the computer. While it booted, she made a list on a legal size pad of paper—all the people related to this case, up to and including Montez Clarke and Anthony Quattro. Even after talking to Montez earlier—she shivered thinking of his two-years hidden feelings for her—she couldn't picture him killing Stone. He didn't seem like he had that much vested in his relationship with Chia Pet Powers. Even in light of Jarvis's new information. Since Chia was the one doing the leaning on Montez, Angie figured she'd initiated their meeting. Whatever he'd said though hadn't 1-pissed her off or 2-elated her. Jarvis said she'd left calmly. What other conversation could've produced that reaction? Certainly not: "Will you give me an alibi?" "Will you take me back?" Maybe something like: "Can I borrow your car?"

Anthony Quattro as a suspect was another story. It wouldn't have been difficult for him to find out Stone was Angie's leading man and put the face with the name. She imagined him on the phone with Amber. And *that* might—probably was—Amber's real reason for coming east: to catch husband Allen in the act—no pun intended, she told herself. Seeing her husband acting and not off doing his salesman thing must've really irked her. She went crying to Daddy, who…what? Researched methods of killing people that would incriminate his daughter, who worked at a hospital? Then again, if arrested, *that* would be his reasoning against being a suspect. "Why would I kill him with something that would point right at my daughter?"

Angie added Jacoby Myers, Fred Saunders, Craig Evert, Caroline Yost and Vic Jason to the list for no other reason than they were in the cast with Stone.

Jacoby admitted having an altercation with Stone. In public. He'd also admitted to not liking Stone very much. But people didn't go around killing people they "didn't like very much." As far as she knew, the others liked Stone well enough. Angie saw no viable motive for any of them to want Stone dead.

She searched online, plugging in each name in turn. In two hours she learned nothing. She had no idea how to search for Stones' aliases. There must be some database Jarvis would know about.

The phone rang. Who could be calling at this hour—it was after eleven. Caller ID gave the answer: Jarvis.

"I hope I didn't w-wake you," he said.

"How many beers have you had?" she asked, amused.

"I...I don't remember."

Angie shut down the computer. "Where are you?"

"In a motel in Nashua. I decided to stay over. I want to interview Montez in the morning. Didn't make sense to go home and come back. Especially since Wilson and the guys left hours ago."

"Are you forgetting you told me all this a few hours ago?"

"Yes. I just missed you. So what did you do after bubble time?"

"I've been researching our suspects."

"How many suspects are there? B-besides the six wives."

Angie read the names from her list.

"Did you learn anything useful?"

"No. Total waste of time. When will you be back?"

"Not till lunchtime probably. After seeing Montez, I'm going to the Alton impound lot to check out Stone's car. Hopefully Chia's will still be there—I tell you she got picked up for speeding?"

"No." The librarian/model drove a black Audi. "Would you like me to go first thing in the morning, before she gets a chance to retrieve it?"

"God, I forgot she'll be making bail. No, thanks though, you have plenty to do. I'll get Wilson to delay its release. Hey, are you telling the truth about finding nothing online?"

She laughed and, as he'd done to her earlier, hung up.

CHAPTER 30

Jarvis arrived at Montez's computer shop at five after nine. Shanda Clarke recognized him immediately. She whizzed around the counter at top speed. She'd gotten a motorized chair since he'd last seen her.

Shanda wore a very classy red pantsuit with a red striped blouse. "Is this a business or pleasure visit?" she asked.

Jarvis gave a gallant bow and kissed her hand.

"Okay, Sir Galahad, I get it." She giggled. "It's business."

"Sorry I don't get down this way very often. How've you been doing?"

She shrugged. "Much better than last time I saw you."

"You had a lot going on in your life at that time. It wasn't that far removed from your accident."

She shook her head. "It was worse having Montez in jail."

"It was only police custody. And it was less than twenty-four hours."

Shanda rolled her eyes. "You should've seen me here in the shop. I'd only been working a couple of weeks at the time. Had no idea where anything was. And I wasn't used to working with the public." She jerked a thumb toward the back room. "I'd always spent my time with my head buried inside people's computers.

"Terrible place for a pretty head like yours. Look at you now, running the joint. I'm really proud of you."

"Thanks." She thumped the arms of her chair with both

palms and gave a broad smile that made her look like her brother. "So, what can I do to help? Do you need technical information or are you on an investigation?"

"The latter. I need to see your brother."

A frown creased her face. Jarvis knew she was thinking about the last time Montez had been involved in murder—a good friend. But, classy lady that she was, she said nothing. "He didn't come in this morning. He went directly to Alton to the theater." She tipped her head and gazed at him from dark eyes. "I bet Angie's very busy with Tyson gone."

"How'd you know he left?"

She gave a wide smile. "I saw the Christmas show where they announced it. The show was grand."

"Angelina will be delighted you said so."

A client came in. Shanda greeted him then turned to Jarvis. "Sorry Montez isn't here."

"That's okay. Maybe you can help with a few things. Did you ever meet Chia Powers?"

She wrinkled her nose—not in confusion, in dislike. Shanda sent a quick glance at the customer who was browsing the video games. "If there's anything I can help with, let me know," she called. To Jarvis, she lowered her voice, "Chia is rather…let's just say insecure and indecisive. I always joked with Montez that she needed help deciding which underwear to put on in the morning." She frowned. "That wasn't nice. Sorry."

"Actually, it was very tactful compared to other ways I've heard her described." They shared a chuckle. "Did you know she was married?" he asked.

This brought a rise to Shanda's eyebrows; they disappeared into her long bangs. "I didn't until a couple of days ago when Montez told me. I promise you, detective, Montez would never go out with a married woman."

"That's what I heard. But here's my problem. I'm not sure you know yet. Chia's husband was murdered yesterday."

Her hand shot up to cover her mouth. "You don't think

Montez did it!" When the customer glanced up, she shot him an apologetic look and turned her chair a few degrees toward Jarvis. "You can't be thinking that. Please tell me you're not—"

Jarvis shook his head. "I pretty much ruled him out right away." He kept his voice low also. "But here's my problem. Montez learned about her marriage to Stone Powers last Tuesday. I have a witness who saw him with her on Thursday night. Then two days later her husband is dead."

She ducked her face and cupped it in her palms. He was pretty sure she muttered, "Not again."

"Shanda, I'm here to see if you can help."

She looked up. "We don't live together so I can't say what he's ever up to. But detective, I cannot imagine him..." She sighed.

Jarvis wished he could put her mind at ease.

"So, you say he went out with her again after he found out she was married," Shanda said.

"Yes, so, unfortunately that pushes him higher on our suspect list."

"You realize it might've been an accidental meeting. Or she forced him to meet her."

"Forced him?"

"Yes, like some kind of blackmail. You know, 'if you don't meet me I'll tell so-and-so something I know about you.'"

Jarvis nodded. "Could've happened. That's why I want to speak to him—to push him back down on the list. I'm returning to Alton now. If I happen to miss connections with him, please tell him to call me." He fished a business card from his wallet and handed it to her.

"I'm sure he'll get in touch with you right away. I know he wants to be rid of that woman."

"Did he tell you that?"

"Yes. Even before Tuesday—he said he was trying to think of a way to break up with her."

"Knowing Montez's strong personality," Jarvis said, "I wouldn't think he'd have trouble breaking up with someone."

"She...well, she's quite clingy. He thought she might be the stalker type. He was trying to find the right way to do it."

Like framing her for murder? suggested Jarvis's devilish side.

"I don't know how he stood it. She drove me crazy with her 'didn't I, Montez' all the time—and I didn't even see her that often. She was always blowing up his phone with texts. Checking to see where he was, I bet." Shanda stopped for a breath and a glance around the shop. The customer was browsing through a row of computers on a long table.

"Did he answer her texts and calls?" Jarvis asked.

"No way anyone could answer them all and get anything done. She kept showing up places he worked."

"So it was like she was stalking him. How did she find out where he'd be?"

"That's the thing, he didn't know. It was like she had a homing device on his car. But he couldn't find it."

That could explain how she showed up at that bar Thursday night. He had to hear the facts from his mouth. Sergeant Wilson hadn't arrived to pick him up yet so he decided to walk around the corner and visit Blanche. He hoped she was over her mad at him for bringing her into the station.

"There's someone coming to pick me up. Could you tell him I'm around the corner at Blanche Powers' shop?"

Shanda frowned.

"What's wrong?" It seemed like a simple enough request.

"Blanche Powers?"

He nodded.

"Chia Powers?"

This girl had a quick mind.

"Yes." She'd hear about it soon enough on the news. "They were both Stone's wives." Before she could question him further, he gave a grin, spun on a heel, and headed to Blanche's.

Jarvis didn't like Montez Clarke. Never had. The man was too strong-minded, too forward, too...

Not to mention the attraction between he and Angelina. Part of him wanted Montez to be guilty, but his logical side couldn't fathom it. No matter how hard he tried, even two years ago, he couldn't think of Montez as a killer.

Blanche was in her store. She sat behind a sewing machine. Its motor was going at top speed, the needle slashing up and down, sewing some large blue silk fabric. It tumbled across the worktable and onto the floor. She shifted it with one hand while guiding the material with the other hand. Though she was facing in his direction, it didn't appear as though she'd seen him come in.

He didn't speak; he didn't want to startle her. After a minute, she stopped the machine to adjust the material. That's when she noticed him.

She gasped and put a hand to her mouth. She didn't smile. She didn't frown. Just raised her head high and stood to approach him. "Good morning."

He stepped forward to hug her. She moved into the embrace. He held in a sigh of relief. She wasn't angry. Thank goodness.

"I wanted to make sure we're okay," he said once she stepped back.

"Yes, we're okay. I know you were doing your job. I'd be pissed if you didn't. I hope you came with good news."

He shook his head. "Sorry." He jabbed a thumb over his shoulder. "I had to talk to Montez."

Blanched nodded. "I got to meet one of the other wives yesterday."

"Is that right?"

"You guys did a good job keeping us apart inside the building, but nobody watched the parking lot."

He grinned thinking he should get hold of the surveillance videos. "Which wife?"

"The Asian—what's her name Miata or something like that?"

"Miata Lin."

"That's right. Hey, come on, sit down a minute."

"Can't stay long. My ride should be here soon, but I wouldn't turn down a cup of coffee if you have one."

She shook her head. "You and your coffee." Blanche glided across to a Keurig machine and in a moment placed a cup in front of him.

"So, what did you and Miata Lin talk about?" he asked.

"In a nutshell, that if we'd known what he was up to, we would've killed him ourselves." She clapped a hand to her mouth. "Oops, probably shouldn't have said that in front of a cop."

"I'm in friend mode today."

She made a dramatic sweep of her hand across her brow. "Whew! Don't want to give you another reason to haul me to the station house."

"I don't want another reason. Are you seeing her again?"

Blanched smiled. "Whatever gave you that idea?"

"Because you act as though you liked her. And because one short meeting in a parking lot…"

"How do you know it was short?"

"Because you wouldn't have wanted any of us to see you. And because I imagine there are lots of questions you want to ask each other."

"You got that right. As a matter of fact, we're having lunch today."

He shook his head. Women!

"You mean if you found out Angelina was married to a couple of other guys, you wouldn't want to meet them?"

"To beat the daylights out of them maybe."

She shook her head. "You might want to but you wouldn't. Any progress on the case yet?" He pulled in a breath, preparing to answer, but she did it for him. "You can't talk about it."

He leaned over and kissed her cheek. "You got that right, my friend."

At that moment Ambrose Wilson entered the shop. "I saw that."

Blanche and Jarvis laughed and got to their feet. Jarvis

polished off the contents of his in one swallow. He kissed Blanche again and told her to keep her chin up. "You going to the theater today?"

She shook her head. "I'm trying to finish a project for the theater in New London. I'll be out that way most of the day."

"I won't keep you any longer."

Out in the SUV—Wilson had brought his personal vehicle—Jarvis told him about the discussions with Shanda Clarke and Blanche.

"That's something I was thinking about last night," Wilson said. "About the wives committing the murder together."

Jarvis chuckled. "Detective Rodriguez and I were discussing the same thing last night." He told Wilson some of the names they'd come up with for the ladies gang. The development of more names helped pass the time back to Alton. "Did you know the wives met outside in our parking lot?"

Wilson made a choking sound that was probably a laugh combined with fear of what the captain would say when—not if—he found out.

"Did you find anything at impound?" Jarvis asked.

Wilson pulled into traffic and headed toward the highway. "Chia Powers' car does indeed have a long scrape on one side. And it has silver paint embedded in it, the same color as that of Stone's beemer. I sent chips out for analysis. There was no evidence inside her car at all." He stopped and let the information settle for a minute.

What did that mean? That Chia was the killer and didn't want the evidence in her car? That she never had any there? If she was the killer and had known about the other wives, might she have planted something in their vehicles? That was a big if. He bounced a few more ideas through his brain, but none stuck right now.

"It was a different story in Stone's car." Wilson drove north on the highway for the hour-plus trip. "His was a veritable smorgasbord. He had two vials of nose drops and two containers of hand sanitizer in the glove box. There was a bag of deodorant and shampoo on the front passenger seat. Wait, before you say that's not a big deal... The odd thing about them was, they weren't recently store-bought. They'd each already been opened. Some was missing from each container."

"Maybe he ran out and a wife gave them to him—to be considerate."

"Why? To put in their own bathroom?"

Jarvis shrugged. "For his trip to Chicago?"

Wilson shook his head. "No, those bottles were too big to take on the plane."

"Not if he was checking through baggage claim. You can take any size you want in a suitcase."

"Right, but why would he, he was only going overnight."

"Good point. What else?"

"There was a distinct smell of alcohol in each one. Wanna know what I think?"

"Even if I didn't. I have the feeling you're going to tell me."

"Damn right. I think somebody poured some out to make room for the alcohol."

He nodded. "I think you're right."

"I sent them for testing. Called the fingerprint team too."

Jarvis was pleased. His sergeant had been busy. He was self-driven, a man who didn't need supervision. A man perhaps aiming for his job. Crap.

CHAPTER 31

Jarvis swallowed down a grapefruit-sized lump. He worked hard, did his job well, had lots of success—shouldn't fear competition. Right? Wrong. He held in the sigh that wanted to clear his lungs. "What did they find for prints?"

"Lots of 'em in both cars," Wilson said. "Haven't ID'd them all yet but we've isolated Chia's and Stone's in both their cars for sure."

"Nice work."

They stopped at the drive-thru for some sandwiches and took them to headquarters. Jarvis was anxious to see what the rest of the fingerprint yielded. Also, some of the evidence testing might be back by now.

The captain wasn't in his office so, no need to check in. There were two pages in the fax machine. Wilson snatched them on the way past. He dropped them on Jarvis's desk; they each took a page.

"What've you got?" Wilson asked. "I have print results from Stone's car."

"I've got Chia's." Jarvis opened his sandwich and munched while Wilson read and talked with his mouth full.

"The Audi had three sets of identifiable prints. Hers and Montez Clarke's on the driver's side. Stone's, hers, and Clarke's on the passenger side. None to speak of in the back."

Jarvis nodded and swallowed. "Makes sense. What I wish is that each print came with a date of application."

Wilson grinned. "Yeah. Sure would help. Ms. Powers' car wasn't any too clean so the prints could've got there at any time. Whadda you got?"

Jarvis popped a bundle of fries into his mouth and, taking into consideration how gross it looked when Wilson talked with his mouth full, chewed and swallowed. "In Stone's car, there's only his prints in the driver's seat."

Wilson nodded. "I had the idea he would never let anyone drive his car."

"The passenger side has several sets: Chia, Blanche, and Miata Lin's. There's a full palm print—Stone's—on the back of one back seat."

"Probably he braced himself while putting something back there. Amber's prints aren't in the car at all?" Wilson asked.

"No. Which leaves me with two lines of thought. One is that since she's just gotten back in town she hasn't been in the car yet. The other thought, and one I like a lot better, is that she's our perp and made sure not to touch anything when she was there. You know—got him to open the doors for her, etc. Has she been interviewed yet?"

"No, the captain said to wait for you to do it."

"Okay, can you have someone pick her up?"

Wilson crumpled his empty bags. "Consider it done. Anything else?"

"Yes." Jarvis scrounged for a pad of paper and scribbled some names on it: Fred Saunders, Caroline Yost, Jacoby Myers, Craig Evert and Vic Jason. "Can you interview each of these people?" He tore off the page and handed it to Wilson.

"I assume they work at the theater."

"Right. Saunders is the set designer. The other three are actors. The three guys are regulars on Angelina's staff so they should be there. The Yost woman was hired for this show only."

"Anything you want to know in particular?" Wilson stood.

"Obvious things: How they felt about Stone. I want to know if he really was as likeable as Angelina thinks. Ask if they saw anyone tinkering with his car or locker at the theater. By the way, did you print the locker?"

"Sure did."

"Good." The rest of the results should be in soon. "Find out also if they saw anyone hanging around who didn't belong. Find out if they'd hung out with Stone outside the theater. Or if they saw him anywhere." Jarvis specifically didn't mention the dispute between Myers and Stone at the skating rink, curious to see if the information turned up during questioning. "It's okay to sit them down as a group. In this instance, it might be the best idea. Get them comparing notes. It might help stimulate the others."

"Kiana Smith isn't on the list."

Jarvis laughed. "You can talk to her if you want, but she's not a suspect. Besides, I hear she's got a pretty mean right hook so you don't want to get on her bad side."

Wilson got up and left. Jarvis phoned Angelina. She didn't answer till the fourth ring, which meant she was busy. She sounded winded, which meant she hadn't been near her phone.

"Hi Jarvis."

"You out jogging or something?" he asked.

"No, at rehearsal. I was on the stage, my phone was in the front row. Are you back yet?"

"Yes. I'm at the station."

"Just to let you know. I picked up Red. She's fine. She's had free run of the theater all day. Made a lot of new friends. One in particular."

"Lemme guess—Montez."

"Right."

"Is he still there?"

"I don't know. Want me to find out?"

"Please. If he is, ask him to stop by to see me."

"Hang on." She didn't cover the phone. "Vic. Are you busy?" she shouted.

There was an answering shout of "No."

"Could you run upstairs and see if the computer guy is still there? If he is, ask him to stop at the police station asap."

A shouted, "Okay," came through loud and clear.

"I assume you didn't catch up with him in Nashua this morning," Angelina said.

"No." Jarvis finished the last of his sandwich, cold now. "I had a nice talk with his sister though. She says hi. I also stopped by to see Blanche."

"Uh-oh."

"No. She was okay. Totally."

Angelina lowered her voice. "Do you have any thoughts that she's guilty?"

"She's about halfway down the list."

Angelina laughed. "I don't know if that's good news or not."

"Good. Oh, the reason I called. I wanted to let you know Wilson is on the way to interview your staff."

"So you didn't call to talk to me?"

He disconnected the call, smiling. Almost immediately his intercom buzzed. "Detective, Amber Powers is in Room 1."

"Thanks."

"Oh…and, sir, her father is with her."

"Thanks."

Why wasn't he surprised? Jarvis wondered if the reason his daughter originally moved to the west coast was to get out from under Daddy's thumb. At the theater, Angelina was having a time staying away from him, but he'd put that down to her mother's interference. Perhaps renting space to him hadn't been such a good idea. Time would tell.

Jarvis disposed of the lunch trash. Then he sat and made some notes about the case. He used a dry erase board to try to connect the suspects visually. Nothing popped off and clobbered him on the head. No wife stuck out above the others. One was possessive. Two had access to the isopropanol—and the knowledge of how to use it. The third wife had no apparent motive, and in Jarvis's experience, those were the most logical suspects. He cradled his head a moment then decided he'd avoided the pair waiting in Room 1 long enough.

He got up and made his way there. Wilson wasn't in his office, which meant he wasn't back from the theater yet. As he twisted the knob to the interrogation room, he wished he'd gone to the theater with the sergeant.

Amber Powers was seated at the small table. Daddy Quattro was pacing the small room—four steps one way, four steps the other. At the sound of the door opening, he whirled around and zipped at Jarvis like a tornado across the Kansas plains.

"What do you mean having my daughter brought here? The thought of her having anything to do with her husband's murder...it's ludicrous. She's just gotten in town. What motive could she have to do such a heinous thing? She loves Allen with all her heart." Now he got directly in Jarvis's face. Jarvis hated the up-close-and-personal method unless he was the perpetrator, but he didn't flinch. "What kind of cop are you anyway?" Quattro shouted.

This time Jarvis did move. He backed a step and walked around the irate restaurateur. He went to the door, opened it and called for an officer.

"Just what do you think you're doing?" Quattro growled.

Heavy footsteps sounded in the hall and a rookie officer shot into the doorway. "Please escort this man from the building," Jarvis said.

The officer put a hand out to take hold of Quattro's arm but Quattro jerked away. "What do you think you're doing?" He glared at Jarvis.

"Removing you from the premises. Your actions so far have broken more rules than I have time to list." Quattro sputtered, about to speak, but Jarvis stuck a finger in his face. "I did not invite you here. I asked your daughter. Now out."

Quattro didn't move. If anything he puffed himself bigger. Jarvis nearly laughed, but he needed to keep this situation under control. "Don't make me have to get physical."

"Take off that badge and I'll show you how to get physical."

Jarvis made a show of looking at his front pocket, proving

he wasn't wearing a badge (though it was in his back pocket). "Do your worst, big man." Jarvis took one step forward.

Quattro whirled away toward his daughter who was sitting there calmly, no emotion showing on her face or manner, even with the threat of violence going on before her. "Don't answer any questions. Just keep your mouth shut."

"I don't have anything to hide, Dad. The longer I avoid this the longer they'll keep me here."

He leaned into her face. "I said, don't talk to them. I'll call Victor. Wait till he gets here. I mean it."

"Just go, Father."

Quattro deflated a bit but couldn't resist a parting command to Jarvis. "Do not question her until her lawyer arrives."

Once again Jarvis checked himself—the urge to salute almost got the better of him. The door shut on the restaurant owner's backside. As Jarvis turned toward Amber he could've sworn she sighed in relief.

He sat in the other chair at the table. "I want you to know you aren't under arrest or anything like that. I'm just trying to put together a picture of the last week of Stone—er, Allen's life."

"To be honest, I'd like a glimpse of that myself." Her voice was wistful.

"I guess the $20,000 question right now is, do you want to talk to me or wait for the attorney?"

"I'll talk. I have nothing to hide."

"Okay, when and why did you come back here?"

"You mean here to Alton or back east?"

"Both I guess."

"I arrived twelve days ago."

Plenty of time to acclimate and learn about the other wives, Jarvis thought.

"First reason, I lost my job as coach for the surf team in southern California—I'd been the Mission Beach coach for three years. Second reason: Allen and I hardly ever saw each other."

"How long have you been married?" he asked, though he already knew they'd been married since 2010. Of the four wives under suspicion, she'd been his first, though of the six marriage licenses they'd found, the two unknowns were prior to these.

"We were married on Mission Beach on August 26, 2010."

"No children, I assume."

She shook her head. "We were both too busy." She lowered her voice. "And frankly, neither of us are very child-oriented."

"Didn't you coach children's surfing?"

"Gosh no. It was an advanced group—adults only."

"My girlfriend's…" He hesitated, unsure how to present Rickie's relationship.

But he didn't have to. She smiled and said, "I know Rickie. Knew. He was a member of the same Mission Beach team but he was retiring just as I got the coaching job. From what I heard at the time, he went back to Hawaii to surf as an amateur."

That was more than Jarvis knew about him.

"Rickie Kennedy was a legend in his twenties."

Jarvis nodded. Time to get back to the subject. "Okay, so why come to Alton?"

She sighed. "Third reason: family. Though, as you can see, my father and I clash, I'd hardly seen him since I moved out west. And I know he's lonely since my mom died. Allen would hardly ever be home, so…" She shrugged.

Some family was better than none. Jarvis understood. He wished he had a better relationship with his brother.

"So you moved in with Dad till you could find a place of your own."

"Right, which happened damned fast." She laughed. "I moved just far enough away that he wouldn't be dropping in too often unannounced. I got a place in Northwood. Of course, it's too big for just one person."

"That's quite a hike to Lakes Region General."

"Yeah. I know but I have an application at a couple of Concord hospitals."

"Excuse me for saying, you don't seem too broken up about Allen's death."

"It's not that. I adored him. I thought he adored me. Now I learn there were other wives." A couple of tears popped into the corners of her eyes. "How much could he have loved me? A girl wants to think she's the only one." The tears escaped and rolled down her cheeks in perfect rhythm with each other. Jarvis plucked a tissue from the box on the table. "Thanks. I thought we were soul mates." She gave a small laugh. "Sounds silly, but that's how it was. How did he die?"

"You don't know?"

"All I know is he was in a convenience store."

"He was poisoned." Jarvis waited for the information to sink in. Why didn't she ask any questions? So, he asked, "Don't you want to know what kind?"

"I guess. I don't know what difference my knowing would help. I mean, the poisons you see on TV usually cause these grizzly deaths, and if Allen died like that, I don't want to know."

"I get the idea you close your eyes when those scenes come on the screen."

She managed a small smile. "You got that right."

"I need you to know that, while we're here, your apartment and car are being searched."

"For the poison?"

"Right? Isopropanol."

"I don't know what that is."

"You work in a hospital…"

"I work as a receptionist."

"But you told Angelina…"

"I wanted the job to seem more important than it is. What is that iso-stuff you mentioned?"

"Essentially, rubbing alcohol."

"I don't have any in my apartment. I just moved in. It's not the kind of thing you pick up when you're outfitting a place."

What did that mean? Was she warning him they wouldn't find anything and thumbing her nose at them? Or just stating a fact? He couldn't read her expression. He wished, not for the first time today, that Angelina were here. She'd be able to tell.

His cell phone rang. He didn't recognize the caller ID number. "We didn't find anything in her car or her place," the voice said.

Damn.

A knock came on the door. It opened. The rookie officer admitted a tall, stick-thin man wearing a bowler hat—really? "The Quattro's attorney," the officer said.

Shit.

"You got that right," Amber said.

Damn, had he said that out loud?

CHAPTER 32

On the stage, Caroline linked arms with Vic. They turned to leave the construction company's office. Vic stopped at the door, blocking the way. He tore off the hard hat and heaved it to the floor. It thudded and rolled, landing someplace out of sight. Vic grasped Caroline's arm and swung her around. She gasped as he bent her back and planted his lips on hers. After a moment, he set her back on her feet.

"Great job, folks!" Angie shouted. "Very good. You can all go to lunch. You don't have to come back afterward, but can you be here about nine in the morning?"

Many shouts of "Sure" and "Yeah boss" came from the direction of the green room.

"Wait!" This shout—a male's—originated from the back of the auditorium that had everyone stopping in their tracks and doing about-faces. A man stood in silhouette at the top of the aisle, but Angie recognized Sergeant Wilson. She liked the big, friendly officer, but couldn't stop the blast of anxiety that shot through her at the sight of him. He hadn't stopped in to bring lunch the way Jarvis usually did. He hadn't stopped to check fire codes. Nor had he come to read any of the growing slush pile of unread submissions.

He started down the aisle. Nobody moved to go toward him. They stood clustered at the left of the stage, on the steps and partway down the dimly lit hallway to the green room. From her spot center-front first row, Angie walked to meet him at the foot of the steps to the stage.

"I'm sorry to disrupt things, but Jarvis sent me to do some interviews."

His comment received surprising reactions from her cast and crew: "That's okay with us." "Sure, come up." "Let's go out back and sit." And one long sigh from somebody.

Angie gestured him up the trio of steps. He followed them to the green room where everyone took seats, leaving the one at the head of the table open.

Angie strode to the far end of the table and leaned against the wall. He wasn't here to see her but she wasn't leaving him alone with her people unless he demanded she do so. Kiana took a seat near the end of the table.

The sergeant stopped in the entryway. He seemed nervous, unsure what to do. She gestured him into their private domain. He lumbered to the head of the table, took out a notebook and pen.

"People," Angie said, "this is Jarvis's cohort—partner in crime as it were. Sergeant Ambrose Wilson. I don't have to tell you to be nice to him."

There was some laughter that didn't set the sergeant at ease.

He opened the notebook. "I'll make this as fast as I can. As you know, I'm investigating the death of Stone Powers."

Sad murmurs all around.

"Yes, it was a very sad thing, and I'm sure you agree that we need to find his killer as soon as possible."

"Before the trail goes cold," someone said.

"Yes. Now, could we go around the table and everyone tell me who's here?"

Each person said their name. He checked them off a list on his pad.

"The only person who doesn't seem to be here is a Fred Saunders."

"That's because he's our set designer," Angie said. "He's out back."

"I'll go get him." Vic jumped up and disappeared in the

direction of the set room.

"And we seem to have an extra person. Am I to assume you're Ms. Kiana Smith?"

Kiana nodded.

Vic returned leading a bewildered Fred.

"Nice to see you Mr. Saunders. Please take a seat." The sergeant clicked the top on the pen and poised it to write. "I'd like to know your basic impressions of Stone Powers as a person."

There were a number of positive responses, the cast repeating silly stories Stone had told them. One said how Stone had brought a special sample painkiller after he'd complained of a sore back.

"How could anyone not like him?" This from a smiling Caroline. "He was funny and considerate and…yeah, okay, I'll say it—gorgeous." Everyone laughed.

Two people, Angie realized, had remained silent throughout: Jacoby and Fred.

Wilson noticed too. He pointed the pen tip at Fred. "How did you feel about Mr. Powers?"

"Er, ah…" Fred started to stand, then elected to remain in his seat. "I, ah, didn't like him very much. I thought he was too full of himself. Telling all those stories to keep people from seeing the real person inside."

Probably an apt description. His self-esteem problem explained why he'd married so many women—he needed constant ego bolstering. Kiana gave a tiny nod of agreement.

When Wilson focused on Jacoby, he cleared his throat. "I didn't like him either. All those women"—he shot a peek at Caroline—"sorry, but you guys fawned over him like he was God's gift to manhood. And all those stupid stories. What a liar. That many things could never happen to one person."

"Did any of you have occasion to see him outside the theater?" Wilson asked.

Vic raised a hand. "I saw him at the Wolftrap in Wolfeboro. He was with a blonde woman. She was tall. Really pretty.

Wearing a fur coat."

This seemed to describe the woman from the convenience store. Angie had a pretty good idea at this point, who it was. She hadn't yet been able to tell Jarvis.

"How were they getting along?" the sergeant asked.

Vic shrugged. "Seemed fine but we were leaving the restaurant. It was about nine o'clock. Stone and the woman were still eating—didn't seem to notice us and we didn't approach them. But outside, as we got to our car, the woman came out carrying a small plastic shopping bag—you know, like you'd get at a department store. While we waited for our car to warm up, she opened the passenger side door of Stone's car—and yeah, she had a key. I know because the headlights flashed. She put the bag on his front seat and then went back in the restaurant."

"Did she lock the car when she was done?" Wilson asked.

Vic nodded.

While Wilson scribbled Jacoby piped up, "You'll find out… maybe you know already. I met up with him at the skating rink. We got into it."

There were some surprised gasps around the table. Probably related to learning that the calm and cool Jacoby had been riled enough to "get into it" with anyone. Wilson nodded, which meant he already knew. Jacoby described the incident.

Wilson turned toward Stone's locker, still covered in fingerprint dust. "Did any of you see anyone—anyone at all—tinkering with his locker? Or lingering around it."

Every face around the table screwed up in concentration, each wanting to be as helpful as possible. Angie didn't see anyone cast a suspicious glance at any of his compatriots. Good.

"Okay," said the sergeant, "what about Mr. Powers' car? Did you see anyone hanging around it? Particularly touching it in any way."

Craig's hand went up. "I saw a woman putting a big black bag in the backseat."

"When was this?" Wilson asked.

Craig wrinkled his mouth as he thought. "I'd say Wednesday in the morning."

"Describe the bag."

"Black, big—like for trash. It had a yellow pull-tie."

"Did she have keys?"

Craig thought again. He shook his head. "The door was unlocked.

Angie felt herself frowning. Stone adored that car—didn't let anyone else drive it. No way he'd leave it unlocked, not even if he expected someone to put something in it.

"Can you describe the woman?"

"Don't need to—it was Blanche."

Wilson scribbled on his pad. "Okay, great. Anyone else?" No replies. "Okay one final question. Have any of you seen anyone lurking around the building? Someone who doesn't belong here."

A couple of voices mentioned Montez and Mr. Quattro, but a discussion clarified saying they "kinda belonged there".

"There was that guy Montez's girlfriend," Caroline said. "Remember Angie—when she came in the theater and you threw her out?"

Everyone laughed. Angie explained to Sergeant Wilson how Vic and Craig had escorted Chia to her car.

"There's also Mr. Quattro's daughter," Fred said. "She wandered around in here a lot."

"Did you see her anywhere near Mr. Powers' locker?" the sergeant asked.

"Well, now that you mention it." Caroline puckered her lips and tilted her head at him. "I do think I saw her near it."

Angie wasn't sure how this could be the truth. How would Amber know which locker was Stone's? Unless she'd been in the building with him at another time. This hardly made sense because she'd supposedly just arrived here from California. Was Fred trying to focus attention on her? If so, why?

Wilson slapped the notebook shut and thanked everyone.

While they filed out, he stepped toward Angie. "You look tired."

"It's been a long few days."

"You got that right."

"So, who's at the top of your list?"

She said, "What makes you think I even have a list?" then stepped around him.

Angie wondered if Anthony Quattro was in the building right now, but it was worth checking. To the sound of Wilson's bark of laughter, she went upstairs.

The construction crew was still hard at work. Montez stood on a ladder about halfway down the hallway stringing cable through the rafters. He smiled down at her.

"You doing all right?" she asked.

His grin widened. "Sure am. Are you the messenger girl?"

"Come again?"

"Sent to remind me to get to the police station."

Now it was Angie's turn to smile. "Sorry. No. I didn't know anything about it. I'm looking for Mr. Quattro. Is he here?"

Montez jerked his head in the direction of the restaurant. "In the kitchen."

"Thanks."

He lowered his voice, "I'd be careful if I were you."

She started to ask why but Quattro's raised voice burst into the hallway.

Montez grinned. "Tell the detective I'll be there in an hour."

"You'll see him before I will then," she called over her shoulder, and followed the restaurateur's shouts.

Angie found him snarling directions at a pair of large men maneuvering an 8-burner stove into place against the wall. No matter what they did, he didn't think it was right. He made them move it an inch this way, then two inches that way. An inch forward, a half-inch back. Angie stood there, surprised at his change in demeanor—was this the real Anthony Quattro? Was his flirty manner a cover-up for this bear? She waited till they got it in place before making her presence known.

Mr. Quattro glanced at her, then at the stove. He grumbled something in Italian that she couldn't understand—and probably didn't want to—then motioned for her to go back into the hallway.

She wasn't sure if she was being dismissed or he'd come too.

"Yes. What is it?"

She gave him a raised-eyebrow look.

"Bad time to visit," he groused. "I have to watch these morons every second. They can't seem to get anything right." He buttoned his camel hair coat that had been hanging open, showing off his expensive silk shirt.

Not sure she wanted to know, Angie's incorrigible curiosity made her ask, "Is something wrong?"

"Wrong! What could be wrong?"

"I don't know, that's why I asked. It seems as though you're angry with me for some reason."

He scowled, looked at the ceiling for a five-count, then back at her. "I'm not angry with you. There's some shit going on at the police station…"

"What kind of shit?" she asked. "And what's it got to do with me?"

He stabbed his left arm in the direction of the elevator. Twice. Good thing no one had been standing there or they would've been knocked over. "That…that stupid detective friend of yours has my daughter in there. Said it's just for questioning, but I know what was gong through his head."

"What's that?"

"He's gonna try to pin Allen's death on her."

"Are you insinuating he'd fabricate a case against her?" Now it was Angie's turn to scowl. Sticking up for him would be useless under the circumstances. "I would've thought you'd be there with her," was all she said.

"I was!"

Montez, who'd been chest deep in the ceiling, bent to look at them. You okay? he mouthed. She nodded.

Quattro turned, spotted Montez and growled. "No f-ing privacy in this place."

Montez laughed, but Angie was pretty sure Quattro missed it—most of the sound was muffled up in the ceiling.

"You ought to know why I'm not there!"

"Me?" What on earth was he talking about?

"Don't try and tell me your lover hasn't called to gloat that he had me thrown out of the place."

Heaven, she prayed, please help me not fall on the floor laughing. "Why would he do that?" she asked.

"So he could put words in my daughter's mouth!" he roared.

"I'll have you know—"

The words were lost because Mr. Quattro had pivoted and headed for the elevator. Angie double-timed to keep up with him. "Why would Jarvis do that to Amber?"

"Because he knows about you and me!"

She stopped short. "What!"

Montez peered down from the ceiling again. This time he was smirking. Probably he was recalling he'd used the same words to her a couple of days ago.

"He knows I've asked you out," Quattro said.

"How would he know that, and why would it have anything to do with the murder investigation?"

Quattro stopped and punched the Down button. "What did you come up her for anyway?"

"I came to see how Amber was doing. With Allen dead, I thought she might want a woman to talk to."

Mr. Quattro gave a scornful laugh. "She can't be doing too well if she's under suspicion for murder now, can she?"

Inside the ceiling, Montez snorted. Almost right away, he turned the laugh into a cough. He bent his face out of the ceiling waving a hand in front of his face. "Dusty up here."

Quick thinking, Angie managed *not* to say. "It's none of my business but I wouldn't recommend going back there," she said to Quattro.

"You're right, it's none of your business." The elevator doors opened without a sound. Quattro darted inside. He held the door from closing. "I just want to make sure that asshole lawyer showed up."

"Why don't you phone him?" she muttered, then added, "Don't drive too fast. Amber will still be there when you arrive."

He frowned. "That's what I'm fucking worried about."

She turned to go back downstairs and bumped into Montez. "Pretty slick, babe. Pretty slick."

"I have no idea what you're talking about."

"How did you not tell him to take his f-ing restaurant and shove it?"

"This will probably make him pull out anyway."

"Especially if the daughter's guilty." He went back and folded the ladder, then leaned it against the wall.

Why say that? Did he know something?

Angie crossed her arms and looked up at him. She almost tapped her foot too but the message got across.

"No. It was a random comment." He gave his characteristic shrug.

"Montez, stop being cryptic. If you know something—out with it."

"I know nussing, nussing."

Who else had imitated the Hogan's Heroes sergeant recently? She grabbed his arm. He stood erect, tools clutched in both hands. "Tell me."

"I heard her threaten to kill him." He bent to fit a hammer into a trunk-sized toolbox.

"Don't stop now. Time. Place. Circumstance."

He whirled on her, a giant pair of wire cutters in his hand. "There's a price for my information."

Uh-oh. Dare she ask? "What price might that be?"

"Have dinner with me."

Angie's pulse jumped into a double-time beat. "You know that can't happen."

Montez broke into his wide Chiclet grin. "Just checking.

Lemme clean up this mess, then we'll talk." He dropped a few more tools in the box, laced a padlock through the hasp, then straightened up. Angie led him toward her office. As she reached the doorway she wondered if they should've talked in the green room instead. Too late to change now. She unlocked the door and went in.

She gestured for him to sit. He shot a disdainful look at Krakos. "I assume there's a story behind that butt-ugly fellow." He sat on the sofa, staying on the front edge. "And I don't wanna know." Now he leaned back, arms resting across the back of the sofa.

She took up her usual position against the desk, hands gripping the edge on either side of her, feet crossed.

Finally he dropped his eyes from her chest, and his arms from the back of the couch. He leaned forward. I was having a beer at JJs. She and"—he leaned a bit further forward—"you aren't gonna like this." He leaned back and let his foot thump to the floor. She almost told him what she'd said the other day to Kiana—pretend it's a bandage, hurts less to just rip it off all at once, but she knew Montez would only spew the information when he was ready. So she waited.

The name that came from his mouth was so much of a surprise her knees nearly buckled. Montez laughed. "I've heard the phrase 'her mouthed dropped open' but never believed it actually happened till now."

Angie closed her mouth and pulled in a breath. Trouble was, the name had crossed her thoughts more than once in the past two days. She just hadn't been able to fit any of the pieces into place so they made any sense.

"Could you hear any of their discussion?" she asked.

"That's why I didn't mention this before. No. And they were behind me so I couldn't keep turning around. All I can say for sure is there was no shouting. They weren't drunk. They acted, I guess you'd say, like friends."

"Friends."

"Best way I can describe it."

She leaned away from the desk. He stood from the sofa. "Time to get back."

Angie locked the office door. "See you tomorrow I guess. Thanks for confiding in me."

He chuckled. "Your problem now—what you do with the information."

"There's no way to know if it's even related to the case."

"Right you are."

They went down together in the elevator. "So, what did you hope to get out of him?"

"Who—Mr. Quattro?"

"Yeah."

"I wanted to find out if Amber has been in town long enough to have wanted to poison Stone."

"Poison?"

"Yes, he was poisoned. Isopropanol."

"Don't know what that shit is." When she opened her mouth, he put up a hand. "Don't want to know either. But I have a question. What difference does it make how long she's been here?"

"Because isopropanol acts more slowly than other poisons. Makes a person appear drunk at first."

"Now I get the thing about Stone. I thought he was trashed all the time. But it was funny, because…" He pinched his lips together. "He didn't seem the type. Y'know?"

She did. Angie had found it hard to believe also. It didn't fit his fun-loving personality.

"'Nother question," Montez said, "Why would the cops think Amber, in particular, did it?"

Angie lifted her chin and deposited some new information on him. "She was his wife also."

This resulted in a rip-roaring guffaw from Montez. He wrapped both arms around himself and fell back against the cushion. Angie tucked hair behind one ear, trying to maintain control but finally couldn't help joining in.

After a minute, he got himself together enough to ask,

"How the hell many does he have?"

"At last count, six."

"Ho-lee crap."

"My thoughts exactly."

"Question. The shit I just laid on you—how does it relate?"

"Damned if I know."

CHAPTER 33

Jarvis accompanied Amber and her redundant attorney to the parking lot. The lawyer hadn't spoken a single word since he realized Amber and Jarvis had wrapped up the interview. Anger rolled off him like aroma from road kill. What the hey...the anger would reflect in Quattro's bill. Probably what was really on his mind was the bawling out he'd get from Daddy-O.

Jarvis waited in the door while Amber got into the car with the lawyer. Jarvis wondered where Quattro had gone when he left here. He'd been pretty mad. A pissed off Quattro wasn't a pretty sight. Jarvis hoped he didn't go take it out on Angelina or the restaurant.

Speak of the devil. Quattro's Lincoln Navigator turned into the driveway, throwing up a spray of gravel from the shoulder. He spotted the attorney's car and stopped behind it to prevent it from backing out. Why he thought his attorney would try to escape him...Jarvis chuckled. With Quattro's mood, anyone would want to escape.

Quattro and the attorney both got out of their cars. The restaurateur was already shouting. In the background, Amber's voice begged him to stop making a scene. He spotted Jarvis standing there and lowered his voice.

Jarvis realized he might get more information if he went inside to watch the monitors. Thoughts of the monitors also reminded him of the video of the meeting between Blanche and Miata Lin. He turned, went back inside, and straight to the room where a bank of monitors flashed scenes from inside and outside the building.

He yanked a chair from under the desk. The wheels protested and the chair creaked when he let all his weight fall into it. He rolled close to the parking lot monitor. Quattro and the attorney were in a shouting match. Neither appeared to be winning. Amber climbed from the attorney's car and got into the passenger side of Daddy's car. She didn't say anything to either of them.

The attorney gave Quattro's SUV a *get it out of my way* motion. Quattro shouted a couple more things at him then did indeed move his car—into a parking space. Jarvis cursed and wondered if he could pretend he'd left the building already.

While he waited for Quattro to come inside and demand to see the captain. Anything might come of that, from Quattro being laughed at to Jarvis being fired—or at least demoted.

In the meantime, he searched for the tapes dated the night the wives had been brought in for questioning and collected all the parking lot videos. He carried them out to the front desk, because when Quattro learned the captain wasn't here, he would be gunning for him. Hopefully not in a literal way. Jarvis checked that the catch on his holster was undone just in case.

Quattro was indeed waiting. Jarvis resisted the urge to search the guy, hit the buzzer to open the door, and wiggled two fingers for the man to follow. He strode to his office with the man practically stepping on the backs of his shoes. Quattro slammed the door.

Jarvis didn't bother sitting. He had no intention of allowing this blowhard to stay longer than a minute. Everything had been done by the book, though there was no way Quattro would look at it that way.

Jarvis planted his feet and crossed his arms in the timeworn message I'm not listening to anything you have to say. Quattro picked up on it right away and opened his mouth but Jarvis stopped him with, "I've been on this case four days. In those four days, I've gotten exactly twelve hours sleep, so I'm in no mood to take any of your"—he couldn't say BS so he said—"lectures. The interview with your daughter was done completely above board and lega—"

"You questioned her without the lawyer being present. I distinctly told you not to do that."

"Mr. Quattro, Amber is over twenty-one, she has the legal right to consent to anything." He took a step toward the angry man—maybe not one of his smarter moves, but he wanted Quattro to know that, just like his attorney, he wasn't intimidated by all the bluster. "As I told you earlier, Amber was not, nor is she now, under arrest. I was merely questioning her, just the same as was done with the other wives." He couldn't help dropping in the information about the other wives—just a little dig to bring the man down a peg or two. It had the opposite effect.

"My daughter had no knowledge of any other wives."

"That's not what she says." Surprise number one to the blowhard.

And it was. His eyebrows blended with the wrinkles in his forehead.

"Look. That's all I'm telling you about this case. Your daughter agreed to the questions. She was very helpful."

"Does that mean you know your killer?"

"I'm not—"

"Yeah yeah, I know, not at liberty to share the information."

"That's not what I was going to say. I was saying I was not sharing the information with you. Period."

"Why the hell not?"

"What your daughter told me is none of your business."

"It most certainly is."

Jarvis sighed, stepped around him and opened the office door. "Don't make me have to have you removed bodily—again."

"Had to have your minions do it though." A smirk popped onto Quattro's face.

In the other room, the fax machine dinged. There was some grinding and paper shushed into the bin like a downhill skier. More than likely, this was the rest of the fingerprint results along with other information he'd sent for. He jerked his head toward the sounds. "Looks like I have work to do."

Realizing he wouldn't get anywhere with Jarvis, Quattro turned and strode to the door. "I'll have you know, I'm going over your head with this."

"Knock yourself out." And he meant it.

Jarvis followed him to the exit and stood until Quattro's Lincoln cleared the parking lot. Then he went to the fax machine to extract a dozen pages. It was indeed what he'd requested—information about Stone's two other wives, and a copy of his birth certificate and the fingerprint results.

Jarvis started for his office with the papers then as he reached the door, turned, photocopied the information, left the originals, took the copies, and beelined for his Jeep. He'd go home and walk Red. After that, he'd sit with a few beers and digest all this new data. The trouble with most of his plans, they were doomed to failure. He did get home and walk the dog, but as he popped the first beer, and sat to read the information on wives one and two, he realized they lived in the Portsmouth area.

It was a nice afternoon for a ride. He phoned Angelina. Hopefully she was done at the theater by now. Maybe she felt like going for a ride. She agreed right away.

"I'm hitting the shower," he said, "then I'll be over."

While letting the hot water blast the suds from what was left of his hair, he thought of the woman who, sequentially, was Stone's wife number one. Darlene Fisher Powers had been brought into James David Powers'—the name on Stone's birth certificate—life in February of 2008. Someone with whom he'd worked at the marina in Portsmouth made the ID that Stone and James were one and the same. There was no notice of a divorce or remarriage in her name.

Chronological wife number two was Anne, no middle

name, Powers. She had married Stone, known as Michael at the time, in 2009, divorced him in 2010 and remarried almost immediately. There was no mention in the paperwork whether this Michael Powers was the same person as their Stone Powers. Right now, it didn't matter. All it would take for identification was a photo.

The fax had also spit out license photos of the women. Both were pretty and seemed to have natural friendly smiles. He dressed in chinos and a light blue button-down shirt. Jarvis smoothed back his wet hair and started to slap on the deerstalker, changed his mind, and heaved it on the bed. He wasn't fooling anyone but himself.

"Come on, girl. Wanna go for a ride?"

At the mention of her second favorite word, Red hopped and leaped and bounced toward the back door. He grabbed a water bottle and a bowl for her, and the folder of information for Angelina. The wind was cold and he almost went back for the hat.

As he pulled out front of her condo, she exited carrying a picnic basket. He got out and ran around to pull her into a kiss that left no doubt how much he'd missed her. He took the picnic basket and held her door. Right away she noticed he wasn't wearing the hat, but said nothing.

"We've both been working too hard," she said. "I thought we could have dinner on the beach."

"Grand idea, but you do realize it's January, right?" He put the Jeep in gear and headed south on Route 11.

"I was hoping we might find a spot out of the wind."

"Stranger things have happened." He experienced a surge of love for this woman. How she'd changed since they met. Two years ago she was very high-maintenance, practically unbending in her attitudes. He hated to have negative thoughts but she'd been much like her mother. But now, she didn't bat an eyelash getting her hands dirty working in his yard, or painting his porch, though she did fret about blood on a two hundred dollar pair of shoes. Which he couldn't blame her.

"So, I see you located the two other wives," she said.

He told what he knew about them. "I'm not a hundred percent positive about the one named Anne. I have no proof Michael and Stone are the same person."

"A photo will fix that. I brought a poster. It's in the picnic basket."

Angelina read the fax sheets about the wives. She flipped to page three. A sideways glance showed it to be Stone's original birth certificate, which matched the one found in his safe. Jarvis didn't say anything as she perused the contents. Something about it had bothered him, but he'd been unable to tell what it was. No doubt her mega-brain would see it right away.

She read out loud. "Born James David Powers, October 2, 1972 in Laramie, Wyoming. Parents: Randall Shore Powers and Annabelle Jasper Grayson."

Angelina was quiet for quite some time. He knew better than to disturb her. Finally she said, "What a lying son of a…"

"In what way specifically?"

"He told me he was born in Secaucus and his parents died when a cement truck ran over their car. I bet you're also going to tell me he wasn't in the marines."

"Didn't check on that. Do you think it's important?"

"Only if he married someone while he was away."

"Very funny."

Just outside Rochester, he merged onto Route 16. That would take them on a straight shot into Portsmouth. Portsmouth police, who'd provided most of the faxed information, had also included the home addresses of both wives. Before leaving home, he'd checked the map. Darlene lived closer to the north side of town.

"Can you plug Darlene's address into the GPS, please?" he asked.

The mechanical voice was soon giving them directions to the first wife's home. It was in a nice neighborhood. Two cars were in the driveway, both newer model Fords. Jarvis's information said that Darlene hadn't remarried.

STONE COLD SOBER

They got out, told Red to protect the picnic basket and headed for the house. A short woman with bright blue eyes behind wire eyeglasses opened the door. The smell of homemade chocolate chip cookies shot out at them. Jarvis identified himself and Angelina and asked if they could come in. She frowned when he mentioned the word police but backed so they could enter.

She led them to the kitchen where indeed, cookies were cooling on the counter. She plated some, long red hair swinging near her waist, and shoved them between Jarvis and Angelina at the table. Then she sat. And waited for Jarvis to speak.

"We're here about your husband James." Jarvis helped himself to a cookie.

The woman's baby blues popped open wide. "Haven't heard from or about him in years."

"So, you're not still together?" Angelina asked.

Darlene shook her head. "I sent him packing two years ago."

"Mind if we ask why?" This from Jarvis.

"Caught him cheating. I'm a one strike you're out kind of girl."

Angelina nodded. Jarvis smiled inside. She was a one-strike girl also. She could identify with this woman so he let her do the talking.

"But you didn't divorce him," she said.

Darlene shook her head hard this time. "Wasn't about to make it that easy on him. If he wanted to get married again, he'd have to come and beg."

And she wouldn't offer him fresh-baked cookies.

"You haven't heard from him at all?" Angelina asked.

"Not a peep." She tipped her head and addressed Jarvis. "What brings you here? You didn't just come to ask if I've heard from the rat."

"No. James passed away the other day."

"Oh, that's too bad." A small smile crossed her face. "Yeah. I called him a rat but I wouldn't wish him dead. Just out of my space. Y'know? What happened?"

Jarvis looked at Angelina, wondering how much they should say. Thing was, if she'd known the name he'd been using, she'd be aware of his death and his multi-wives; it had been all over the news. So, he told the Stone Powers story. By the time he finished she was gripping her chair and rocking back and forth laughing.

After a minute, she recovered herself. "Like I said," she sniffled and wiped happy tears, "I'm not glad he's dead but he sure got what was coming to him, didn't he?"

CHAPTER 34

There didn't seem to be much more to say. Jarvis snatched one more cookie, said they were delicious, and made their exit from Darlene Powers' home.

Angie programmed the GPS for the home of wife number two, Anne Powers Watson. She was the only one of Stone's wives who'd divorced and remarried. Angie couldn't wait to hear her story. Had she too caught him cheating? Was it possible she was the one Darlene had caught Stone cheating with?

Angie's cell phone rang. Rickie's number came up on the caller ID. "Hi, how's tricks?" she said.

"Fine. Wanted to let you know your mom and I patched things up. We actually sat down and talked yesterday. She understands about my trust fund and is going to loan me the money for the car until next year."

What the heck was he talking about? As far as she knew their troubles stemmed from a lack of sexual desire on his part. Shoot. It was all more information than she wanted so she said, "I'm glad to hear that." Jarvis was staring at her with a question on his face, so she mouthed Rickie's name.

"Where are you?" Rickie asked.

"In Portsmouth, following up on two more of Stone's wives." Rickie's laugh was so loud Angie had to move the phone from her ear. Why did everyone think this travesty was so funny? "What did you call for?" she asked.

"To find out how the case is going. I just got back from my class and I'm psyched to put what I'm learning to use. Wish you'd told me you were going. I would've tagged along."

"You would've been wasting your time today. So far this trip is a bust. The first wife hadn't seen him in years."

"You sure about that?"

"Yes. I'll tell you about it when we get home."

"I'm just so excited to get into some action."

She grinned. "You come home from each class that way. I'm glad to hear that though, I can't imagine Mom's going to be happy once you're ordained." She laughed. "I guess I should've used the word licensed, shouldn't I? What was the class about today?"

"Following up on leads. How to decide which ones to do first."

"Sounds important. It's not always an easy decision."

"That's what the instructor said. Where are you going now?"

"We're on the way to the second wife's place, but she's moved on—divorced him and is remarried so I don't expect much to come of this."

"What time will you be back?"

"Probably late. We're diverting for a picnic."

"Okay then, I'll talk to you tomorrow. Want to get together for breakfast?"

"Sure," she said, "but it'll have to be early. I have a nine o'clock rehearsal."

"Seven thirty?"

"Works for me. Seeya." Angie hit End and put the phone away. "Rickie's going to drive me crazy with this detective school stuff."

Jarvis laughed. "Yeah, he's been hitting on me every chance he gets too. I guess it's a good thing. He needs something to do but follow your mom around all the time. Besides, I'd bet money he can't talk to her about it." When he laughed, Red stuck her head between the seats and licked Jarvis's cheek. He fluffed the hair on her ears and told her to get back in her seat. Red tried to lick Angie too but she leaned away. She hated doggie kisses.

"Oh forgot to tell you. Had a run-in with Mr. Quattro this afternoon."

He laughed. "So did I."

"He was shouting at a guy moving a giant stove into place. Gosh, Jarvis, I thought he was going to hit the man."

"Was this about one o'clock?"

"Yes, why?"

"I had his daughter at the station for her interview." He told how Quattro had raised such commotion at the station he'd had to have him thrown out.

"Wish I could've seen it."

"I think you got the fallout."

That made sense. It was the something over which Anthony Quattro didn't have autonomous control.

"Unfortunately," Jarvis added, "I'm afraid there might be some domino effect regarding his restaurant."

She sighed. "Wouldn't surprise me. With Stone's death, there's two strikes against the theater anyway. What else is going to happen?" She raised both hands high. "No! Forget I said that. I don't want to know. So, how did the interview with Amber go?"

He told how she'd agreed to speak without her lawyer, which enraged Daddy Quattro no end.

Angie laughed. "I can only imagine."

"I feel for the lady moving back here."

"I have the sense she'll be heading out west quite soon."

"Does that mean you don't think she killed Stone?"

"It does mean that," she said.

"Neither do I. Do you have any idea who did?"

"Yes."

"Not talking?"

"Not quite yet."

They arrived at Anne Powers Watson's home. It was the

right half of a duplex in a less than affluent part of town. Two cars were in the yard. Both older models. The door was answered by a man of average height with long curly hair and a mustache in need of trimming. Jarvis identified himself then asked if he could speak with Anne. The man's eyes narrowed but he led them into the apartment. The living room was clean but cluttered with children's toys. He shoved some onto the floor so they could sit.

"I'll go get her. I think she's downstairs doing laundry."

There was a low hum of voices from the basement then soon two sets of footsteps climbed up. At the same time, many footsteps could be heard on the second floor. The couple seemed to have an army upstairs.

Anne entered the room carrying a basket of clean laundry. She set it on one of the two overstuffed chairs and came forward. Jarvis made introductions again. She walked back and began folding clothes. Some were very small—newborn size. Man, Angie thought, if this woman just had a baby she sure looked great.

The husband took the other chair in the room. He sat on the edge, leaned slightly forward, forearms on his thighs.

"We are investigating a case where your name came up," Jarvis began.

"Mine?" Anne asked.

"Yes. Do you know a James David Powers?"

She frowned. "I don't think so, why?"

"How about Michael Frederick Powers?"

The frown eased. She nodded. "I was married to him a long time ago." She set a folded pair of baby blue jeans on the coffee table, moved the basket to the floor, and sat. "What's going on?"

"I guess you didn't see the news. Your ex husband was murdered in Alton the other day."

"Sorry to hear that, but what's it got to do with my wife?" the man asked.

Jarvis explained the case and that they were following up

on the multi-wife leads. Anne was the first person who didn't react with raucous laughter about Stone's many dalliances.

"Do you mind if I ask why you separated?" Angie asked.

Anne shrugged. "I'm not really sure. Sounds silly but…I owned a business, a gift shop at the intersection of Market and Bow. Great tourist location. Well, the economy and a hurricane hit me bad. I didn't have enough insurance and couldn't afford to open back up. He was making enough at the marina, but somehow things went downhill from there. On top of that, he didn't want any kids."

"How many do you have?" Angie asked.

"Three and a fourth on the way." She patted her tummy, which was flat as a pancake so she must be in the early stages. "We just drifted apart. He started working more and more hours." She shrugged and gave a wide smile at her husband. "It all worked out for the best."

Angie wouldn't be surprised that with enough digging, another wife would turn up about this time.

Angie and Jarvis stood in unison, thanked the couple and left them to their laundry. They drove to the ocean. It was late afternoon; the sun was going down. Wind blustered off the water and dashed all thoughts of a picnic. So they ate in the Jeep, heat blasting, waves bashing the shore and dodging the dog's head poking between the bucket seats. Angie hadn't had this much fun in a very long time.

On top of that, the sperm of an idea she'd had a few days ago, sadly, had caught up with the egg and formed into a living, breathing suspect.

CHAPTER 35

Angie rose early, trying not to wake Jarvis. She dressed to head out for her jog. Red would not be deterred. Though she didn't sleep over that often, she knew the routine and yipped once before Angie could shut her up. "Wait," Angie said, "Quiet," and sat to put on her running shoes, hoping the goop in the road had melted. She hated running with wet feet. Jarvis had suggested several times that a nice pair of army boots would keep her dry.

She slipped into the blue parka with the yellow reflective stripe, hooked on Red's leash and they slipped outside.

Knowing the identity of the murderer was a great burden. This more so than the last cases she and Jarvis had worked on. Repercussions from the Stone Powers—she couldn't think of him with any other name—murder were sure to affect the theater, and just possibly, her personal life.

When seeking a killer, professional detectives sifted through evidence and applied them to a category—means, motive, and opportunity. She'd cleared two of the three as related to her prime suspect. One still had her a bit baffled.

Angie ran, keeping the dog against the guardrails, though traffic this time of morning was rare. She let her mind roam free, sorting and categorizing the clues and evidence. At the turnaround on Route 11, she stopped to gaze over the northern end of Alton Bay. Still frozen. Bob houses dotted the panorama. In the daytime you could see across to the other side where affluent houses on 28A dotted the shorefront. One of them HeavenScent, owned by Tyson's parents and currently rented by Angie's mother.

Red gave a tug on the leash. Time to head back. She was right. Suddenly Angie was anxious also. There was work to do. Adrenalin pumped into her limbs and they took off.

She knew without a doubt who had murdered Stone Powers.

Where and how to begin proving it though?

Jarvis was awake when they arrived back at the condo. The aroma of fresh ground coffee greeted her first, then Jarvis took Red, cleaned the big Irish setter's feet, and let her free. She dove into her food dish. Jarvis hung Angie's jacket.

"Gosh, do you always sweat like this when you run?"

She grinned at him. He broke into an even wider grin and slapped her on the back—harder than necessary. He tugged her into the kitchen, poured coffee, and leaned across the coffee still grinning.

"So?"

She knew what he wanted her to say. Should she drag it out? Usually she made him wait. Let his frustration grow. Today she wouldn't torture him but needed to ask a few questions first.

"Tell me what you've been thinking about this case."

His smile died. He sat on the adjoining stool.

"Do you have fingerprint reports back?" She took a long sip from her cup.

"I do. Want me to get them?"

"Yes. Later. Let's talk about the suspects first."

"Of the wives, like Amber the best." He held up his hand. "I know you said you weren't focused on her. But I think she realized what he was up to, and that's why she came back east."

She nodded. The theory made sense.

"She has access to the medical stuff first-hand."

"So does Miata Lin. Remember she's a gynecologist."

"I know. But Amber's prints are the only ones not found in any of the other places."

"That could be because she wore gloves."

"Could be."

"And then," he said, "Chia's got the violent personality."

"Poison isn't a violent person's reaction to a problem."

"You mean, she would've beaten or stabbed him."

Angie smiled and patted his arm. "Right. Now you're thinking like a detective."

"Humbug. That doesn't rule her out though, does it?"

"No, but I think it pushes her down the list. What do you think about Blanche?"

"I hate to think of a friend doing such a thing."

"Won't be the first time that's happened," Angie said.

"True."

"Something bothers me about the way she reacted to the news of the multiple wives."

"You mean you think she knew. About all of them."

"I do. Whether she'd do anything about them, I can't say. We talked the other day but I wasn't able to get a read on her."

"You're usually really good at that."

"I might be too close to the situation. Wish you'd been there. Your input would've been good."

"Have you been looking at people other than the wives?" he asked.

"Of course."

"Anyone in particular?"

"You first."

"Montez Clarke."

"Because…"

"He's way too laid back. Too poker-faced. You never know what's going on behind that face."

He was so wrong about that!

"What makes you suspect him? You think he was getting Stone out of the way so he could have Chia?" Angie didn't mention Jarvis's jealousy over this man's presence in her life.

And neither did he bring it up. "No. I don't think he was that serious about her. I think his morals focus in a different direction—he'd be more pissed about what Stone had been up to. More likely to try and right the wrong.

Angie nodded. Jarvis made a good point. No matter what Montez did in his past, he was loyal to certain beliefs and, as Jarvis said, moralities. He'd know how to keep his prints from being found as a scene. Angie had no way to know for sure, but she'd bet he could enter a home and deposit the poison without anyone knowing.

"What about Anthony Quattro?" she asked.

He chuckled. "After his behavior yesterday, I can definitely picture him killing someone. Especially Stone—for hurting his little girl. For taking her away from him."

So could Angie. But again, it would be more of a physical killing.

"I think he'd be more of a spur of the moment, in-your-face killer. He wouldn't bother planning something as elaborate as this. Gun or knife. That'd be my choice for him."

Angie shook her head. "Not a knife. Too messy. Gun or maybe a well-placed punch to the throat."

"More likely he'd pay someone to do it for him."

"You got that right," she said but realized killers were unpredictable. Emotions and situations could drive them to do the oddest, most out-of-character things.

A few moments of silence passed. Angie mulled over what they'd just discussed, adding and discarding information in her brain. The longer she juggled the pieces, the better they fit.

Jarvis grabbed the corner of the newspaper he'd picked up at the bakery and scribbled. *Going to get fingerprint reports.*

She blinked a couple of times to bring his scribbles into focus, and said, "Can you bring the evidence reports too?"

He went to put on his jacket and came back jangling his keys. Red peered up from her bowl, wagged her tail, but otherwise didn't move. Jarvis bent and kissed Angie under the ear. "Will you at least tell me who did it?"

She kissed him back, planting a delicate one on his lips. Then she pulled him down and whispered in his ear.

The information clearly came as a surprise. A deep frown marred his face as he turned and left the house.

Angie finished the coffee, left the mug on the counter, and went to shower. When she came out, Red was sitting outside the bathroom door wagging her tail. Angie shrugged. "If you were lonely you should've gone with Dad." She finished dressing.

Her cell rang. Rickie's number on the caller ID made her groan. Hopefully his call didn't mean the problem with her mother had re-occurred.

"Hi Rickie."

"Any news on the case?"

Should she tell him? "Yes. We know who the murderer is."

Silence a moment. Then he said, "Are you going to tell me?"

She laughed and lied, "No. I haven't even shared the information with Jarvis yet."

"Where is he?"

"He went to pick up some information at the station. How's Mom doing?"

"Okay. She's making pages and pages of notes about the summer thing you're going to do."

"Glad she's excited about it. Mom needed something to do."

"You got that right." Rickie laughed. "So...I can't believe you've figured out another one."

She didn't reply. What was there to say? If you took all the information and fitted the pieces together, anyone could figure it out."

"Even me?"

She laughed. "Of course."

"Could I come over and look at the information? If you show me how you put things together in your head maybe it'll help me learn."

"Sure. Come on over."

Angie hung up and went to put together something for

lunch. She had no idea if her mother was coming too. Didn't matter. Maybe better if she did.

Red's head popped up, ears pricked. "Who's here?" Angie asked.

Red raced to the door, head tilted to one side. Jarvis entered, ruffled the top of her head and came in to hand Angie the folders. Then he ruffled the top of her head too. She was too busy looking for what she wanted to bother smacking him like she usually did.

He plopped a box from the bakery on the counter. Inside were two fresh bear claws. "Thanks." She grabbed one, took a bite and set it on a napkin.

He shoved a folder in front of her. Angie ate and read the very long report, which included prints taken from each of the four wife's homes and vehicles, along with prints from the theater—Stone's locker in particular. The prints of her murderer appeared in two places—Amber's car. Which she'd expected. And Stone's locker, which she hadn't

Jarvis set two coffees on the placemats.

Offhandedly, she said, "Rickie's on the way over."

"That right?"

"He wants me to show him how I put the pieces together."

"I'd like if you could show me too."

"There's nothing I can show you…" Angie deliberately left the sentence hanging, which made him chuckle. "Will you make a call for me?" She jotted a message on the corner of the newspaper.

He read it, crumpled it, and tossed it in the trash. Then he left the room, phone in-hand.

She opened the folder that contained results of the evidence collected from the wives homes and cars, and Stone's locker at the theater.

The doorbell rang. Jarvis ran down the hall and opened it. Rickie entered.

"Hi," Angie said. "Mom didn't come with you?"

"No, she was busy on the internet. I think she was looking

up tent prices."

The three of them settled at the dining room table, paperwork spread everywhere. Jarvis outlined the way the case had gone so far. He gave a thumbnail on the interviews with the wives.

"Were you able to formulate any ideas about them from those interviews?" Rickie asked, a blank notebook page spread in front of him, pen in-hand.

"Yes and no," Angie said. "It's important to watch their reactions as information is given or surprise questions are asked. Few people are able to completely control their facial expressions. But it's important to watch without them knowing you're watching."

Rickie grinned a white-toothed smile. "I already figured that out. I don't know if you realize it or not but you do that with your mother all the time."

She hadn't realized it, but it made sense. Throughout her life Angie had furtively examined the relationship between her parents. Especially her father, who, when he'd been drinking, took offense if he saw anyone watching him. Now that she was older she knew his reactions were due to his feelings of guilt and inadequacy. As a child, she only saw a man who brutalized her, her brother and mother.

Rickie poked her in the arm. "Are you okay?"

Angie shook herself physically to douse the memory. "Yeah, I'm fine." She went back to the evidence folder, recapping what she'd found. Angie spoke mostly to Jarvis, though Rickie scribbled away, taking notes. "Isopropanol was found on Stone's person, in all his hand sanitizers and containers of nose drops. He kept containers everywhere—in his car, locker, bathrooms and in a couple of cases, dining rooms. Almost all showed evidence of tampering. It was found in his shampoo and shower gel in his bathroom at Blanche's"—she flipped pages back and forth collecting information—"and in his things at Chia and Miata Lin's. It was found in his travel gear."

Rickie looked up from his notes. "Perp wasn't taking any

chances, was he?"

Angie pointed a pen at him. "Did you notice where it *wasn't* found? This can be as telling as where it *is* found."

Since Rickie hadn't seen the notes, Jarvis answered, "Only at Amber's—her home and her car. That's one of the reasons I'd focused on her as our killer."

"But if you don't find her prints, doesn't that tell you she wasn't there?" Rickie asked.

"It could mean she wore gloves. Or was trying to make us think that way."

"She might've expected that since she just got to town she wouldn't be a suspect at all," Jarvis added.

"Makes sense," Rickie said.

"Just before you phoned, we were talking about the murder. We know who killed Stone Powers," Angie said.

Rickie clicked his pen, prepared to write. Eyes wide, he asked. "Who?"

"You."

CHAPTER 36

Angelina flipped to Amber Powers' page in the fingerprint folder. She sat there reading for quite some time. Rickie Kennedy hadn't moved except for blinking his blue eyes several times. Then he broke into loud laughter.

"I know you're watching me for a reaction," he said, "even though you're pretending not to."

"No, I'm not," she said.

"That's what you said a minute ago."

"Yes, but Jarvis is watching you for me."

Indeed he was. He kept expecting the shock to wear off and reality to set in—then Rickie would react. Jarvis wasn't sure what he'd do, but he had a pretty good idea Rickie wouldn't stick out his wrists and wait for the handcuffs to be snapped on. Good thing because after the phone call to have HeavenScent searched, he'd left them in the bedroom.

"So," said the confused ex-surfer, "what are you looking for?"

"I found it." She turned the page and stabbed a pink lacquered fingernail so Rickie could see. Jarvis recognized the page. It was the one set of prints they hadn't been able to identify in Amber Powers' car.

"What do you want me to see—those prints?"

Angelina looked up. "Would you like to bet your new car that I know whose these are?"

A smirk blossomed on his face. He leaned back in the

chair. "Yes."

"I bet we discover they're yours."

"Couldn't be."

"Well, I have a witness who saw you with Amber last Tuesday night."

The smirk disappeared so fast from Rickie's face that Jarvis thought it made a sucking sound.

"Easy enough to check, don't you think?" Angelina said.

"I guess." Rickie leaned forward now. "Just because I was in her car does not mean I killed her husband."

"That in itself doesn't mean it. You're right."

"You know, Angie, I always thought you were on the ball. Now you have me disappointed."

She smiled up at him. "Not really worried about that. I'm worried how my mother's going to take the news."

"I expect she'll take it a lot better than you think."

"That sounds suspiciously like an admission of guilt."

Rickie shook his head. "No. Our relationship has about run its course. This morning I told her I was leaving her."

That was probably why Gloria hadn't come with him. Too busy crying. Or throwing things.

"Did she give you the money for the car yet?" Angelina asked.

Rickie shook his head.

"Keep an eye on him, would you?" Angelina stood and left the room. She returned carrying a plastic evidence bag Jarvis hadn't seen before. She placed it on the table between the two men.

Jarvis couldn't help smiling at the lock picking kit—a quite expensive one. "Where did you get this?"

"Rickie's glove compartment."

"How'd you get in my car?" He was indignant. "I keep it locked all the time."

"That's true but you didn't hide the second set of keys. I was at mom's yesterday. I pretended to go to the bathroom but sneaked outside. I knew you wouldn't keep anything in the house just in case..."

She didn't sit down, which meant she had more to show them. Admiration for this woman flooded Jarvis's veins.

"I'll be back," she said.

Jarvis didn't speak to Rickie while she was gone. Neither did he take his eyes off Rickie, whose attention was focused only on Angie's hallway.

There were some sounds in the guest room. A moment later she returned carrying a bagged laptop computer, which she also placed on the table. The label on it clearly said the date, Rickie's name and the location of her 'find'.

Rickie sat up straighter. "Where did you get that!"

"Don't be dense. You know where I found it."

"I thought Tyson said Gloria was working on the computer when he left," Jarvis said.

"He lied. I got the computer yesterday. Want to know what I found on it?" she asked, looking at Rickie. "I won't bother booting it up. For Jarvis's benefit: I found internet searches about isopropanol poisoning. Aaaand"—she drew out the word and faced Rickie again—"a search for how to pick locks. I assume that's how you got into all their houses."

"I did do the search for the alcohol. When you mentioned what kind of poison was used, I wanted to know more about it."

"Good try," Angelina said with a tiny grin, "but the dates on the searches are from before Stone got sick."

Rickie jumped up so fast he surprised Jarvis, who'd been expecting it. Jarvis leaped up, tipping over his chair. He launched himself at Rickie who landed facedown in her white carpet. Jarvis caught both Rickie's hands and held them tight.

"Angelina, get my handcuffs in the bedroom then telephone the captain."

She left at a run. While she was gone, Red came to help. She sat on Rickie's feet.

When Angelina returned, she burst out laughing and snapped a photo. "Can you guys say YouTube?"

"You'd better not!" Rickie's shout was muffled in the white carpet. Jarvis hoped like hell Rickie wasn't bleeding. He'd never hear the end of it.

She handed Jarvis the cuffs, dialed the captain's home number, and explained the situation. She set the phone on the dining room table. Jarvis shoved Red off Rickie's feet and helped him up.

"Captain Folsom will meet you at the station."

Jarvis aimed Rickie toward the door. They stopped short seeing a scowling Gloria standing there. "There are men in my house...tearing it apart. Angelina, tell me they were joking when they said Rickie killed that man?"

"Mom..."

"Why?" This question Gloria turned on Rickie. He shrugged. All he said was, "Amber."

Gloria reared back and, before Jarvis could stop her, slapped him so hard she almost toppled both of them to the floor. Red took a stance beside him, barking at her.

"Red. Quiet."

The dog shut up. But she didn't relax. She kept her cocoa colored eyes glued to Gloria.

Angelina went to the closet to get Rickie's coat. She slid it over his shoulders. Plopped the hat on his head harder than necessary. "There's a third reason we might not've found Amber's prints on anything: because you wiped them off so she wouldn't be a suspect."

"I only wiped them off Stone's car."

"How did you get in his car?" Jarvis asked.

"Internet."

"Shit." This from Jarvis and Gloria. Jarvis nudged him into the foyer.

"Where are we going?"

"Jail, stupid." This from Gloria. Then she softened a bit. "So, all those times you disappeared, you were seeing Amber?"

"No, Gloria, I was escaping your perpetual nagging. I didn't know Amber was in town until Tuesday. We happened to meet up at the theater the day you had me bring the mail. I met her for coffee that night. She told me she thought Allen was cheating on her. Then, when we were here for dessert I saw the poster and realized Stone and Allen were the same person." He stopped for a breath. "And when you"—he jerked his head back to indicate Jarvis—"were talking about him having two wives, I realized Amber made it three. I did some research and found another one in Rhode Island." Rickie shook his head. "Made me sick to think about it."

"So you decided that, rather than call the cops and turn him in for bigamy, you'd kill him," Gloria said.

He nodded.

"You sick bastard." Gloria struck him again.

Jarvis nearly smiled. Angelina's face said she'd been about to hit him also. Even so, she said, "Mom, stop it," the same time Jarvis said, "That's enough, ladies, we can't have him going to the station all bruised. Can we, Red?"

Red barked.

Jarvis urged Rickie toward the door. Rickie stopped and turned toward Angie. "Please know that I tried to keep the theater out of it."

"Your prints were found on his locker."

"I guess I might've touched it but out of respect for Angie I didn't put anything there."

"Thanks a bunch, Rickie. I'm sure that killing my leading man didn't bring us any attention at all."

Jarvis kissed Angelina on the cheek. "This could take a while. I think I'll head home directly after. I haven't gotten much sleep lately."

"You can sleep here."

"No, I can't."

As soon as the door closed behind them, Angie went to pour some wine. She shut off all the lights except the one over the stove. She and her mother went to sit in the living room.

"You okay?" She asked Gloria.

"Yeah. It hasn't really sunk in yet." They sat in silence a

while. Then her mother said, "Was he really sick in the head?"

"Honestly, I don't think so. I think he—no offense to you at all but I think he had gotten all he could out of your relationship—"

"And decided he wanted to start one with Amber."

"That's what I think."

"He said they weren't seeing each other in California."

"They probably weren't. I think his nose was put out of joint when she got appointed as coach instead of him."

"I don't give a damn either way." They sat through another glass of wine, not talking, both lost in private thoughts. "I think I'm ready for another world tour."

Thank God.

"I figured you'd think that."

Oh damn, had she said it out loud?

ABOUT THE AUTHOR

Cindy Davis recently relocated to Florida from New Hampshire. She spends most of her time at the computer, either editing or writing. She enjoys the outdoors, whether hiking, camping, gardening or bringing the computer to the swing in her herb garden.

Cindy has been a full-time editor for over fifteen years. She's had the pleasure of working with more than two hundred authors on almost five hundred manuscripts. Many of her authors have gone on to find agents and big publishing contracts. Most all her authors are now published. See the My Work page at www.ficton-doctor.com.

Cindy is a multi-published author. She pens mostly mystery but has dabbled in fantasy, adventure, women's fiction, non-fiction and yes, erotic fiction. Check her out at :
www.cdavisnh.com.